"You don't know the meaning of emotion!"

Denial rushed to Hilary's lips, faltered and was lost in the crushing impact of his mouth upon hers. By the time she sought to recover her shattered senses, he was drawing back.

"I have a mind to teach you that meaning, my cool English miss," the *conde* said smoothly. "But you tremble! Surely one kiss is not so great a shock!" His voice was soft with amusement, and the suspicion flared in Hilary that he was considering future shocks.

"I—I certainly didn't expect such a shock from *you, señor.*"

"Me? Do you think I am impervious to the call of the senses?"

"I just did not expect such a practical demonstration of word definition," Hilary said shakily, wishing her heart would stop its wild capers!

Dear Conquistador

by

MARGERY HILTON

Harlequin Books

TORONTO • LONDON • LOS ANGELES • AMSTERDAM
SYDNEY • HAMBURG • PARIS • STOCKHOLM • ATHENS • TOKYO

Original hardcover edition published in 1972
by Mills & Boon Limited

ISBN 0-373-01610-7

Harlequin edition published August 1972

Second printing September 1972
Third printing September 1980

Printed in Canada

CHAPTER ONE

WHEN Hilary Martin was born the Fates bestowed on her two very precious gifts: a loving heart and honesty. For good measure they threw in the bloom of health, an aptitude for languages, and a spoon which, if not silver, maintained its lustre throughout a happy and uncomplicated childhood. But there was one gift for which, when she counted her blessings, she was to sigh and beg forgiveness for her greed: the gift of dissemblance. If only she were able to pretend!

It was not until the day of her thirteenth birthday that she became aware of this particular omission in her personality, and it was inevitable that this occasion should coincide with her first experience of the shattering effect the masculine sex was capable of accomplishing without any apparent effort.

Long afterwards she realized that he was quite an ordinary mortal. He was no more immune to the miseries of a streaming cold or the vagaries of life which try the frailty of human temper than any other mortal, but through the rosy haze of romance which veiled her eyes she saw him only as the shining centre of this wonderful new experience which was transforming her entire vision of living.

He was a colleague of her father, a few years younger than Mr. Martin, and it seemed the most natural thing in the world to blurt out an invitation to her birthday celebration, which, after understandable surprise and a querying glance at her father, he accepted with some amusement, and then forgot to come.

While the new record player blared out the new records and the teenage gang screamed and swooned and laid bare the buffet table and sidled out in search of niches suitable for little experimental forays into human relationships Hilary mooned through her party with an expression which would have inspired an Ibsen. That the cause of it remembered belatedly two days later and hastily forwarded a box of chocolates made no difference; he was guilty of betrayal, and all the chocolates in the world would not bring consolation.

5

Finally her father took her aside late one evening and launched into what the family called 'one of Father's little philosophies'. After a dissertation on being reasonable, and growing pains in the young female, and a few diversions into sidetracks that didn't really have anything to do with the matter, he said on a note of despair:

'Darling, you must learn not to let people see!'

There was a lot more in this strain, about it being a hard world, and an honest trusting nature being a drawback at the times when the carapace of a crustacean was a better asset, and while he had no desire to see her become tough and insensitive he didn't want her to get hurt. And that sometimes blurting out the truth led to more trouble in life than a tactful evasion at the right moment.

Yes, it all came back to the gentle art of dissemblance, an art, not a gift, and this was just the beginning of realizing what life could mean to a girl who wasn't very skilful at disguising her feelings.

Hilary began to think about it and to learn, painfully, what seemed to come like second nature to her feminine friends. She still suffered the relentless force of honesty, however. She still risked missing her stop on those odd occasions when the bus conductor missed taking her fare and she had to hunt for the right change to drop into the little box beside the driver. She would still confess instantly if she made a slight error at work, even if her confession resulted in wrath descending on her fair, silky head. She still blurted out the whole unvarnished truth to anything she was asked, but she did gradually learn to be a little more reserved when her path began to intertwine with that of the opposite sex.

Until she reached the age of nineteen and fell in love with her new boss.

For three months the dividing line between heaven and earth was a very blurred borderline. He took her dining and dancing, initiated her into the thrills of sailing, and all the while told her things that made her flower into tender, awakening beauty, and finally he took her to Rome on a business trip, where for the first time he was truly honest with her and she was more honest than she'd ever been. She told him in no uncertain tones that she didn't want to be seduced, that she couldn't dream of having any sort of relationship with a married man, even if she loved him and his wife was an absolute bitch to him, and finally, at the end of the disastrous trip, she told him she didn't even want to work for him any more. After which she cried quite a lot, until she acknowledged that disillusion could contribute quite a lot to heartbreak, and somehow it didn't hurt quite so bitterly once she faced that sad little truth.

When the ensuing family uproar subsided and Hilary reached the point where she'd scream if one more word was spoken on the subject, her father said wearily: 'You didn't have to throw up the sponge altogether. You could have requested a transfer to another department. What are you going to do now?'

'I'm going abroad,' Hilary said simply.

'*Abroad?*' Mr. Martin cried.

'Abroad . . .' Mrs. Martin faltered. 'For a holiday, darling?'

'No. To work.'

The shocked silence which followed this statement was almost as intense as the one which had greeted her account of the cause of it all. Before they could gather breath and marshal objections she said firmly:

'Listen. I've always wanted to travel. My French is supposed to be good and my Spanish was good enough to deal with the correspondence from the firm's South American agencies. So why should I waste it?'

'But what kind of a job?' her mother asked anxiously.

'I don't know yet, but I've been to a bureau and talked it over and they're going to let me know when something suitable comes along.'

'There was another silence, then Mr. Martin said: 'You're set on this?'

'I am, and I've thought it over very carefully, so please don't try to talk me out of it. Try to understand,' she said pleadingly.

'Hm, well, I don't see why not. You mightn't get the opportunity when you're older and settle down,' he said slowly, and she could have hugged him. 'I wonder if old Jameson could help,' he went on musingly. 'I believe he has connections with Heatherly's continental side. He might know of a secretarial opening. I suppose you're thinking of Paris?'

Hilary looked steadily at him and shook her head. 'I wasn't. Actually I was thinking of North Africa, or the Canaries, or even,' she hesitated, 'South America.'

Mrs. Martin sat down weakly and echoed this somewhat startling announcement. Hilary cut in quickly: 'But don't you see, it all depends on the job, and the people. I've got to be prepared to be fluid. It's no use picking on one particular place and refusing to consider anywhere or anything else. I might wait ages for the right thing to turn up, if it ever does.'

For a week or so it seemed as though Hilary was going to be unlucky. She had several interviews, but each time either Hilary didn't have the exact qualifications the prospective employers required or *they* lacked the qualifications Hilary required, and gradually the family began to breathe more freely again. It wasn't that they wanted to hamper her freedom or keep her tied to home-strings, but they could not help suffering the qualms natural to loving, responsible parents when a much loved young daughter suddenly decides to remove her place of residence to a strange land across the seas. And the mention of South America had been a little too overwhelming for Mrs. Martin.

Then one morning there was a telephone call from the bureau asking Hilary to call that afternoon.

Lunch was unusually quiet that day. There was an unspoken conviction that 'this' was going to be 'it', even though Hilary smiled and assured them that it would probably prove to be another false alarm.

But all the same she dressed with care and took particular pains with her grooming. Her gold-spun silky hair fell sleek and shining to the small collar of her apricot-toned suit. Four big pearly buttons closed the jacket and matched the plain bronze patent pumps which enhanced the shapeliness of her long slender legs. Her eye make-up was rather more discreet than usual, and a light film of apricot lip-tint emphasized rather than hid the candid sweetness of her mouth.

The room in the bureau was light enough with its pastel decor, but Hilary brought a freshness into it that made the

8

rather blasé-faced woman at the desk look up more closely at her and smile with sudden warmth.

'It looks as though it's turned brighter outside?'

Hilary said, 'Yes', smiling, and took the chair indicated, composing her hands in her lap and trying not to betray her inward twinges of nervousness while the woman scanned a paper on the desk. She looked up.

'Now, Miss Martin, this post . . . It's an exciting opportunity for the right girl, although not exactly a secretarial job. How do you feel about working with children?'

Hilary forgot her anxiety. 'Children?' she exclaimed. 'It – it's not an *au pair* arrangement?'

'Far from it.' The woman shook her head. 'There's a boy of six, and the main requirement here is practice in English conversation and some French. There is also a girl of seventeen to whom you would be a companion. The salary is generous and I'm sure you would receive every consideration. This is a very good family of the highest repute – the Conde's ancestry can be traced back to the days of the Conquistadors. Needless to say,' the woman smiled reassuringly, 'we would not dream of sending you so far away unless we were assured of your welfare. We have our own high reputation to maintain. But of course you also must be prepared to furnish references as to your own suitability.'

'Yes, I realize that, but . . .' Hilary hesitated, 'you said, "so far".'

'Oh, yes, I'm sorry. I'd merely mentioned that it was a Spanish family. You would be in residence with them at their home in Lima. Peru.'

She waited a moment, obviously prepared for some signs of withdrawal.

Hilary betrayed none, except for a sudden sparkle of interest in her hazel eyes, and the woman continued: 'Also, you would have to be very sure, because you would have to undertake to remain there, barring genuine illness, naturally, for at least one year, and be prepared to travel with your two charges should the necessity arise, otherwise you will forfeit your air fare – a considerable sum, as you will realize. So if you have the slightest doubt say so before we proceed any further.'

'I haven't, so far.' Hilary met the woman's gaze levelly.

'But I presume I will be given further information at an interview with this prospective employer?'

The woman inclined her head. 'There wasn't any point in sending you along until we'd got the preliminaries over. Now . . .' She reached briskly for the phone, consulting the open book on her desk as she did so.

Hilary drew back, turning her head and pretending a tactful interest in a flower print which was remarkable only for its colourless insipidity, while the woman spoke briefly into the phone.

Presently she replaced it. 'Now, if you go along to this address, Miss Martin, before four-thirty, and take this card with you . . .' she paused to write quickly on one of the agency's introductory cards, 'Señora Alvedo will have a talk with you and make her recommendation accordingly.'

'I won't be meeting the – the actual person who will be employing me?' Hilary asked.

The woman smiled. 'Good gracious, no. Lima is more than six thousand miles away. Señora Alvedo is acting as the family's representative – it's quite often done in a case like this. Now don't be nervous, you'll find her most charming and understanding.' She stood up. 'You'd better hurry. Good luck!'

A taxi was dropping a fare as Hilary emerged from the building. On impulse she waved and ran towards it, reflecting that as the hotel was at the other side of town she might as well take the cab and save time.

She felt excitement quickening her heartbeats, and a distinct stirring of butterflies in her stomach as she paid the driver and stood for a moment outside the hotel entrance. Thank goodness she'd taken pains to appear her very best . . . so this was where the other half dallied while in transit! Taking a deep breath, she advanced into the warm, quiet opulence of the London Luxor.

Across the half moon sweep of the gleaming reception desk the polite mask of the reception clerk did not flicker. 'Señora Alvedo? First floor. Number nineteen. Take the lift, madam.'

There seemed to be about half a mile of deep blue carpet to cross. Hilary decided to take the stairs; the lift would only stir the butterflies to renewed frenzy. Room nineteen. Her age. It seemed a portent . . . She trod softly, counting down to zero until she stood outside the white and gilt panelled door.

There was no immediate response to her tap, then the door opened and a dark-haired girl in a scarlet coat looked out and grinned, 'Another one? Come and join us.'

Hilary had not expected to see other applicants – a ridiculous notion, she thought as she entered the ante-room and glanced at the other occupants. It was supposed to be an exciting opportunity; why should she be the only applicant?

There were four of them: an older woman whose pale face and taut mouth betrayed her inward tension; a plump cheerful girl who looked about Hilary's age; a teenager, and the girl in the red coat. The very young girl looked little more than fourteen or fifteen. She caught Hilary's glance and pulled a grimace of resignation, putting up her hand to push back her mane of thick, ash-blonde hair. It immediately flopped forward again as her hand fell and the tiers of gaudy bangles jingled down to her wrist. She giggled nervously, and the girl in the red coat said: 'The suspense is killing, isn't it?'

The other two made no response, but the young girl said: 'I bet it turns out to be another *au pair* swizz. If it is I shan't take it. Talk about slavery! I know, I've had some. But just think of it. Flying to South America. Isn't a Conde a sort of Spanish count? I'll bet—'

The inner door opened and a rich foreign voice queried: 'Miss Marilyn Jones .... ?'

The teenager grabbed her bits and pieces and bounced in jauntily.

After three or four minutes she emerged, not quite so jauntily, giving a gallant little thumbs down as she opened the outer door.

The older woman lasted a little longer, and the plump girl almost ten minutes, then the girl in the red coat was summoned and Hilary was left on her own.

She took the opportunity to check that her appearance was still immaculate. Hilary was not vain, to the contrary, she had never fully comprehended the attractive picture she made as seen through other people's eyes, and a natural fast-idiousness made her dislike a careless, ungroomed appearance.

She was dropping her compact into her bag when the dark girl came out and she became aware of how tight was the coil of tension within her. The dark girl whispered wryly: 'Don't ring us – we'll ring you,' and shrugged. 'I think I've missed that plane after all.'

Once more Hilary was alone, waiting now for her own voice of fate. A minute ticked by, then another ... and another ... There wasn't a sound from the inner room. She stood up, frowned, and hovered uncertainly. They couldn't have forgotten her ... She heard the clatter of a tea trolley passing the outer door, faint muffled voices beyond, then silence again. Abruptly she moved forward and tapped lightly.

There was no response. She bit her lip, then tapped again and opened the door a little way. She looked round it, the tentative, 'Excuse me', hovering on her lips, and blinked with puzzlement. The spacious sitting-room of the suite was empty.

Frowning, she withdrew and gently closed the door. Slowly she went back to her chair near the outer door and hesitated uncertainly, debating her next move. Was it worth waiting any longer? But the whole day would be such a waste. She sat down and took the agency card from her bag. She was definitely at the right place. She had an appointment. They must be expecting her. Aware of a distinct sense of disappointment, she looked at the blank closed door. Perhaps Señora Alvedo had been called away for a few minutes. Perhaps she wanted to take aspirins, or wash her hands, or make notes, or something ... One had to allow for the small unexpected things which were so easily explained. She would wait another five minutes, then she would knock again. Perhaps the elusive Señora Alvedo would have returned. If not ... she would call it a day. After all, there was no guarantee that she would land the job, and something else would come along.

Hilary bent to retrieve her glove and the next moment she saw stars. The glove fell from her hand and she straightened dazedly, straight to the dark stare as startled as her own.

'*Santo*—! I beg your pardon!' The door which had just made painful contact with Hilary's head swung back and a tall man in an immaculate pale grey suit towered over her. 'Are you hurt? I had no idea . . .'

'It's all right.' She shook her head. 'It's my own fault for sitting so near the door.'

His dark brows flickered. 'Oh no, not at all. You are sure you are not hurt?'

'Quite sure.' This was, as always, the truth. A bump on the head soon dropped to a losing place against the competition of a masculine force like this one! With some difficulty Hilary broke free of the compulsion so unaccountably present in what was, after all, merely a politely concerned regard. 'Quite sure, *señor*,' she repeated.

An alertness flashed momentarily over the dark, imperious visage, then he inclined his head with polite finality and turned towards the inner door. Hilary relaxed, then the stranger checked his stride and swung round.

'You were wishing to see me, *señorita*?'

'No, *señor*.' She smiled a little, knowing she had made no mistake over his nationality. 'But please . . . I do have an appointment with Señora Alvedo. I wonder if you . . .' She had taken a step forward as she spoke and suddenly felt absurdly diminutive against his height. Then her expression faltered at the puzzlement in his face.

He said, 'But I thought they had all— How long have you been here?'

'Almost three-quarters of an hour,' she said ruefully.

'And Sanchia is not here . . .?' An imprecation she had no difficulty in translating escaped him, and she hid a smile. It looked as though Sanchia had a masterful one here – if she were his wife. But he was gesturing with a strong, well-shaped hand, and with a murmur of acknowledgement she passed through into the sanctum from which her fellow hopefuls had emerged with such doleful expressions.

Strangely, it no longer appeared so spacious a room when the tall, grey-clad figure took possession. He indicated a chair, then crossed to the adjoining room. Moments later he reappeared and now there was annoyance in the handsome, aristocratic features.

He said, 'I regret that Señora Alvedo is no longer here.

Please accept my apologies for your inconvenience.'

Hilary stood up. In face of this obviously genuine concern she could not display her own annoyance at a wasted afternoon. But she could not hide a note of disappointment as she said quickly: 'Please don't worry – it's not your fault. Thank you for – for checking for me. I might have waited in vain if you hadn't turned up.' She held out her hand, then let it fall as he apparently failed to notice the gesture.

He said, 'One moment. I'm correct in assuming that you are here in connection with appointment of a *compañera-maestra* to Juanita and her brother? It is all down here . . .' He was consulting papers on a flower-laden table.

She nodded, watching him thrust the great bowl of blooms impatiently aside. He glanced up. 'There have been four young ladies here this afternoon, all of whom have been marked as completely unsuitable. Let me see . . . Miss Jones, Miss Chater . . .' He scanned the notes, his firm mouth compressing as he flipped over the page. 'Mrs. Bulmer . . . and Miss Marchant.' He glanced sharply at Hilary. 'That is not your name, *señorita?*'

'No – it's Martin. Hilary Martin.'

He studied the list again and shook his head. 'Your name does not appear to be here, Miss Martin.'

'But it must be!' She felt dismay. 'I definitely have an—' She stopped, exclaiming with relief as she remembered the card. Hastily she looked in her bag. 'I have a card from the bureau – here it is.'

He took it, frowning, and glanced down again at the appointment book. Then his frown cleared. 'I think there has been what you would call a mix-up. Martin and this other name – Marchant – could sound alike over the telephone, and I'm afraid Sanchia tends to be rather excitable when using that instrument.'

He regarded her thoughtfully for a moment, then said abruptly: 'So it seems, Miss Martin, there is nothing else to do but interview you myself, and ask you all these extremely personal questions.'

'Oh, but . . .' she bit her lip, 'will it be all right? I mean—'

Suddenly he seemed taller, and the light in his dark piercing eyes more quelling. 'Of course it will be all right. I can assure you that if *I* do not have the authority, then . . .' He paused at her expression of bewilderment and his tone softened slightly. 'Do not fear, *señorita*, I am well acquainted with the family of Romualdo Pacquera – better so than Señora Alvedo.' He shrugged. 'It was simply that it was considered more suitable to enlist a woman's judgment.'

He gestured, and Hilary sunk back into her chair. It seemed she was to have her interview after all. Though what would come of it she couldn't begin to comprehend. Oh, well, in for a penny . . .

He seated himself at the other side of the table and again that enormous bowl of flowers became an obstruction. He shifted his position, and Hilary sprang up impulsively and moved the bowl to a nearby side table. He stayed silent until she sat down again, then said rather sardonically: 'Thank you – you seem a very helpful person, Miss Martin.'

Instantly a blush of confusion turned her cheeks deep rose. She felt foolish, and that sense of feeling small rushed over her again. Worse still, for some reason his dark gaze was making her aware of her girlhood in a way no man's regard had ever done before. She tensed, trying to shield her embarrassment, and then he smiled, in a way that instantly banished the awkwardness and brought a shy responding curve to her mouth. He said in Spanish: 'Have you ever worked with children, Señorita Martin?'

'No,' she admitted, taking her language cue from him, 'and that is one thing I must make clear. I am not qualified to teach children, if that is what you require. Although I had a good education, I should not like to mislead you in that respect.'

He shook his head. 'No, Miss Martin. Joaquin already has a tutor who is excellent, except that his English and French are a trifle stilted, and Juanita's education is being taken care of. The main requirements are improvement of her English and a companionship not at present available.'

'Has she no friends of her own age?' Hilary asked, puzzled as she considered this statement from a wholly British angle. It seemed rather strange to import an English girl from so far away. Surely Lima was not entirely barren of girls suitable for this purpose?

As though he read her thoughts he made a negative gesture. 'It is not as simple as that. Juanita has not yet had time to form suitable new friendships. Six weeks ago she and Joaquin suffered a sad loss. Their parents were lost in that air disaster in Chile – perhaps you remember reading of it? There were no survivors.'

'Oh, how dreadful! I'm so sorry,' she exclaimed, instantly distressed.

He inclined his head. 'Naturally their grandmother insisted that they be brought to Lima, where they will stay until Juanita marries and Joaquin completes his education.' He paused, a certain intentness coming into his expression. Abruptly he reverted to English. 'I wonder how much understanding you have of the convention and tradition which govern the upbringing of a girl such as Juanita.'

'I have heard a little of what we think of as the Spanish *grande* way of life,' she said slowly. 'I know that Juanita will have little freedom of the kind we know. Her life and her friendships will be arranged for her and she will accept that it should be so without question. I also know that her marriage will be arranged for her, regardless of whether love enters into it, and that she will be obedient to this as to all other things,' Hilary finished quietly, not letting her gaze falter from the strong stern features of the man who had taken charge of the interview.

'You understand quite a lot,' he said coolly. 'Do you disapprove of the Spanish *grande* way of life?'

'Since you ask, *señor*, I do. This is the twentieth century, not the Middle Ages. You may be shocked that I express such an opinion, but that is a privilege of *my* freedom, *señor*,' she said firmly.

She had spoken defiantly, despite his air of autocracy, and she did not regret voicing her conviction, even though it might cost her job. Then she saw a flicker at the corners of his strong mouth as he leaned back.

'You speak frankly, Miss Martin. Good, I prefer honesty to sanctimonious lip service, even though we can never agree. Yes, I think that you, even with the somewhat questionable aura of this famous permissive swinging London round you, may prove the diversion of which Juanita is in need.'

16

So you admit she needs a diversion,' said Hilary, beginning to feel more and more sorry for the unknown Juanita who was already taking on a sad, shadowy picture in her imagination.

The sardonic flicker appeared again. 'I am not denying it. We are not, in spite of our apparently tyrannical outlook, entirely devoid of understanding.'

'Aren't you afraid I might have a – a questionable influence on her?' Hilary betrayed a trace of annoyance. 'I may whet her appetite for a taste of the freedom I enjoy.'

'Not in the least,' he said calmly. 'The odds are stacked too highly against you, and there is even the possibility that you might find Juanita influencing you yourself to question some of the conceptions you hold so dear.'

'Never!'

'No?' he gestured mockingly. 'Where is that open-mindedness for which the British are reputed? Live and let live, I believe is the way you express it.'

She said nothing, and he went on: 'We will see. However, we digress. Now I must ask you some of these tedious questions. Why do you wish to seek employment abroad?'

'I like travel and strange places.'

'So. But liking travel and strange places is not quite the same as making a new life there for an extended period. Is your home background a happy one?'

'It is. I'm not trying to escape an unhappy home life, if that's what you mean.'

'You are not trying to escape anything else?' The dark gaze was penetrating.

'No!' she flashed. 'And my personal life is no concern of yours.'

He held up his hand. 'Do not protest. You have told me what I want to know.'

'Have I?' Her lips compressed. 'Then perhaps you need ask no more questions about my personal life.'

'You have an extremely good character reference from your former employers. Why did you resign so suddenly for the flimsiest of reasons?' he asked sharply.

She was startled by the abrupt change of angle. 'I wanted a change, that's all.'

For a moment his dark head bent over the card bearing

the agency's details. Then he looked up. 'Very well, I will not press what is obviously a painful matter. Oh, yes, Miss Martin, when a certain fire enters a woman's attitude we may be sure of one thing; that somewhere a man has been responsible. Am I not right?'

Hilary had had enough. She stood up. 'I don't think we have anything more to discuss, *señor*. I wish you luck with your quest and would advise you to employ a little more tact in future if you *must* find an English girl to suit your requirements. Good afternoon, *señor*. I can find my own way out.'

He allowed her almost to reach the door, then he said quietly: 'One moment, Miss Martin. Please hear me out, after which I trust your national repute for fair play will make you desist from hurling accusations of tactlessness at my head. And perhaps I may admit that my approach erred somewhat on the side of tactlessness.'

For a moment she stayed where she was, then slowly she came back. He was standing, his proud carriage very straight, and he did not move until at last she sat down unwillingly on the edge of the chair. Only then did he resume his own seat, and relax slightly, taking a slim, finely engraved cigarette case from his pocket and flipping it open towards her.

'Not at the moment, thank you.'

Without speaking he closed the case and returned it to his pocket. He leaned back. 'Try to be impartial, Miss Martin, and visualize the practical viewpoint; ours. If you were seeking a charming Peruvian girl to assist in the education of your young brother and sister, and you found one who promised to embody all the qualities you sought, and she came to settle in your home, gained the confidence of your family, and then suddenly changed her mind and told you she was returning to South America,' he paused, 'you would be indignant, would you not?'

'Naturally,' Hilary said, 'but a charming, intelligent girl would not undertake a contract unless she was prepared to fulfil it.'

'Not intentionally' he said calmly, 'but if she'd decided on a change of scene because of a broken romantic entanglement her subsequent actions could be unpredictable. Quarrels can be mended, and the call of the heart extremely strong – the feminine heart in particular.' He paused. 'I am not attempting to pry into your personal life, *señorita*, merely to establish that there won't be a man beckoning you back across the seas five minutes after we thought our arrangements had been settled to everyone's satisfaction.'

'Believe me,' he went on, 'that is the sole reason for these very personal questions. Is it not understandable, *señorita?*' He smiled, a smile of such singular charm, totally transforming his sternly cut features, that Hilary felt her earlier resentment melt away. It was perfectly logical, put that way, and perfectly understandable. So much so that . . .

'Yes,' she said flatly, 'and I can assure you that there will be no recall of *my* heart across the sea. Or anywhere else.'

His brows went up. 'It is easy to say. You are sure?'

'Sure.' She looked down at her hands. 'Will it satisfy you if I tell you the man in question wasn't free? And if he was it wouldn't make any difference.'

There was a long silence, then he said briskly: 'Good. Now, there are several matters to be cleared. Visa, vaccination, formalities. And there will be the matter of wardrobe. I think it would be best if—'

'Please!' Hilary half rose and stared. '*Señor*, does this mean you are offering me the job?'

'Of course!' He stared. 'What else? I presume you are still wishing to accept it.'

'Oh, yes. But . . . what about Señora Alvedo? I understood she was to—'

He waved his hand impatiently. 'It is of no consequence. I will tell her when she returns that it is all settled. Tell me, how soon can you be free?'

'I – I—' Hilary struggled against dazedness. 'When will I be required?'

'As soon as possible. Next week, if the arrangements can be completed.' He looked amused at her startled expression. 'It is quite simple. We will make all the necessary arrangements for your flight. You will require suitable clothing additions. Remember that our climate will seem like perpetual summer to you after this . . .' A moment of silence and a frustrated gesture expressed his inability to convey his opinion of Britain's notorious atmosphere, 'and there will be certain formalities with which our Embassy will assist. I will forward you an advance on your first quarter's salary along with your flight ticket and if anything occurs to puzzle you we will deal with it.'

Hilary nodded, more to convince herself that she was taking it all in than to add her contribution to the interchange.

'Regarding your visa; there will be no difficulty in arranging this speedily. Should there be any questions you are unable to answer, keep this by you. I trust it will help.'

He took a card from his pocket-book, wrote on the back, and handed it to her.

She looked down at the black copperplate engraving of the name inscribed there and then turned it over, her lips parting as she read the message he had written. *'Please give every assistance to bearer, Miss Hilary Martin,'* and beneath it the flowing black signature: Romualdo de Pacquera y Zaredopenas.

Dawning comprehension struggled with disbelief as Hilary looked up at the dark eyes in which devilry and amusement glinted. She said slowly: *'You ...* you are the Conde himself?'

He bowed. 'Forgive me for omitting to introduce myself until this late stage. Are you now convinced that all is in proper order?'

She shook her head, then her lips parted to contradict the unconscious negative. She said weakly: 'It seems to be so. I – I wish I had known.'

'You would have been less outspoken, perhaps?'

'Perhaps.' *Or less unguarded!* the small voice of instinct whispered. She sighed, suddenly not trusting herself to remain poised if she tried to hold that perceptive gaze.

'But that was not how I wished it, *señorita.*'

Her lashes drooped like soft silken shields as she opened her bag and tucked the card carefully into the inner compartment. She took a deep breath and stood up, trying to form the suitable phrases for leave-taking. 'Is there anything—?' The tentative beginning died away as she looked up and met the regard that had eroded her poise far more thoroughly than she had suspected.

He had also risen to his feet, to stand motionless with his

fingertips resting along the edges of the folder. His cool regard did not flicker as he said slowly: 'You will forgive me if I make a somewhat personal observation, *señorita*?'

Almost imperceptibly she inclined her head, unable to break free of that invisible bond forged by the sheer magnetism of his personality.

'You are blunt beyond the bounds of discretion, *señorita*, and I suspect you are quick to temper, slow to submit, and outrageously stubborn.' His brows rose, as though defying contradiction, then relaxed as the barest suggestion of a smile touched his mouth. 'But you have a quality of honesty that is rare in a woman. It is for that quality mainly that I make my decision. I trust it will prove a happy one.'

The little silence lengthened and once again Hilary felt that strange constriction robbing her of the ability to make the smooth, guarded responses she wanted to make.

'And now,' the Conde said gravely, 'you will take tea with me.'

CHAPTER TWO

THE quiet reassuring voice of the captain completed his landing announcement and Hilary groped for the clips of her seat belt. The hour of four-thirty was not the most auspicious of the twenty-four, she decided; it was the hour when even the most hilarious of parties tended to falter, the worst time to wake trembling and afraid from the grip of nightmare, the time when the world seemed at its most unfriendly and uncaring, and the spirit at its lowest ebb. Certainly, it was the worst time to be landing at a strange airport, in an unknown land, after a long airborne night extended unnaturally by the crossing of five time zones.

The confusion of the end-of-flight rush for the washrooms settled suddenly. Somehow, everyone slid back into their places, hastily stubbed out cigarettes, and a tense air of order prevailed as the jet lost height and skimmed down towards the runway lights of Lima Airport.

Hilary took a tighter grasp on her personal luggage and tried to convince herself that the tight coil of tension in the pit of her stomach was due simply to the excitement of the longest flight of her life and not to the fact that she'd had the twenty-two hours of that flight with nothing to do except think of the future at the end of it and the whirl of the week preceding it.

Was it a mere ten days since that afternoon she had walked into the Luxor – and into a change of scene drastic enough to delight the most travel-thirsty of fresh-field-seekers? Somewhat to her surprise she had not seen the Conde again after that formal yet delightful afternoon tea she had partaken of with him; his instructions had been lucid and comprehensive, and she had not encountered a single snag in her preparations for the journey. He had telephoned her at her home, only once, and she had been out shopping, and her father had taken the message. Rather disappointingly, it had not required either answer or querying, so there had been no valid reason at all to ring him back, and she knew that he was leaving London the following day to visit Madrid en route for South America. The thought had occurred, quite inconsequently, that if he hadn't had the business detour to make, or if she could have completed all her preparations in a shorter time, she might even have travelled with him. But she had dismissed the idea as fanciful and rather silly; if he considered it necessary to escort her he would suggest it, and if he did it wouldn't reflect much confidence in her ability to assume responsibility . . . all the same, she hoped he wouldn't forget his assurance that she would be met at the airport, even though this was the most ghastly hour to expect anyone to turn out to meet a stranger.

She expected to shiver when she left the plane, but the air was warm and humid, and slightly misty, and the airport buildings held little more individuality at that time of morning than any other international airport. Glass and concrete streamlining did not have nationality, and as she went through the clearance rigmarole dear to officialdom she reflected wryly that reality was proving less exciting than the anticipation of imagination. She passed into the ken of whom she hoped was the last grey-uniformed official.

Briskly he scrutinized her papers, reached for his stamp, frowned, then scrutinized them again. He looked up, and Hilary's heart quailed; what was wrong?

'You are Miss Martin? Miss Hilary Martin?'

'Yes.' She looked anxiously at the stamp which had not descended to make its vital impress.

He looked down again at her papers, stamped them with a flourish and closed her passport. Relief came, only to vanish again as he stood up, her papers still in his hand, and said politely: 'Will the *señorita* come this way, please?'

Now what? Was he going to impound her? And papers and luggage and all? Her imagination working overtime, she followed him along the concourse to a side door which he held open, motioning to her to enter.

There seemed to be only one occupant of the small lounge, and as that occupant rose to his feet Hilary gasped 'Thank goodness!' and made no effort to disguise the fervency of her exclamation.

The Conde came forward. 'There is something wrong?'

'N-no – at least I—'

'Everything is in order, Señor Conde,' the official announced briskly. 'The *señorita*'s papers . . .' He held them out to the Conde and then turned to the door, snapping his fingers smartly. A porter materialized like magic, holding Hilary's cases, and despite her tiredness she felt fresh respect for the Conde. This; after all she'd been warned about . . . *Ah*, mañana . . . *Tomorrow* . . . The official bowed. 'I trust the *señorita* will have an enjoyable stay in our country,' and with a deferential nod to the Conde he departed.

'Well, so you are here at last,' the Conde smiled. 'Have you had a pleasant journey?'

'Yes, thank you.' Suddenly she felt uncertain, and quite unable to say anything else.

'You sound unsure.' His smile faded into an expression of gravity. 'Something is worrying you?'

'No. I thought something was wrong.' She looked up. He seemed to expect some sort of explanation. 'When he – that man – kept my papers and – I didn't expect to see you here.'

The dark brows arched. 'But surely, *señorita*, you did not imagine I would allow you to arrive here at this hour of the night and not meet you to escort you to the villa?'

She said nothing, suddenly aware of weariness now that the tension of the long journey was over and she was actually here at last. He looked down and noted the faint violet shadows under the hazel eyes and the lids that wanted to droop their shadowing fans of dark silky lashes. His own tawny-dark eyes softened.

'You must be very tired after that long flight. Come,' he tucked one hand under her elbow and took her blue airline bag from her, 'my car is outside and it isn't a very long journey.'

Afterwards, she retained only a blurred impression of that car ride through an alien darkness, of a garden scented by blossoms unseen, of a vast salon with gilded frescoes and huge mirrors, a wide staircase opening upwards like a great ivory and gold fan, and the Conde handing her into the care of an elderly, grave-faced woman. Her refusal of refreshments was not countered, but a tray holding milk and biscuits was brought into her bedroom, and when the woman withdrew Hilary lay for a little while, reflecting on the un-expected appearance of the Conde at the airport. It was kind of him to turn out himself to meet her in the middle of the night . . . rather comforting . . .

Her lashes fell against her cheeks and she sighed softly, letting her contours relax and settle into the cool silken comfort of a deliciously soft bed . . . She stirred once or twice, blinked towards the light showing at the edges of the venetian blinds, thought she should check on the time, and slept again before she could reach for her watch, until sud-denly she was wide awake with the uncanny sensation of being watched.

She sat up, and a small voice said solemnly: 'It is twenty minutes after eleven. Are you going to wake up soon?'

Hilary blinked and rubbed her eyes, trying to see the speaker through the dimness as she groped for a not yet familiar lamp switch. The small voice said: 'Shall I undo the shades? I know how they work.'

She located the lamp switch in time to see the little figure carefully sorting out the cords of the blinds. Suddenly they slid open and the bright bars of sunlight spilled across a turquoise and white carpet and the figure of a small boy who turned and regarded her solemnly. He said, 'Is that enough, or shall I send them – *pouf*!' He raised his hands upwards.

'They will do as they are for the moment.' She looked at her small mentor and smiled. 'Did you say it was after eleven?'

He nodded and came to the bedside. 'You are the English *señorita* who flew all the way from England yesterday?'

'I am. And you are . . .?'

'I am Joaquin.' He held out his hand. 'How do you do, Señorita Martin.'

'How do you do, Joaquin.' Equally gravely she accepted the proffered hand and shook it. 'Thank you for coming to wake me.'

'You do not mind?'

'Not at all. I might have slept for—'

There was a movement outside the door Joaquin had left partly open. A light, slightly anxious voice said queryingly: 'Joaquin, where are you? Joaquin – you're not—' There was a small silence, then a tap, and 'May I come in?'

As Hilary called assent the door was pushed open and a piquant oval face topped by glossy, raven dark hair looked round. The tentative smile on the young mouth faded abruptly, to be replaced by indignation. 'So you *are* in here! You are one very naughty boy. You know what you were told.' The rest of a very attractive girl appeared as she advanced into the room. 'Come at once. You are disturbing Miss Martin and she is very tired after her long journey.'

'No, don't scold him,' Hilary said quickly. 'It's high time I got up. If he hadn't—'

The girl came forward. 'No, you are not to get up, not yet. Joaquin, go tell Concepta – the breakfast tray, immediately.'

Looking rather mutinous, Joaquin obeyed, and the girl turned back to a still sleepy Hilary. 'I'm sorry he disturbed you. You are to have breakfast in bed this morning. It is an order.'

Hilary hesitated. 'Are you sure? I have come here to do a job, not to be waited on like – like a special guest.'

The girl gestured. 'It is the Conde's order; that you were not to be disturbed this morning until you felt sufficiently rested, and then breakfast was to be sent to your room. Joaquin has been very naughty and disobedient, and he will have to be punished.'

'Oh no, not for . . .' Hilary got out of bed and searched for her wrap among the things she had taken from her case earlier that morning. She found it and slipped it on. 'I'm very glad he came and wakened me. How do these work?'

'I will show you.' Joaquin reappeared and went importantly to the window to cope with the gaily coloured blinds. 'You just do this, so, and they – *pouf*!'

'Joaquin! You know you are forbidden! Already you break them in your own room. Now come and leave Señorita Martin in peace or she will want to return to England on the next plane.'

His small brow petulant now, Joaquin was escorted from the room, reminding Hilary of a little grandee who discovers that his subjects will not bow to his rule as he hopes. She smiled to herself, suspecting that her new job might be many things but dullness would not be one of them.

Concepta arrived with a beautifully set breakfast tray and the request that the *señorita* must ask if there was anything she particularly wished to her taste. Hilary assured her that it was all perfect and when the little maid had gone she settled down to enjoy an unaccustomed luxury. For several years now she had made it her job at home to take her mother an early morning cup of tea, ever since the attack of pneumonia which had come near to costing Mrs. Martin her life when Hilary was fifteen. Verging on the mid-teen years which all too often produce an impatience towards parents that is more thoughtlessness than lack of affection, Hilary had suffered a salutary lesson and never forgot the vow of thankfulness she took the night when the crisis was passed.

She poured herself a second cup of the delicious coffee and wandered over to the wide french window, wondering inconsequently if her father was remembering the small morning ritual with the tea. She found the window catch and gently pushed one side open, drawing a deep breath of pleasure at the vista before her.

There was a balcony to her room, a traditionally styled one of lacy wrought iron, and it overlooked a garden like a corner of Eden. Immediately below was a terrace, and shallow steps to a path winding between smooth lawns flanked by scarlet verbena and trailing vines of small waxen bell-like flowers. Dreamily her gaze roved on to the sunken rock garden and the pool in which enormous waterlilies swam, to the arbors and the flaunting bougainvillea, the shrubs which cascaded with golden blossoms, the jacaranda trees beyond which the path meandered from sight, and farther away to the left more lawn and a superb swimming pool . . . Hilary leaned over the balcony and sighed again, revelling in the sensuous pleasure of being able to linger on a balcony in a thin nylon wrap, the warm scented tendrils of breeze caressing her throat, and not having to retreat from a sudden squall of rain or the biting attack of an English nor'easter. It was too good to be true; there must be a snag somewhere!

Reluctantly she turned away. She must shower and dress and unpack, and then see about commencing her duties.

An hour later she left her room and looked over the balustrade of the stairway at the great hall below. It seemed deserted, and there was no sound to give a clue to the whereabouts of Juanita and Joaquin. Slowly she descended the shallow stairs and looked uncertainly at her reflection in the big gilded mirror. *Lost?* the girl in the mirror seemed to ask, and Hilary turned away, towards the big double doors opening on her right. She tapped, twice, received no response, and opened one a fraction. It swung soundlessly to her touch and she paused on the threshold, still uncertain and feeling like an intruder. Wishing someone would come and wondering if she should return to her room and wait, she became aware of being watched. It was the second time this morning, and she exclaimed aloud at her silly fancies as she located the cause. Yes, she was being watched, but the eyes were painted!

On the far wall of the room she was looking into hung a large portrait in oils. She stepped forward, instantly recognizing the dark, aristocratic features, and was drawn by those compelling eyes until she was standing beneath the great portrait.

The resemblance was quite unnerving; the smouldering, full-lidded eyes, the lean, slightly aquiline nose, the well-shaped mouth with ruthless determination in its sensuous lines, and the tangible air of authority that would brook no questioning of its domination were the depiction of the living Conde – except for the differences which the strange power of the painting had made nebulous in its first overall impact on Hilary.

Only now did she consciously note the small pointed beard, the stiff cream ruff, the pewter-silver tones where the breastplate caught the light, the warm alizarin crimson of the doublet sleeve and the fall of lace over the strong hand resting on the sword hilt . . . This Conde had been captured in oils all of four hundred years ago. Captured . . .? Hilary frowned. No, that was the last word with which to—

'So you have discovered my ancestor.'

Hilary gasped as the deep tones spoke at her shoulder. She spun round and met the dark living eyes, and the smouldering impact of the reality was infinitely more compelling than that of the painting.

If the Conde noticed her loss of composure he gave no hint of it. His regard intent, he did not allow it to flicker as

28

he remarked coolly: 'You find him interesting?'

'Yes, he – he's very like you.'

The moment the words were uttered she would have given anything to reclaim them. How naïve they must have sounded. But the Conde threw back his head and laughed outright. 'So they all say. Sometimes they go as far as to define the resemblance even further.'

'Oh.' She glanced back to the portrait, perceiving some ambiguity in his words but knowing the hidden foundation for it must remain unknown until she became better acquainted with her new employer – if ever she should become acquainted with him, she reminded herself abruptly.

'May I ask who he was?'

'But of course! We are very proud of him. He served with Pizarro and became a law officer, one of the founders of this land as we know it today. See,' the Conde touched her shoulder lightly, 'here is his helmet and sword.'

She had recovered from her moment of startlement at his unexpected advent and the loss of composure at the unguarded naïvety of her remarks. Interested now, she turned her attention to the other objects in the vicinity of the painting, and their growing significance.

The sword, a wicked tapering blade of Toledo steel, was mounted on the wall and beneath it, on a heavy old cabinet of ebony and bone inlay, rested a finely engraved and polished armoured helmet. She looked up into the dark eyes of the Conde.

'He was one of the Conquistadors?'

The Conde inclined his head.

She reached out and touched the chasing of the helmet. 'There were only a score or so of them at the beginning, weren't there? Pizarro drew a line in the sand with his sword, on the Island of Gallo, and challenged his men to cross it, and so they came to the empire of the Inca,' she said slowly. 'Only a tiny band of soldiers, yet they conquered it.'

'Less than a score crossed that line and made that first venture into unknown territory, facing sickness and perils to discover the land of riches Pizarro was convinced against all argument was there. And when he finally succeeded in surmounting opposition and raising a force it was with less than

29

two hundred soldiers that he toppled the might of the Inca and claimed Peru for Spain.' The Conde turned as he finished speaking and lifted the sword from the wall.

He held it out for her inspection and ran his hand under the length of the blade.

There was something of a caress in the touch of those long, well-shaped fingers, and as he raised his head and looked at her she felt a tremor pass through her. Beneath that polished twentieth-century urbanity ran the fire of Conquistador blood, and the arrogance of his forebears. Hilary was silent. Tales of the Conquistadors were legion, of their valour, their ruthlessness, and their cruelty. They scythed through resistance and took what they desired, whether it was life, or love, or gold.

He said, 'You do not care to be close to such weapons, señorita?'

'Not if there is blood on them, Señor Conde,' she returned, and averted her glance to the painting.

'History is filled with bloodshed. One cannot escape it.' He replaced the sword carefully. 'How well are you acquainted with our history, señorita?'

'Well enough to know that Pizarro and his soldiers raped this land and subjected a brave, cultured people.'

'Who had subjected many others to thralldom,' he reminded her. 'And some of those cultures embraced cruelties such as you would not credit. Practices to make your blood run cold and sicken your heart.'

'In Mexico, yes.' Defiance tinged her tone and she refused to allow herself to be intimidated. 'The Aztecs practised a vile religion, but the Incas were wise and just rulers, even of the tribes they conquered.'

'Not always. They still enslaved them and robbed them of their independence and their possessions, tore them from their homes and territories if they dared to attempt revolt, and bound them within a harsh, rigid régime.'

'But there must be discipline in all ordered societies.'

'True,' he nodded gravely.

'Then you tore up all their roads and destroyed their temples. Wonderful things which can never be built again. Why?' The heat of argument rose in her and her voice quickened. 'Why must conquerors loot and pillage and de-

30

stroy? Is the triumph of conquest itself not enough?'

'You feel very strongly about the sins of my ancestors, señorita,' he said smoothly, apparently unmoved by her vehement outburst. 'Do you feel as strongly about the sins of your own Empirist fathers? Or is that different?'

'Yes, and no. We realize now that we did a great deal we are not proud of, but at least we admit it. We also realize the dreadful ills of our industrial revolution. But we also tried to do some good. We built communications instead of destroying them, we took medicine where it was needed, and we tried to protect minorities.'

'Ah, yes. Philanthropy, even if somewhat misguided. May I remind you that we also brought the Church to dark paganism.' He inclined his head gravely. 'We must have further discussions on the misdeeds of my renowned ancestors, and I must take you to visit the Pizarro chapel where the names of the first Conquistadors are engraved on a memorial tablet. But for the moment we had better return to more mundane matters.'

'Oh, yes.' She recollected the little fact that she hadn't been here much more than five minutes and already she was lecturing her new employer on the sins of his fathers! Suspecting that he was laughing at her, despite his grave expression, she said: 'Yes, señor, I came in search of someone, to inquire about my duties.'

He nodded, touching a bell. 'Please sit down, señorita. Would you like coffee? Or would you prefer something cooler?'

'Coffee, please.' She sat down, choosing a chair where she was out of range of those painted eyes, suddenly aware of shyness, and lapsed into silence.

When the coffee was brought the Conde glanced at a letter the maid had also brought, then put it down and leaned back. He crossed his elegantly clad legs and studied Hilary with musing eyes. 'I do not think there is much more to discuss, señorita. Joaquin is with his tutor each morning, a routine I do not wish to change. Three afternoons each week are occupied by his lessons in music, fencing and French; and most mornings he rides, which does not leave so much time. I should like him to spend the alternate afternoons – after his siesta, of course – and his *meriendo* hour each day with you, during which time I trust his conversational English may improve.'

The Conde paused, his mouth pursing thoughtfully, then he went on: 'It is mainly my niece with whom you will concern yourself.'

Hilary nodded, recalling their original discussion. 'She has finished with school, *señor*?'

'She was in her last term when my sister and brother-in-law were so tragically killed. There was a plan to send her to Europe later this year to a Swiss finishing school, but she was so bereft and distraught at the idea of going so far away from us all that we abandoned the plan, for a while, anyway. Which is partly why you are here.'

Again he paused and a trace of a frown narrowed his dark brow. 'There is one point I must emphasize. I forget if I mentioned the fact that Juanita is heiress to her mother's personal fortune. When she is twenty-one she will be a very wealthy woman. You, *señorita*, will be acting as her *dueña*, and as such will always bear this fact in mind.'

Hilary must have betrayed her puzzlement, for he said firmly: 'You will use your discretion and ensure that she forms no undesirable acquaintances during your outings. Is that quite clear?'

'Oh, yes, *señor*.' Comprehension came to Hilary and an imp of humour bubbled up. 'You mean we mustn't pick up any strange young men while she's in my care.'

His mouth twitched. 'Such a phrase! Pick up. But you have grasped my meaning. Also' – his head went back, considering her – 'you yourself will take care not to pick up any strange young men on any occasion when you are not in *our* care.'

'Yes, *señor*.' Her mouth quivered, but she maintained a suitably serious air and waited.

He fingered his chin. 'I see no other difficulties. Should you have any problems you will come to me, no one else. The children's grandmother is away at present and I do not wish Doña Elena to be worried as she is not in very good health at the moment. Is there anything you wish to ask me?'

'I don't think so,' she said demurely.

'Good. I hope you will be happy with us, *señorita*.'

'Thank you, Señor Conde,' she said formally, 'I'm sure I shall. And I hope your niece and nephew will be happy with me.'

He inclined his head, and she stood up. Obviously the interview was at an end. The Conde moved to the door, then checked. 'There is just one other small point, *señorita* . . .'

She stood very straight and slender, for the moment utterly off guard, and smiled, 'Yes, *señor*?'

'It is the little matter of parading on your balcony *en deshabille*.'

Her smiled died. 'I beg your pardon?'

'I regret that your balcony does not afford quite that degree of privacy. You will forgive me this indelicate reminder?'

Memory filled the blankness and colour flowed into her cheeks. 'Oh—! This morning . . . I didn't think . . . Oh, no, *señor*! It never occurred to me that—'

'That you were observed?'

'No.' Her face felt stiff. 'I'm sorry. I quite understand your objection. I forgot that here it is—'

He held up his hand. 'Please do not apologize. Objection is a harsh word – in this particular context, *señorita*. Personally, I thought your joy of the morning most charming to behold. But a charm, none the less, which I should prefer all and sundry of my household *not* to behold. *Entiendo?*'

'Perfectly, Señor Conde.'

No one could fail to notice the wicked glint in his eyes that marred the otherwise perfect gravity of his composure, and as the full significance of his remarks dawned on her she went scarlet.

He held open the door and she made a decidedly flustered exit.

For a long time she would not forget the eyes of a conquistador, and this time they were not the painted ones!

CHAPTER THREE

HILARY was not sure whether to be thankful or sorry when business took the Conde away from the *quinta* later that day and kept him away almost a week. When she discovered his absence she was suddenly aware of the disquieting sense not unlike that experienced by the novice swimmer when first pushed into the deep end! On the other hand she did not regret the short respite in which to acclimatize herself to her new surroundings and recover from the equally disquieting effect of those final minutes of that interview on her first morning in Lima.

She accepted as natural the trace of stiffness dominating the atmosphere during those first few days. Although she was treated with scrupulous courtesy by family and servants alike, she could not help feeling strange when faced with the confliction of rather aloof formality and emotional excitability which seemed to colour the Latin temperament. The vivid and exotic land of Peru fascinated her, and though shy at first she soon discovered that a smile was an open sesame, that Lima was an attractively laid out and well-kept city, and that the people were open-faced and friendly to the stranger in their midst.

But at the *quinta* it was slightly different.

Joaquin and Juanita were patently on their best behaviour, instructed thus, Hilary suspected, by the Conde himself or their great-aunt, Doña Elena, who was suffering with her arthritic hip at the time of Hilary's arrival and remaining in her own apartment.

Several days passed before Hilary was summoned to present herself to Doña Elena, and, conditioned by Joaquin's and Juanita's awe of their great-aunt, she went prepared to meet an autocrat and discovered a fragile, diminutive old lady whose gracious beauty and manner was completely disarming.

Despite this the charming inquisition was thorough. Doña Elena sat erect, a small indomitable figure in a high-backed carved ebony chair, soft silvery lace at her throat and snowy hair beautifully dressed, and dark eyes which had gained the shrewdness of age without losing the fire of their youthful beauty. First she encouraged Hilary to broach her impressions of her new surroundings, and then proceeded to draw from her quite a lot about her own home and family back in England. She studied the few snapshots Hilary had brought with her, and lapsed into silence for a few moments after she handed them back. At last she said:

'Yes, I think my nephew has chosen well. I was extremely doubtful when I heard of your youthfulness. Oh yes,' she smiled, 'you are very young, a mere two years older than my grand-niece, but two years in youth can effect as great a change as two years in the age of senility. I trust you will use those two years' seniority with wisdom and not allow her to override your discipline.'

'I'll try to do that,' Hilary said seriously, 'but I hope to be friend as well as companion, if she will accept me as such.'

Doña Elena nodded. 'I am sure she will. But there is one thing I would mention concerning yourself.'

Hilary tensed, wondering if it was warning she read in those dark, shrewd eyes.

'You may find our customs strange,' Doña Elena went on, 'and you may meet problems which you have not foreseen. Should you do so, please remember that we will try to understand and advise. We wish you to be happy and contented here.'

'I'm sure I shall be. Thank you – you're very kind.' Impulsively Hilary moved forwards and stooped to kiss Doña Elena's soft cheek. As she straightened she was already wondering if she had offended, but when she looked at the old lady she saw there was a faint glint of amusement in the fine dark eyes.

'I hope I do not need to remind you to be cautious where you bestow your careless English gestures of affection.' Doña Elena smiled. 'Our young men are not accustomed to receiving them from, shall I say, acceptable feminine acquaintances other than family and, of course, elderly matrons like myself. Should you forget, I must warn you that their response might prove more overwhelming than you expected.'

Hilary could not repress a smile. She had a feeling she was going to like Doña Elena very much. She said as gravely as she could: 'I shall remember that warning, Doña Elena.'

'Yes,' the twinkle had disappeared, and Doña Elena sighed, 'I am forgetting; you may not feel inclined for bestowing your affections anywhere for some little time. Forgive me, my dear, for presuming to issue my ill-placed warning. But ...' she sighed again and her eyes held the cynicism that the years can bring, 'times are changing, even here. The old standards are fading, and tradition is becoming something to which one pays lip service but does not always obey. Sometimes I wonder—'

She stopped as a brief tap came at the door. Almost immediately it opened and a tall girl entered. She paused, gave one brief glance at Hilary, and then swept across the room.

It was difficult not to stare a little at the newcomer. Her dark, flamboyant beauty was striking, and her smooth complexion was like amber satin against the dazzling white silk dress that caressed her full, shapely form. There was a regal quality about her and obviously she was someone close to Doña Elena, for warmth sparked instantly in their greetings, whose volubility Hilary had no difficulty in following.

Hilary drew back, hesitating until she could break in to take a polite leave, but Doña Elena turned and gestured, looking at both girls.

'Consuelo – you have not met Miss Martin, have you? She has come from England to help the children with their studies. Hilary, Señorita Navarre is the youngest daughter of my dearest friend.'

Slim cool fingers brushed Hilary's and fell away. The dark eyes made their assessment of the cool, fair girl in ice-blue and shuttered over their conclusion. Consuelo turned back to Doña Elena and smiled with a trace of condescension. 'Yes, Sanchia told me that the Conde had decided to make his own choice. She was a little concerned about this, but I must admit that Miss Martin's accent is excellent.' Consuelo paused, then gave a shrug of dismissal. 'I only hope that she will not influence Juanita to be any more foolish than she already is. Do you know? I saw her riding alone with Ramon last week. I can't believe it was with the Conde's sanction.'

'Is this so?' Doña Elena betrayed shocked surprise. 'Are you certain of this, my child?'

'Certain, even though neither of them saw me,' Consuelo said firmly. 'It is time Juanita realized she is no longer a child and Ramon was reminded that he should not abuse the privilege of his position here.'

Doña Elena shook her head. 'I had no idea that Juanita was in the habit of riding alone with my nephew's secretary.' Her fine brows narrowed over the almost accusing glance she turned on Hilary. 'Is this so?'

'I – I don't know,' said Hilary with some bewilderment. 'I don't even know who Ramon—'

'But of course you don't!' Impatience helped to clear the accusation from Doña Elena's eyes. 'How could you? You have not yet had the opportunity of meeting the young culprit of whom we speak. A most personable young man, but . . .' Doña Elena frowned again and her thin fingers tapped against the silver and ebony cane that lay against her knees. 'Hm, we must speak of this later, when my nephew returns. Now tell me, my dear, what brings you here today?'

'To ask you when Romualdo is returning,' said Consuelo. 'We had no idea he intended to be away so long. Almost a week. You know that Sanchia returned from Madrid yesterday. She is still sad, the poor *querida*. We are hoping the celebration this week-end will lighten her heart. You will all be coming, I trust. You *are* recovered, dear Doña Elena?'

'Why do you think I have nursed this accursed infirmity of mine for almost a fortnight?' the old lady exclaimed. 'Not to be subject to its mercy or otherwise this week-end. I will most surely be with you all. But I speak for myself,' she added wryly. 'For Romualdo I cannot speak, my dear. Who can?'

Yes, who can? Hilary thought with faint amusement when she was able to withdraw a little later and leave Doña Elena and her young visitor deep in discussion over the forthcoming party at the Navarre hacienda, to which some forty guests had been invited. It promised to be quite an

37

affair – even if the Conde failed to return in time to attend. But he would, Hilary decided, unless he was proof against a barrage of feminine outrage. For, from the way Consuelo had spoken, it seemed that his presence was vital to ensure Sanchia's enjoyment of the festivities.

This must be the Señora Alvedo of the interview sessions back in London. The Conde had referred to someone called Sanchia when he had taken over the vetting himself, Hilary remembered, culling from a surprisingly vivid recollection of that entire afternoon's events. So Sanchia was a widow, presumably still very young, and the customary time had arrived to draw her gently from her period of mourning. And her sister Consuelo was naturally concerned for her happiness. But not concerned about Juanita, Hilary decided, making her way along the terrace. There had been a trace of vindictiveness in the way she had informed Doña Elena of her great-niece's apparent misdemeanour.

Juanita was still reading by the pool where Hilary had left her an hour previously when summoned to Doña Elena's presence. She looked youthful and curiously vulnerable as she sat there, a small slender figure in white, her dark head bent over her book. Hilary paused at the end of the terrace, her eyes wondering. What was Juanita up to? She had never even mentioned Ramon, although Joaquin had made a careless reference to Ramon's swimming skill the first time Hilary had swum in the pool. Apparently this Ramon had taught Joaquin to swim during a holiday the previous year.

Hilary had thought nothing of the reference, but now she thought back she remembered Juanita abruptly changing the subject. So far the Spanish girl had been both friendly and amenable towards Hilary, but now Hilary began to wonder if the subdued air of shyness was actually secretiveness. So Ramon was a member of the household, and apparently not a suitable riding companion for Juanita. Spanish convention!

Hilary shrugged off her preoccupation as she glanced at her watch and discovered it was later than she had realized, long past the time to rouse Joaquin from his afternoon siesta.

She went indoors again, her smile reflective. During these

38

early days she had found the new way of life much as she had expected, more leisurely in pace, a different mealtime routine, and a totally different attitude to time, but already she was discovering that in its way it conformed to a pattern as equally regular as that of home, even if disconcertingly alien at times. Now it was lesson time for Joaquin, until about six-thirty, when he would partake of his *meriendo* – a kind of chocolate drink with rolls, which he adored – before being put to bed.

'Joaquin – time to—' She stopped at the door. Joaquin was missing. The small curled-up impression of him still ruffled the counterpane, and there were traces of his having made a hurried if dutiful small-boy toilet, while the much maligned Venetian blinds had been partly opened and now hovered slightly drunkenly two-thirds of the way up the windows.

Hilary juggled them until they completed their run, restored a damp towel to its rail, and turned off a dripping tap in a hand-basin still securely plugged, and went in search of her charge.

'No, I have not seen him.' Juanita put down her book and sighed. 'I'm afraid the novelty has gone thin now he has come to know you. It did not last very long.'

'You mean Joaquin is back to being himself.' Hilary smiled. 'He's done very well to stay on his best behaviour for five whole days. That's a long time for a six-year-old.'

'As long as all the next five days of the future are going to seem to us.' Juanita gave another sigh and stood up. 'Come, I will help you find him. There are three places where we may find him. The stables, the little hut with the generator motor which controls the fountains, or the Conde's library. They are the three forbidden places,' she added resignedly.

The little pump house was empty, and the garden fountains played serenely in the sun, untroubled by the experimental fingers of a small boy, and Juanita turned to Hilary. 'I will go and look for him at the stables, if you like, while you see if he is in the library.'

Hilary hesitated, stables and riding adding up to two immediately, until she remembered that the Conde and his secretary were still absent. 'All right – and *you* keep away from that new horse with the uncertain temper while you're there,' she added warningly. 'Meet you back at the pool.'

She made a purposeful way back indoors, meeting no one but hearing the voices of the servants as they prepared to resume their duties. All seemed silent as she approached the library, but the big double doors were heavy and solid enough to drown any sound within. She opened one and a sharp, guilty scuffle greeted her.

Joaquin was almost but not quite concealed, and she walked briskly down the long room. 'Come on out. I can see you, Joaquin.'

Slowly he emerged from behind a high carved chair, and Hilary's amusement faded abruptly as she looked at him. The conquistador's helmet was now reposing on Joaquin's small dark head, almost obscuring his eyes, and the sword gleamed dully in hands far too tiny to hold it safely.

'Joaquin, for a fine soldier you are badly in need of discipline.' She started towards him. 'Put those back where you found them. Instantly!'

For a moment he hesitated, then mischief sparkled in his black eyes. 'No! I am in command. I shall capture you. Yes! You shall be my prisoner, Señorita Hilary. My Doña Marina, like—'

'Oh no, you villain!' Hilary made a dive for him and knew even as she did so, that she was making a mistake. This was exactly what Joaquin wanted. With a squeal of mirth he darted away, a small boy daring her to pursue him.

He was fleet and nimble, and Hilary bit her lip as he dodged behind a tapestry screen and peeped out tauntingly. He was still brandishing the sword and Hilary stopped, terrified lest he trip and injure himself on the blade. She said as calmly as she could, 'What would your uncle say if he caught you with those?'

'Nothing – because he isn't here.' Joaquin made another triumphant scurry across the room, only to be betrayed by the helmet slipping down and obscuring his view altogether. He stopped to adjust it, and Hilary made a lunge for the sword, her one thought to restore it to its place out of reach.

But she wasn't quite quick enough. Joaquin grabbed at

the same moment and Hilary felt a sharp stinging pain in her arm. She gave an involuntary cry and the sword clattered to the floor as she saw the thin line of scarlet welling on her forearm.

Joaquin stared at her, his merriment ebbing, and she covered the wound with her other hand. She shook her head at him and an expression of fright crept over his small face, incongruous under the deep peak of the helmet. 'It was a good game, yes?' he whispered.

She smiled shakily. 'Yes, my little grandee, and you've won. I surrender. Now, I think we'd better stop playing and put the sword back where it belongs.'

She stooped to pick it up, and Joaquin backed a pace. 'Are you wounded? Really?'

'Yes, really.' The steel felt cold under her hands and the wound burned, but she tried to ignore it, knowing that Joaquin was hovering between fright and guilt, and that it hadn't been entirely his fault. 'Come on, take off that helmet. Then we'll have to get Juanita to play nurse and bandage me.'

But he did not giggle. He sidled round and came close to here, to grasp her wrist with fingers which held that remarkable strength children possess. His eyes enormous, he whispered: 'But I didn't really stab you? That isn't real blood!'

'It most certainly is!'

The chilling tones almost startled Hilary out of her wits. But it was nothing to the effect they had on Joaquin. He stared up at the angry figure neither he nor Hilary had heard enter and cowered back.

'*Tio!* I didn't know! I did not mean—'

'I will hear your explanations later,' the Conde said icily. 'Send Concepta to me, then go to your room.'

The little conquistador quailed, became a naughty small boy faced with retribution, and fled. The Conde turned to Hilary.

She was trying to reach the hooks from which the sword normally hung, and with an impatient gesture he took it from her, closing his other hand round her arm.

'How did this happen?' he demanded.

He looked so furious she recoiled. 'It was an accident. I'm

sorry about your things,' she began quickly, 'but please don't blame—'

The long glance from his dark eyes quelled her, much as it had quelled Joaquin. He was still holding her wrist, staunching the cut with a snowy white handkerchief, then inspecting it with frowning intent.

'It – it's only a scratch,' she said desperately, suddenly aware of a most disconcerting warmth flooding over her. 'Please don't worry about it. I'll—'

'I will hear your explanations also – later,' he said grimly, 'when we have— Ah, Concepta . . .'

The little maid hurried into the room, hastily drying her hands on her apron. 'Yes, *señor?*' she said anxiously. 'We did not hear you arrive, *señor*. We – *Sacramento!*' Concepta saw the sword lying on the creamy rug, the blood-stained handkerchief, and Hilary's flustered face. She threw up her hands and launched into a frantic spate of Spanish.

'Stop – forget it. Go and make the *señorita* a pot of her English tea. At once!' the Conde snapped impatiently, and turned his back on the wildly gesticulating Concepta. He bound the handkerchief about Hilary's arm and steered her firmly towards the door.

Aware that it was futile to argue, she submitted to being led to a small cloakroom near the terrace door. There she was bidden to sit down while the Conde himself ran water into the basin and took a clean towel from the cupboard. His dark features still stern with anger, he bathed the wound and applied a pad soaked with antiseptic.

She could not help wincing slightly at the sudden sting, and his fingers tightened about her wrist with an almost soothing touch until the smarting ceased. Despite this, the strange warmth she did not consciously recognize as pleasure continued to flow over her, along with the sudden, quite uncalled-for activity of her heart.

The Conde was remarking that he had never approved of the adhesive type of dressing because of the impossibility of removing the rubbery residue they left on the skin and with calm dexterity was binding her wrist with bandage.

She shook her head, as though to dismiss the odd little spell of enchantment, and said again, 'It's only a scratch – you don't need to bother.'

42

'It is sufficiently deep a scratch to disfigure your wrist and stain your dress,' he said calmly. 'And why should I not bother?'

'Well, it's – I don't know.' Her composure was lessening every moment. 'I didn't expect it. I—' Again she stopped, aware she was saying all the wrong things. She made herself look up at him and all her old honesty came to the fore. 'You're all so kind. I expected to have to just do my job and – and look after myself when little things like this happened. But you're all just the same, after all.'

He snipped off the two ends and smoothed the neat knot. 'How do you mean; just the same after all?'

'Well, friendly and – and homely. It's just as it might have happened at home. My father always used to make a bit of a fuss when I was a little girl and fell down and hurt myself, and—'

She tailed off. He had straightened, was leaning back against the pale green marble shelf that stretched from the fitted basin to the wall. A shaft of sunlight was catching his lean cheek and throwing the other side of his face into dark shadow, making it difficult to read his expression. 'You mean,' he said coolly, 'you were not sure whether we were going to treat you as a servant or admit you into the atmosphere of a family.'

'Something like that,' she admitted.

'And you are surprised to find we are not as different as you expected? In fact, we are still considerably more tightly knit within the family framework than in your own country.'

She made no response, and a glimmer came into his eyes. 'I trust you are agreeably surprised. I too am agreeably flattered that you realize we are quite human at heart. But I'm afraid I do not feel in the least fatherly in my administrations,' he added sardonically.

Hilary went scarlet. She stood up, knew she was going to flounder in whatever she said, and avoided his gaze. 'Thank you for – for the first-aid, and – and please don't scold Joaquin. It wasn't his fault.'

'No?' He held open the door for her. 'I know my young nephew; and my young nephew knows he is not allowed the freedom of my personal *sala*.'

'Yes, I realize that. I would have stopped him, only I was with your aunt and he wakened from his siesta before I—'

'There is no need of any further explanation,' he broke in firmly. 'I suggest you go and have that cup of tea Concepta should have made ready by now.'

'Yes . . .' she recognized the note of finality in his tone and hesitated by the foot of the main staircase, 'but you are not going to punish Joaquin because of—?'

'Because of you?'

She nodded, and his brows went up.

'If you have forgiven him, then I must. You are the one who has suffered.'

'Thank you.' She smiled at him, unaware of her radiance and filled with a quite inordinate affection for the small cause of her 'suffering'.

The little maid appeared at that moment with the tray and Hilary sighed. She turned away reluctantly, and came face to face with Consuelo.

The Spanish girl looked puzzled and disturbed, and had obviously heard of the small incident. She stared at Hilary, then at the Conde, and finally at Hilary's bandaged arm. 'What happened? You are not hurt?'

'Not in the least.'

Consuelo looked taken aback, almost disappointed. Then she laughed shortly. 'That idiot girl had me believing you were in danger of bleeding to death!'

Hilary said nothing, and a slight smile flickered round the Conde's mouth. He shook his head. 'Not at all. The Señorita Martin has merely crossed swords with a Conquistador and come off somewhat the loser. Is that not so, Miss Martin?'

'That is so.' She returned his smile with a composure she was far from feeling. 'But next time I trust I may be more fortunate, *señor*.'

'Till the next time, then, *señorita*.' He inclined his head mockingly, and she turned away, but she could not help noticing that there was no answering amusement in Consuelo Navarre's expression. In fact, there was born there suddenly a patent dislike.

* * *

44

Remembering this, Hilary was surprised to be summoned to the phone the following morning, to be greeted by an affable-sounding Consuelo. Her surprise increased when Consuelo, after brief, polite preliminaries, issued an invitation to Hilary to join the hacienda party.

'You will forgive me the informality of this invitation,' Consuelo said sweetly, 'but being English you will not mind, I'm sure. It is all the casual approach with you these days, is it not?'

'Sometimes,' Hilary admitted, holding some caution in reserve. 'But I will have to make sure I have the week-end free before I can accept.'

'That is arranged. I have spoken with Doña Elena, and so it is left to you to accept or decline as you wish.'

'Thank you.' Hilary paused, thinking quickly, then made her decision. Why not? 'I should like to accept,' she said formally.

'Then we shall look forward to renewing our acquaintance. Good-bye, Miss Martin.'

Somewhat thoughtfully, Hilary made her way back to the pool and told Juanita of the invitation.

'I am glad,' said Juanita. 'It would have been lonely for you left alone here. Although I believe Tio has changed his mind about going. Some business associate is coming to Lima on Saturday and he must see this man.'

So the Conde would not be at the hacienda. Hilary's spirits did an odd little whirl and settled, rather dully, before she had had time to realize they had even begun the flutter of elation. But how stupid to think that mattered! She must be ... She banished thoughts of the Conde as Juanita started to speak, and experienced fresh surprise.

'Did you say you wish *you* weren't going, Juanita?'

The younger girl nodded, and Hilary noticed she was still wearing the subdued look she'd worn for the last two days. She hesitated, sensing that something was worrying Juanita and wanting to offer comfort, but aware that the budding friendship was still young and that certain reticences must be observed for a little while to come. She said lightly, 'Cheer up, Juanita. It is sure to be a gay affair.'

'I do not like Consuelo, nor do I like their parties,' Juanita said flatly. 'They still treat me like a child and I am seventeen years old. It is ridiculous. They seem to think I am still a *nena*, like Joaquin,' she finished indignantly.

Hilary looked thoughtfully at the beautiful, small oval face. She could see both points of view. At times Juanita glowed with the assurance of a fully mature young woman, at others the childhood so recently left behind was very perceptible. But, thinking of Consuelo, it was not difficult to imagine her being daunted by the older, more domineering girl. Not for the first time Hilary recalled the conversation in Doña Elena's *sala* the previous day. Perhaps Juanita's dislike of Consuelo was not unfounded. The impulse that came then would not be denied. She said casually:

'I am looking forward to meeting Ramon. When will he be back?'

The tension in Juanita's shoulders was instantly discernible. She touched the petals of a flower. 'He should be returning today. Tio sent him to Huaroya where we have our coffee plantation.'

'Do you often go riding with him?'

The reaction to this seemingly casual question gave Hilary an answer before Juanita even spoke. She turned like a startled fawn, dark rose suffusing her cheeks, and gasped: 'How did you know?'

Gently, Hilary told her. 'I've been wondering since yesterday if I should warn you,' she said softly, 'but I didn't want you to think I was being inquisitive.'

'I don't know how she knew,' Juanita said bitterly. 'Only three times have we been able to meet alone, away from prying eyes, and with the luck of Diablo himself *she* is in our path.'

Juanita's slender hands twisted together and her lips showed white as they compressed tightly. 'What are we to do? She will tell the Conde and he will send Ramon away. I know he will. We must think of something,' she said feverishly. 'We must say that we met accidentally, that – that Ramon was riding alone and – and—'

'Have you been forbidden to ride with Ramon?' Hilary asked, worried by Juanita's distress.

'No,' Juanita shook her head and looked up tearfully, 'not exactly. But I knew it was not wise to do so in secret.'

'Secrets like that have a habit of leaking out,' Hilary said

46

flatly, 'but I still don't see what it has to do with Consuelo and why she should go out of her way to tell Doña Elena.'

'Because Consuelo is mean. And she is – how you say? – bossy. But both Doña Elena and my grandmother – the Condesa – have always hoped that the Conde and Consuelo will make a match and unite the two families. Once we thought he might choose Sanchia, but she married another, and now that she is a widow . . . we do not know . . .' Juanita shook her head. 'But because of this Consuelo thinks she can interfere in all our affairs. She has even been heard to refer to him as Ruaz, which only the Condesa is allowed to call him,' Juanita concluded somewhat indignantly.

'I see.' Hilary gave a sigh almost as heavy as Juanita's. 'Do you want to tell me about Ramon?'

'I have loved Ramon in secret for two whole years,' Juanita said mournfully, 'and I shall love him till eternity.'

There seemed little to say to this all-encompassing statement, except for the one question Hilary hesitated to ask. A moment later it was answered. Juanita turned suddenly and seized Hilary's hand. 'Please,' she begged, 'will you help us? Will you promise not to betray us? It means so much to us. You see, Ramon is poor. He comes from a good family, but they are impoverished. And because of this money I will inherit when I come of age they will never allow me to marry Ramon. He himself is desperately conscious of the fact he has nothing to offer me, and that he must work for another. But if I cannot marry him I will marry no one. I will remain an old maid until I die,' she finished dramatically.

'Old maid!' Hilary could not help smiling at the quaint expression. 'How can you *remain* an old maid when you are scarcely seventeen?'

But the glisten of tragic tears in the dark eyes quickly banished her amusement. She said softly, 'Of course I'll do what I can, but you mustn't ask me to deceive your uncle. Not if he's expressly forbidden you to see Ramon.'

'He hasn't, because he doesn't know. No one did, till now.'

'Are you sure that the Conde will be as unsympathetic as you imagine?' Hilary asked, after a moment's reflection. 'Surely he, not Consuelo, is the one to judge if Ramon is a

47

suitable friend—'

Juanita's impatient exclamation checked her. She gave a small gesture and smiled. 'Yes – friend. There's plenty of time before you need think of marriage. Surely you're not barred completely from contact with the opposite sex.'

'I may as well be,' said Juanita despairingly. 'You can't understand, can you, how we must abide by tradition? Oh, why could we not have a liberating influence in this family? Someone with the courage to break free as others have done. We are still living in Doña Elena's youth, not today,' she added bitterly.

Hilary was silent. There was a modicum of truth in Juanita's lament, but on the other hand there was the exaggeration of despair. It was obvious that Juanita had been gently nurtured from birth. Her schooling had been strict but sheltered, she had never been thrust into the fast pace of the average English teenager's life, therefore it was unlikely that she had developed the ability to make judgments or a decision that would not bode heartbreak. She said slowly: 'I still don't think you should try to keep this friendship a secret. After all, you tell me that Ramon taught Joaquin to swim last year. You've obviously enjoyed holiday pursuits together, when Ramon must have been permitted to join you *en famille*, so to speak.'

'That is not enough. I want to marry him.'

'Does Ramon wish to marry you?' Hilary asked dryly, still not convinced that Juanita wasn't enjoying indulgence in an adolescent day-dream built round her uncle's young secretary.

'Of course, but he knows it is useless to ask permission for our marriage. If anyone knew of this he would be sent away.'

For the moment it seemed an impasse. Sighing, Hilary returned Juanita to the diversion of English literature, but she could not help feeling curiosity about the person of Ramon, who had obviously enslaved the young Spanish girl. So she was conscious of a stirring of excitement when she heard that Ramon had arrived back that evening.

At first she experienced disappointment when the moment of meeting came. Beside the Conde, Ramon seemed slight and almost insignificant. He had not the Conde's height and breadth of shoulders, nor had he the Conde's arrogant, assured bearing. But on acquaintance it emerged that Ramon was possessed of a certain charm that might well enchant a young feminine heart.

He was softly spoken, with the liquid dark eyes of the true Latin and the whimsical smile that flashed suddenly – the kind of smile that makes a woman believe it is intended for her and no other woman in the world. His manners were impeccable and his personal grooming immaculate. But was he sincere? And if he was, how would it all work out for Juanita? Certainly he was quite a proficient young actor. There was no trace of a passionate secret lover in his mien as he talked to Hilary in the mellow golden light of the *sala* at sunset that evening.

But the same could not be said for Juanita. Her dark eyes glowed with inner fire and her whole being radiated joy. Hilary felt a wave of concern and impatience. If all were as Juanita stated why did she virtually cry her secret to the world? The old saying, *her heart in her eyes*, flashed into Hilary's mind and at the same moment she felt the presence of other eyes.

The Conde had entered the *sala* and there was a slight frown between his brows.

He moved across the room and it seemed plain he intended to show disapproval.

Acting on impulse, Hilary began to say the first thing that came into her head, mentioning a well-known flamenco singer, and trying to interpose herself between Ramon and the starry-eyed Juanita.

Ramon seized the cue instantly, and the next moment Hilary found herself being invited to attend a flamenco performance with him and some friends. She could do little but accept and settle an evening the following week, but she did not know which was the most daunting: Juanita's hurt expression, or the flash of sheer arrogant disapproval that darkened the Conde's face as she turned to him.

CHAPTER FOUR

THE Navarre hacienda lay in one of the rich, fertile valleys that split the dry coastal plain and provided yet another contrast in a land filled with fascinating diversity of terrain.

The drive took slightly less than two hours and gave Hilary her first real sight of the countryside outside the city. Joaquin was full of excitement and appointed himself chief pointer-out of landmarks he considered of main importance, and Doña Elena nodded approvingly as he identified the distant snow-capped peak of Cerro Huascaran, the highest mountain in Peru.

Only Juanita remained silent and withdrawn, responding in a small voice when addressed but showing no joyous anticipation of the week-end ahead. It was plain she had not yet forgiven Hilary's small intervention the previous day and when the party reached the hacienda and were greeted by Consuelo and Señora Navarre she slipped away afterwards with barely a word of excuse.

Doña Elena frowned slightly and Hilary gave a small inward sigh. Courtesy forced her to remain in the group until Doña Elena was drawn away by her old friend, Joaquin was claimed by two small boys somewhere near his own age group, and she was left to face the delicately arched tilt of Consuelo's brows.

'Sanchia will be with us soon,' the Spanish girl said smoothly, 'and you need not worry about your young charge. He has visited with us before.'

Hilary nodded, aware of the subtlest allusion that she was not quite a guest, and waited politely for Consuelo to make the next move. They were standing on the shaded terrace, overlooking a broad lawn edged with brilliant flower beds, and behind them the big terra-cotta tiles stretched like a checker-board under the old Spanish Colonial style balcony of the floor above. The cases had been taken indoors by the chauffeur, and the small flurry of the guests' arrival had now dissipated.

Consuelo turned. 'Pepita will be here in a moment and

she will show you to your room. If there is anything you wish she will attend to it.'

The other girl sounded faintly bored and again Hilary could only nod and murmur an acknowledgment. She could hear the voices of Joaquin and his companions from somewhere at the side of the house, but the children themselves were not in sight. Hilary hesitated, then said: 'I wonder where Juanita is. Perhaps I should find her.'

'Ah yes.' Consuelo's brows arched again. 'The *pequeña* appeared to be somewhat upset today. She is not indisposed, I trust.'

'I'm not sure,' Hilary said guardedly.

'She is at an excitable age,' the other girl said in an off-hand manner. 'No doubt she will soon be imagining herself in love with every attractive young man she meets.'

'I don't think so.' Coolness entered Hilary's tone. 'You must remember that it's little more than two months since she lost her parents.'

'How could I forget?' Consuelo said softly. 'Ah, here is Pepita. We will see you in the *sala* later. *Adios*.'

'*Adios*,' murmured Hilary under her breath as she followed the little maid to the small bedroom she had been allotted; already she knew her initial wariness of Consuelo had not been misplaced.

She was not surprised to discover that her room was a considerable distance from those of Joaquin and Juanita, or that it faced the full heat of the sun and was stifling and airless. She was not going to allow that to worry her unduly; it was only for two nights and then she would be back in her own delightfully comfortable room at the villa. After a quick freshening of her face and hands she went in search of Juanita. As she had suspected, she found her sprawled on her bed, a tray with biscuits and an iced drink at hand, and an opened magazine face down on the pillow. She turned her head when Hilary entered, then returned her sombre gaze to the ceiling.

'Have you got a headache?' Hilary asked softly, standing by the bed.

'No.'

'Is there anything I can do?' Hilary asked after a brief pause.

'No.' Juanita turned her head. 'Why do you not have a siesta like everyone else? You always wander out even on the hottest days.'

'Mad dogs and Englishmen . . .?' A ghost of a smile curved Hilary's mouth. 'I couldn't go to sleep in the middle of the day even if the weather was like a furnace. Besides, we've only just got here. I'd feel as though it was bad form to retire to my room straight away.'

Juanita made a small movement of her shoulders and did not reply. After a moment or so Hilary sat down on the edge of the bed.

'It isn't that, and you know it,' she said bluntly. 'I upset you last night by trying to help you. Won't you believe that? I did it for the best.'

Suddenly Juanita sat up, and her oval face was bitterly accusing. 'You have been here less than two weeks and already you have made a date with Ramon. The very first time you meet him. Is that how you try to help me?'

'Oh, no!' Hilary was so surprised she could have laughed, had not the situation been so sad for Juanita. Her expression gentle, she tried to explain a motive that should have been instantly clear to Juanita and the reason so obvious for her acceptance of Ramon's invitation.

'If I'd refused it would have made it even more awkward with your uncle being there,' she went on. 'Don't you see? Ramon knew instantly that I was helping to cover up.'

'Cover up?' Juanita frowned, plainly wanting to be convinced but not sure. 'I do not understand.'

'It's a very old ploy, or trick. If two people are in love and wish to conceal it for any reason they pretend an interest in someone else. Ramon certainly didn't intend to ask me out anywhere,' Hilary said firmly, 'but it just happened because you were looking so starry-eyed, and your uncle was watching, and I remembered what Consuelo had said about the riding, and so . . .' she shrugged. 'That's how it was.'

'I see. So you and Ramon will pretend to have an affair so that my uncle does not suspect us.'

'Well, not exactly.' Hilary experienced a flutter of alarm. 'It was a momentary impulse. I don't intend to have an affair with anyone, certainly not Ramon.'

'You don't like Ramon?'

'Not that way. He's very charming and very attractive, but I could never fall in love with him.'

'He is wonderful.' Juanita heaved a sigh and wrapped her arms round her knees. 'I shall love him for ever and ever.'

'Yes, but it's going to be difficult to keep it secret if you go around looking like you did last night,' Hilary said dryly. 'I've heard about the language of the eyes and how a Latin can enchant without words, but I'd never realized just how telling it was. However, that wasn't what I was going to say. I've had an idea.'

Juanita glanced at her, looking more hopeful. 'Yes? About us?'

'Why shouldn't you come with us to the flamenco?'

'Tio would never allow it?'

'Have you asked him?'

'It would be useless.'

'Well, *I* will ask him.'

'His answer will be no. In fact, he may object to you going with Ramon.'

Hilary's mouth tightened. 'He'd better not. Your uncle is most kind and charming, but he must not dictate to me what I do in my free time, or there'll be sparks flying.'

'Sparks?' Juanita giggled, having regained her good humour. 'But you do not know my uncle. He is very wise and he does not like to be defied, and he can be very very angry if he is not obeyed.'

'I suspect that, but with all due respect to him my situation is somewhat different from yours, *querida*. As long as I do my job, for which he pays my salary, exactly to his satisfaction, he can't criticize my actions in my personal life.'

'That is how you look at it,' Juanita said steadily, 'but you will find that it is different, so don't say I did not warn you.'

'I won't,' Hilary promised, and dismissed the serious little warning immediately as born of Juanita's still childlike awe of her uncle, the Conde. But she herself was different, Hilary decided, the prickles of indignation still sharp at the idea of the Conde trying to impose the same standards of conduct and restrictions on herself as on his young niece. He would never dream of questioning her personal affairs.

53

Perhaps if she had pondered the thought a little more deeply she might not have dismissed this outrageous idea quite so quickly, but the sudden squeals of childish voices raised in argument distracted her attention. With a murmur to Juanita she went to the french windows which gave access to the balcony.

Below, three small flushed and excited boys were wrestling fiercely for possession of a large ball. As she smiled and Juanita came to her side the little group broke apart leaving Joaquin the victor, triumphantly clutching the ball.

'I tell you no!' He sprang back and bounced the ball. 'Not that way. Pele would do this! This way!'

He aimed an almighty kick which sent the ball soaring over the boys' heads and the scarlet hibiscus hedge that bounded the lawn.

'Olé!' Hilary applauded, then stifled her laughter as an angry cry came from beyond the hedge.

The smiles of the three small football enthusiasts also faded as Consuelo appeared. Her dark features were furious as she brushed at a smudge on her hitherto immaculate cream dress and a torrent of rage broke from her when she saw the culprits. Joaquin stood his ground, his small face defiant, and said stiffly: 'I did not mean to hit you, Señorita Navarre. We did not know—'

But Consuelo ignored him. She had seen Hilary on the balcony. She glared upwards and cried: 'Can you not control these children? Do you see what they have done? It is a disgrace! My dress is ruined! You—'

'I'm sure it isn't.' Hilary kept her voice even. 'I can't even see any mark on it.'

'You can't?' Consuelo gestured. 'You are not even trying. Why are they not having their siesta instead of behaving like young *picaros*?'

Hilary sighed. Perhaps the ball *had* left a trace of dust on Consuelo's person, but did she have to go on like this? Joaquin was gazing up anxiously while the other two culprits were quietly stealing out of the way. She said placatingly: 'They've had their siesta. You can't expect three healthy children to sit and twiddle their thumbs all day. I'm sure they didn't do it on purpose – in fact they didn't – I saw it.'

The placating quality disappeared from Hilary's tone and

54

she added firmly, 'I'm sure it'll brush off if you—'

'It will not! The dress is ruined and I shall never wear it again,' Consuelo declared dramatically. She swung round. 'And it is all your fault, Joaquin. Your uncle shall hear of this. Go indoors instantly, all of you. I shall see that you are punished.'

'I think not!' Suddenly Hilary lost patience and began a rapid descent of the stairs at the end of the balcony. The pink flush of annoyance was in her cheeks as she faced the angry girl. 'It was entirely accidental. I doubt if they even knew you were there. But they will apologize, and *I* will personally remove the mark from your dress. And that will be the end of it. Children!'

They came meekly, to Hilary's secret surprise, and Joaquin apologized meekly, giving a small bow as he did so, and the other two followed his lead. Hilary suspected that imps of mischief lurked in the dark eyes, but when they glanced up at her, as though to seek her approval, their faces were so utterly solemn as to disarm the most suspicious disciplinarian.

But Consuelo was not mollified. She seemed about to break into further upbraiding, then muttered something that Hilary could not catch and flounced away. The moment she was out of hearing Joaquin moved nearer to Hilary.

'Will she tell Tio to punish us? I did not mean to hurt her, Señorita Martin.'

'I know you didn't. But if she does tell him then *I* shall tell him the truth. I'm sure he will understand that it was an unfortunate accident.'

Joaquin looked slightly less worried and in a very short time he had become his normal imperious little self. Not so Consuelo. When she reappeared, having changed into a superb white and black outfit, her expression made no secret of her dislike when she saw Hilary.

She was accompanied by a slender, graceful young woman whom Hilary had not seen before. Juanita whispered: 'That is her sister Sanchia. You will find her more pleasant than Consuelo – sorrow has made her sweeter.'

Whether Juanita's terse little surmise were true or not, the sad-eyed young woman was entirely different in temperament from her sister. Sanchia was softer-voiced, more restrained in her gestures, and with a graciousness entirely devoid of arrogance.

Hilary warmed to her, and almost straight away discovered that Sanchia was the Señora Alvedo with whom she should have had that well-remembered interview weeks back in London.

Sanchia was rueful, smiling with recollection. 'I was so excited that day – I had only two days in your city and I wanted so much to see your wonderful shops, and it was the first time I had been to Europe since – since my husband . . . You understand?'

'Yes, I do understand,' Hilary said gently.

'And of course my English is not so clear as your way of mine, and I was wondering what I should say to Romualdo that there was no one suitable.' Sanchia sighed. 'They were all so hopeless. That child with the bangles and beads, and then she had the chewing gum as well . . .'

'Miss Jones?' Hilary remembered the jaunty young hopeful with her fears lest the job should prove another *au pair* 'swizz'. 'I think she'd had an eye-opener with her previous job.'

'Eye-opener?' Sanchia looked puzzled, then nodded. 'I know – surprise. If only I had seen you first then I could have saved nearly all my afternoon. And to think that I went away and left you to Romualdo's tender mercies! Have you forgiven me yet?'

'Nothing to forgive – anyway, it wasn't quite as bad as that,' Hilary laughed.

'I am not so sure.' The amusement faded from Sanchia's dark eyes, leaving the lingering sadness that was never far from her face. 'The Conde can be quite – how would you say it? – intimidating to those who are not *intimo*. Sometimes I am thankful that he is not head of our family, but I dare not say this to Madre!'

She was silent for a moment, then exclaimed quickly, 'But I talk too much of myself! You are happy here?'

'I'm loving every minute of it,' Hilary said without an instant's hesitation.

'*Bueno!*' Sanchia clapped her hands and glanced round. 'We must drink a toast to that. Where is Consuelo?'

But Consuelo was not to be seen. The little maid came

56

from the house and Sanchia asked her to bring wine, then turned to Hilary. 'You must not mind my sister. She is one of her – how do you say it? – Tizzy? No, pique, because I will not let her manage me again. It is different for me now. She has never escaped from the family, but for three years I travel and live all over the world with Carlos. We became – cosmopolitan. So marvellously free. And now,' she sighed, 'I must conform again, or live alone, unless I marry again.'

There was a small silence of understanding. Then before either of them could speak a big station wagon swept into view down the long curve of the drive. Sanchia sat up rather abruptly, and from nowhere Joaquin and his two small friends rushed down the drive to greet the big, broad-shouldered man getting out of the station wagon.

'It is Señor Gilford,' said Sanchia, relaxing back again. 'He is from the neighbouring hacienda. It is – oh, three times larger than ours. He—'

Her words faded as the boys and the newcomer approached. He was deeply tanned, pleasantly featured, and his fair hair was bleached to pale gold with hours spent in the hot sun. Joaquin was demanding: 'Are you going to the *corrida* today, Señor Gilford?' and the fair man was responding: 'We are all going to the *corrida, amigo.*' His smile changed as he saw Hilary's companion.

'Hello, Sanchia,' he said quietly.

Hilary's impulse to cry out: *You're English!* was checked. She waited till Sanchia returned his greeting and made a normal introduction, and Bruce Gilford made the exclamation instead.

'I might have known – one look at that complexion,' he said delightedly, holding both her hands in his. 'I'd heard the British colony had increased by one a few days ago. Now what part? Let me guess.' He narrowed brilliant blue eyes and pretended to think hard. 'London?'

She smiled happily. 'Surrey.'

'So we're still neighbours.'

'Señor Gilford is what is known as a true man of Kent, I'm told,' Sanchia put in.

'Is that born north or south of the Medway?' Hilary asked. 'I can never remember.'

57

'Neither,' he grinned. 'It's east. A Kentish man is born west.'

'I think perhaps your geography is not quite as good as your languages, Hilary,' said Juanita teasingly, who had come quietly to join the group.

'Well, who cares about geography?' Bruce Gilford laughed. 'This is wonderful.'

Hilary thought so too. Suddenly the day had become alive. Only one thing worried her, and a little while later she was able to confide the worry to Bruce Gilford during a moment when they were alone.

'It's the *corrida*,' she said uncertainly. 'I dread it.'

'A lot of Englishwomen do. But you don't have to go.'

'I'm not sure,' she said slowly. 'I had no idea that it was on the agenda today – I thought there was just going to be high jinks after dark – you know, dancing and eating and drinking.'

'That comes later.' He grinned. 'I can see you've still got quite a lot to learn yet. When we get back from the *corrida* there'll be a tremendous party feast, then the singing and high jinks. It'll go on half the night.'

'Yes.' She frowned. 'But I wish I could get out of the bullfight. It's horrible.'

He was silent, and she knew there was little he could do to help her avoid an entertainment she found distasteful. Already she had got off to a bad start with Consuelo; she could not risk giving further offence by refusing to fall in with her host and hostess's arrangements. Besides, she was bound to accompany Juanita and Joaquin.

They were preparing to leave now. Already some of the guests were getting into the cars and driving off, and Joaquin and his friends were waiting impatiently, having been promised that they could ride with Bruce in the station wagon.

Hilary's faint hope that perhaps Juanita might have wished to cry off was quickly doomed. Juanita seemed to be looking forward to it, judging by the smile of anticipation in her eyes, and Hilary could do nothing but try to repress her misgivings and follow Juanita into the car.

The *plaza de toros* radiated its taut, smouldering excitation long before the Navarre party assembled in the tier

58

almost immediately above the *barrera*. Music blared from the speakers, music as martial and fiery as the blazing colours of the matadors' suits and the golden sunlight pouring through the slight haze hanging in the air, a thousand voices sounded and made a curious high-pitched babble that stretched like an intangible canopy above the great yellow circle of sand, and a smell compounded of dust, heated human bodies and animals invaded the nostrils to exhilarate or evoke the sickness of revulsion.

Bruce Gilford was at Hilary's side for a few moments before the crush at the entrance separated them. He said softly: 'It's an excitement you have to experience once in a lifetime – if only to have a sound basis to argue from. You're not going to let the flag down, are you?'

'I'm not thinking about the flag,' she said sharply, 'I'm thinking about the bull.'

He put an arm lightly between her shoulder blades to guide her up the steps. 'I'll sit next to you and hold your hand if it gets too much for you,' he said softly.

But it didn't work out that way.

Joaquin wriggled between them, his young voice shrill and excited, and Sanchia moved nearer, with an elderly man and his son who had been later arrivals at the hacienda that morning. Consuelo was with Don Alonso and his wife, from the neighbouring ranch of which Bruce Gilford was manager, and Juanita was moving on ahead with two other guests. When eventually they were all in their seats, strung in a long row of faces mostly unfamiliar to her, Hilary was sitting between strangers. She leaned forward, saw Bruce sitting between Joaquin and Sanchia about five places along, and then settled back, taking off her dark glasses. Almost immediately she replaced them. They provided a symbolic if frail guard against that which she had no desire to see. Suddenly the music stopped. The crowd was silenced, and Hilary saw the gateway to the *toril* was opened. The hush in the vast *plaza* gripped and imprisoned the senses, and the bull ran into the centre of the great yellow circle.

There was the audible sighing sound of a thousand breaths expelled, and a strange stab of fear and fascination ran through Hilary, as the massive black creature wheeled to face its persecutor.

It began; the play of scarlet and yellow capes, the picadors and the sweating horses, the *bandilleros* with the tawdry ribbons, the cheers and jeers of the crowd, the rising blood-fever of spectacle and the glittering, weaving, dancing figure of the matador, and the central dominant power of the enraged bull.

Long before the second barb was quivering, transfixed, Hilary knew she had to get out or make a fool of herself. The sight of scarlet on the glistening black hide did not induce the feminine weakness of sickness or fainting; it roused in her an anger of humanity and an anger of impotence because she could do nothing to stop the barbaric spectacle. Thankful that she was within a couple of places from the end of the row, she rose and slipped past the knees of her neighbours, murmuring, '*Perdone . . . Siento mucho que . . .*' until she reached the gangway and passed the sweetmeat sellers, the favour purveyors, the uniformed duty officials, to reach the comparative peace of the outer grounds.

There she halted, taking a deep breath and looking about her, before she began to walk slowly in the direction of where the cars were parked. Her head was throbbing with the effect of the heat and the noise and her hatred of a sport to which, despite her wish to understand impartially the many aspects of the Latin temperament, she could never reconcile her hatred of all inflicted suffering. She raised her hand to the soft chiffon bandeau which held her hair drawn tightly back from her face and slid it free, letting it loop over her arm while she ran her fingers through her hair, sighing softly at the release it seemed to give as the soft fair cloud flowed free about her face.

She slowed to a standstill, the question of what she would do next not yet occurring. Not one of the party had noted her precipitate flight, no startled comment had followed her and no hand reached out to check her, and she was conscious only of thankfulness to be alone and out of it all. Through her distress the first practical thought began to form, telling her of an intense need for a drink, only to be banished by the sound of footsteps. The last voice in the world she expected to hear at that moment said sharply:

'*Señorita – are you ill?*'

She spun round and came face to face with the Conde.

'You!' she gasped. 'But I thought you were away!'

'I was, but my business colleague was summoned to deal with a personal emergency.' His dark patrician features tightened with impatience. 'You have not answered my question. I saw you leave the *corrida*. Are you ill?'

'No, just sickened.' The shock of seeing him was subsiding and anger returning. 'I couldn't stand it a moment longer. It's inhumane. I don't know how anyone can sit and enjoy, *applaud*, such a barbaric entertainment. Sport!' she cried fiercely. 'It isn't sport! It's an anachronism. It belongs to a medieval mentality, along with bear-baiting, and cock-fighting, and—'

'One moment.' His dark brows drew together. 'You are speaking of the *corrida*?'

'What else? I think—'

'I think you know nothing at all on which to base such sweeping condemnation of something which is not merely a sport. It is an art, and a symbol of man's supreme courage.'

'Courage?' She made no attempt to disguise her scorn. 'Whose courage? Man's supreme egotism, you mean.'

'Would you care to face one of those creatures?' he asked, his composure remaining controlled. 'There is no pretence for the sake of showmanship, and the bull does not always lose. The *corrida* can mean death, *señorita*.'

'And that's why I hate it,' she flashed.

'Can't you see, it panders to the worst element in human nature? People go with the same secret dread they go to a circus. There is always the risk that the trapeze artist will crash to the ring. This is the excitement, the attraction, but very few people will admit it.'

'And this would blind you to the grace and the skill?'

'Yes.' She took a quivering breath and turned away. 'But not because I do not admire that skill and courage. I do, and grieve to see it squandered. Man is given the priceless gift of reason, Señor Conde. He can make the decision to squander or risk his life, but an animal is not given that choice. It fights, or kills merely to survive, and if man chooses to inflict pain on it then it has no choice but to defend itself. And man calls it sport!' she exclaimed bitterly. 'I loathe violence and suffering, whether of man or beast, and there is

61

more than enough of it in the world without deliberately causing any more.'

There was a brief silence, and the air seemed filled with a curious hush. From a long way off she heard the sound of the crowd within the *plaza*, and with a dull stab of pain she knew what it signified. *El Toro* was dead.

She felt light but firm hands on her shoulders. Slowly the Conde turned her to face him. He said quietly: 'For a cool little English maid you feel very deeply and with a strange perception, do you not?'

She could not reply or look up to the hot revealing light of the sun. All the anger was purged from her now, leaving sadness, and a feeling of being alone and without defence in an alien sphere. There was only the outline of the man who towered above her, the dark brown tie of fine silk with the narrow bar of gold glinting level with her eyes and blurring a little against the oyster silk of his shirt. A movement blotted out the glint of gold, and a hand tipped at her chin, warm round the delicate bone structure that protested obstinately against the light pressure.

He studied the small set oval with the flush of apricot tinting the soft roundness of her cheeks and with one long curved forefinger he brushed lightly at the single big sparkling diamond of moisture that had escaped the lowered veil of lashes.

'I think you have something in your eye, *chiquita*. A speck of dust, perhaps. If you blink hard against this handkerchief it may come out.'

The soft white lawn feathered below the shielding lashes and the big sparkling drop vanished. She blinked, and her chin tilted proudly without any further assistance. 'Thank you, *señor*. It has gone now.'

'I am glad.' His dark head inclined slightly to one side. 'I think perhaps this is not the moment to continue our discussion of the finer ethics concerning the *corrida*. Permit me, *señorita*.'

He placed an escorting hand beneath her elbow and turned towards the long line of cars. Automatically she walked forward, then stopped, turning a puzzled glance up to the dark chiselled profile. 'But the others, *señor*? Should we not wait for them?'

'I think not. It will be some time before the *corrida* is over.'

'Yes, but the children. I should . . .' She still hesitated.

'I have instructed Ramon to ensure that they remain close to the party. Do not worry, *señorita*, all will be well.'

'But – don't you wish to return to the *corrida*? You *were* there, weren't you?'

'So many buts!' The Conde snapped his fingers and a small urchin appeared as though by magic. While the Conde produced car keys and in a leisurely manner opened the passenger door and handed Hilary into the interior the urchin went into action with duster and leather on the windscreen. The Conde flipped a coin and the urchin grinned a perky, '*Gracias, señor*', as he caught it neatly.

The luxurious American limousine purred into action and the delicious coolness of its air conditioning began to fan gently against Hilary's flushed face. She wondered where he was going and stole a discreet glance sideways, but the coolly arrogant profile was remote, intent on the driving scene, and she stayed silent. For a fleeting space she allowed her gaze to rest on the hands which held the car in effortless control. They were well-shaped, as immaculately kept as a woman's, but there any effeminate comparison ended. There was too much suggestion of supple steel in their lean lines and a dexterity that would not fumble at whatever skill their owner might command of them, whether it be of craftsmanship or control – or the finessing of a woman.

She must have sighed, for he said, 'You are feeling recovered now?'

'Yes, thank you.' She relaxed, a wry smile curving her mouth. Why did he have the power to disarm her so easily? Even as he left her in no doubt as to who held complete mastery, no matter what the situation. Somehow it wasn't fair!

In a very short time she recognized the outskirts of the city and wondered if for some reason he was returning to the villa. But he drove directly into the city centre, eventually pulling up outside the Hotel Bolivar. He turned to her, and now there was a hint of devilish amusement in his eyes.

'I believe I detected the first trace of a little nostalgia this afternoon, a certain *anoranza*, which I must deal with.'

'Oh . . .' she bit her lip, taking in the façade of Lima's premier hotel and suddenly conscious that she must be looking anything but her best. 'Señor, I appreciate your thoughtfulness, but—' she gave a soft rueful laugh, 'I feel dreadfully untidy to go in there.'

'Nonsense. You look charming.' With arrogant eyes he surveyed her. 'And I am sure the powder room mirror will not have the effrontery to contradict me.'

She steeled herself to remain unconvinced in face of this blatant Latin chivalry and slipped from the car. The Conde escorted her into the hotel as gravely as though she were a princess and paused. 'I will await you in the main lounge – but please do not argue *too* long with that mirror, *señorita*.'

Small tremors of excitement started to bubble up within her as, outwardly calm, she quickly dealt with dust and stickiness. The day had come right again; it held anticipation again – pleasurable this time.

Four of the five minutes she had mentally allowed herself had elapsed when she had applied touches of fresh make-up and combed her hair into sleek shining order. Instinctively she delved in her bag and swore softly under her breath when her missing hairband failed to come to light. She must have dropped it outside the *plaza de toros* – unless she'd dropped it in the car. She would have to leave her hair loose and remember to look on the car floor afterwards . . .

But long before she stepped back into the car she had forgotten the bandeau. The certain emphasis behind the Conde's observation earlier about nostalgia took on fresh meaning. As though with a wave of a wand he transported her from the sultry hot colour of sub-tropical Latin America to the peaceable leisure of tea in an English spa hotel. The English tea-room in the Bolivar recaptured it very aptly. Pink and white marble, flowers, waitresses wheeling trolleys of delicious cakes, scones and strawberry jam, real English tea from a silver teapot, the buzz of chatter in the background, and the Conde at his most urbane; elegant, a faultless host and companion, superb as only he could be . . .

Hilary was silent with content when it was time to leave. Her eyes smiled as he put her into the car, and there was the tiniest suggestion of laughter lilts at the corners of his mouth

64

as he took his place at the wheel. They lingered there for quite a while, until the city limits had been left behind and the spread of the city lay like a Cubist serration of white concrete and glass outlined against the great backdrop of the Andean foothills.

The Conde was the first to break the silence. Without allowing his attention to flicker from the road he observed calmly: 'You see now that we do not entirely neglect the more restful aspects of life.'

'Yes,' the smile still softened Hilary's eyes, 'I see also, señor, that you never do things by halves.'

'By halves? In what way, señorita?'

'By half-measures.' Her voice was cool, giving no indication of the small bubbling tremors that were beginning to effervesce again. 'You do not do things in a careless way as we sometimes do, agreeing or taking a half-hearted course of action because it's less bother than refusing.'

'Ah, you mean that we are more positive in our reactions? Or more obvious in our approach?'

'Not exactly. Positive, yes,' she said carefully, 'but obvious – no.' She watched a large flock of birds flying in darkening waves across the sunset and thought that 'obvious' was the last epithet to apply to the enigmatic Romualdo de Pacquera y Zaredopenas.

The dark flight of the birds diminished in the westering sun, and the silence in the car seemed to wait for Hilary to break it. Suddenly she was uncertain of herself – and her autocratic companion. Had she offended? She had been extremely outspoken after the *corrida*; only now in the cooler realm of retrospect could she realize how outspoken. But he had been aloof rather than angry, almost patronizing had he not too ingrained a courtesy ever to betray such a lapse of behaviour. And he had taken her to tea, during which not for one single second had his impeccable manner wavered – nor the mocking charm with which he had masked her giveaway emotion. *Something in her eye!* None of it added up to the behaviour of someone angry or offended, or both. Unless ... An appalling possibility suggested itself and filled her with horror. What if he had been teaching her a lesson in manners? When in Rome ...

She turned her head to seek the gravely composed profile,

fully expecting to read there some unguarded indication of what he really thought.

As though in response to the small silent seeking, one dark brow lifted.

'So you believe you are beginning at last to understand us?'

She skimmed her gaze back to the road ahead, a strange sense of relief coming now that it seemed she had let her imagination run riot. She said carefully: 'No, I don't think I would presume to understand anyone, not after too brief an acquaintance, señor.'

'Is that how you think of us – of me? As an acquaintance?'

His tone had changed. She knew she had not imagined the clipped note that had entered it and she said hastily: 'I – I wasn't defining it specifically – not as any one person. Certainly not yourself, señor.'

There was a silence. The Conde slowed behind a cart heavily laden with cotton bales and waited until he had pulled out to overtake before he remarked coolly: 'I find that rather interesting.'

She restrained the obvious little prompting when he paused, and waited.

'It confirms something that I have long suspected of the English,' he continued in the same cool tones. 'You will never commit yourselves emotionally to strangers, or acquaintances, except in anger.'

'I think that's a fairly universal failing,' she defended. 'It isn't confined to us.'

'We will leave the universal aspect out of it for the moment, I think, and confine the discussion to us.'

'Us?' Her glance swept sideways.

He gave an almost imperceptible nod. 'Narrowing our canvas, metaphorically speaking. I am interested in the exchange of comparisons regarding our diverse temperaments.'

'Do you think we should exchange such comparisons?' she said after a long hesitation.'

'You mean on a personal basis?' He took a bend at fifty and the car held the road effortlessly. 'You object?'

'N-no, I don't object.' She stared straight ahead, 'But

I am not very sure what you mean by a personal basis, *señor*.'

'Our assessments of – I shall say "foreigners", although I dislike the term – must be based on our reactions to them and their culture, and coloured by the impression we gain of their behaviour. Impressions which can be misleading. You agree, *señorita*?'

'Oh, yes. Entirely.'

'Good! Then you realize that discussion and exchange of viewpoint between differing nationalities is essential to promote clearer understanding. True, *señorita*?'

'Yes, *señor*,' she said after a moment's hesitation while the suspicion came that he was indulging his sardonic humour at her expense. Suddenly she twisted round to face him and burst out impulsively: 'You consider me too outspoken, don't you, Señor Conde? You are trying to tell me tactfully not to opine in anger but adopt a more rational attitude, because of this afternoon. Well,' she added firmly, 'I did not intend to give offence to you personally, but I haven't changed my mind.'

Not a flicker disturbed the aristocratic lines of his profile. He said, 'I should be disappointed if you had.'

She was startled. 'Disappointed? I don't understand.'

'I dislike sycophancy, almost as much as I respect honesty,' he said calmly, 'therefore, although your views constitute sheer heresy, I endeavour to understand that you are quite genuine in your wish to avoid personal offence.'

'Oh, I do!' she cried. 'It's all a matter of principle. I—'

'Yes. The principles of life, particularly when the underdog is concerned. That is the one thing guaranteed to set the most stolid of Englishmen aflame. He will remove his blinkers, set forth for foreign shores and proceed to point out the errors of his hosts' way, completely oblivious to the fact that equal injustice exists at his own front door.'

'Oh, no! I'm sure we don't!' she said hotly. 'I'm sure that is exaggeration.'

'Is it?'

'It's biased, put like that.'

'I am not so sure, even though I am not disputing your genuine belief in your motives. If you will consider it you will find there is truth in what I say.'

67

The impulse was strong to deny and protest, but she caught in his tone an echo that recalled a discussion between her parents only a short time before she left home. For a moment the phrases came back as clearly as though her mother were there at her side, frowning over her sewing as she exclaimed: '*I don't see why we can't mind our own business for a change and keep out of international troubles,*' and her father immediately launching into explanations of just why Britain was committed to following her current foreign policy at all costs. Hilary had giggled, as she often did when her parents had their comfortable little domestic differences, and promptly forgotten it – until a quirk of memory unexpectedly turned it up in somewhat different circumstances. Now it had the same effect on her, making her forget touchy national pride and want to laugh. Biting her lip, she denied *that* impulse as well and assumed a sober expression.

'*Señor*, is this a declaration of war?' she asked gently.

'It hardly seems a declaration of better understanding! Nevertheless, it appears to be causing you some amusement,' he observed dryly.

'Actually, it isn't.' She risked another sidelong look, safe in the assumption that his attention must be occupied mainly by driving. 'We're nearly there, aren't we?'

'A few miles, three at the most,' he said. 'Why, is something concerning you?'

'No, not really.' She subsided back, aware now of the people at journey's end crowding back upon the scene of her thoughts and wishing that she could push them away for a little longer. 'I – I hope they won't think my behaviour too bad this afternoon.'

'Because you fled the *corrida*?'

'Not exactly. But perhaps I should have gone back, or waited for them.'

'I have already taken care of that,' he said coolly. 'And it has also occurred to me how remiss I have been.'

'In what way?' She was surprised.

'We have made no formal arrangements for your free time. You should have reminded me,' he added with a touch of unconscious arrogance that made Hilary smile secretly to herself.

'We did leave that in the air,' she recalled. 'It was to be arranged to our mutual agreement.'

'We had better leave it in the air no longer,' he said firmly. 'When do you wish to have your free time? At the week-end?'

'If that is convenient, but it seems to have worked out already that I have a great deal of leisure. Joaquin spends half of each day with his tutor, and being companion to Juanita isn't like work at all,' she added.

'Nevertheless, I insist that you have time when you feel completely freed from any demands we may make of you. We will work out a suitable time-table when we return to Lima.'

'Thank you,' she said, then forgot formality. 'But I don't object in the least to it being elastic, *señor*.'

'Elastic?'

He sounded puzzled, and she said quickly: 'I mean that if I was needed any special week-end I'd be quite happy to fit in with the family arrangements. Equally, if the occasion should arise when I especially wanted some free time in the middle of the week I should like to think that I could ask you let me re-arrange the routine. Not that it's likely to happen,' she added, 'but just in case.'

'Just in case you form a rather special friendship in Lima? Yes, I quite understand, *señorita*.' He paused, and swung the car into the narrow side turning that led to the Navarre place. 'But I feel I must warn you before you venture forth in your impetuous British way to seek out new friends. There is this proposed visit to the flamenco, to begin with, which my secretary suggested. It would have been wiser if you had not accepted it.'

A small cold shock ran through Hilary. 'You do not approve, *señor*?'

'I do not.' His voice had gone crisp. 'I am well aware that you consider it perfectly all right to accept an invitation from a total stranger to accompany him alone. But not with Ramon, and here.'

'And what's wrong with Ramon?' she demanded. 'I'm sure you don't employ anyone of a disreputable nature.'

'I do not speak in a personal way of Ramon. Of course he is of unquestionable integrity, but I am trying to tell you

69

that what would be perfectly acceptable in your own country, or even here with someone of your own or American nationality, is not acceptable in our society. We do not respect a young woman who forms casual relationships with one of the opposite sex and frequents café society.'

She sighed. 'Yes, I know. Doña Elena also warned me about this, only the other day.' She hesitated, looking towards him. '*Señor*, I do appreciate your concern for me, but unless I get to know people and mix with them how am I to see the real country and understand the people? I want to get behind the façade the tourists see, not be cloistered so safely I will know little more of this fascinating country when I get home than I do now. And I *can* look after myself, *señor*,' she added softly.

'Can you? I wonder.'

There was an abstraction in his tone that surprised her, and she realized that his concern was something more than courteous responsibility for a new member of his household. He sounded genuinely worried, and the thought made Hilary forget her hard-won ability to dissemble. She said hastily: 'Oh yes – don't worry. I have an instinct about people and as long as I follow it I'm all right. It only let me down once in my whole life,' she added with a wry smile, 'and I think it was because I wouldn't listen to it.'

'It would have to be a man, of course, this isolated instance?' he said dryly.

'How did you guess?' In the shadows, her mouth curved with bitterness, then relaxed into resignation. 'So I'm not likely to be deaf a second time.'

'I should not be so sure of that, *señorita*,' he said coolly. 'There is wisdom in logic but rarely in instinct.'

She sighed and stayed silent, thinking sadly of Juanita and the promise she had made to her, a promise that was going to be more difficult to keep than she had imagined. But for once the antagonism the Conde so often invoked was slow to spark. It was easy to tell herself that he had no right to play the autocrat with her and criticize what she chose to do in her personal life. But she couldn't deny that he was proving a man of integrity who held himself responsible for the welfare of his family and household, and he had chosen to extend that responsibility to herself. Her parents would approve, she knew. In fact, they would feel a great deal happier if they knew just how strictly she was going to be protected – if the Conde had his way! She said in a musing voice: 'You see, *señor*, I instinctively thought of Ramon as part of the life here, and so I was delighted when he suggested taking me to the flamenco. I'm looking forward to it immensely.'

'You care for our music and dance, *señorita*?'

'I love it.' She did not have to instil false enthusiasm into her tone, for it was true, she did love the fire and colour of the flamenco. She turned to glance at him, wondering if she dare make the suggestion that Juanita might come with her, but before she could venture to do so he was braking the car to a halt and turning to face her.

'Why did you not mention this to me? I would have made arrangements for you to visit the flamenco. For that matter, I would have escorted you myself.'

'You, *señor*?' A small thrill of pleasure was unexpectedly intense. He nodded gravely, and she could not help smiling at a sudden prompting of the logic he apparently wished her to employ. 'But how could I ask you, *señor*? I would have offended convention again, quite unwittingly.'

'It would be somewhat different in this case,' he told her with unconscious arrogance. 'Meanwhile, please take care in future over your acceptance of invitations, particularly from whom you accept them.'

To her own surprise she found herself meekly acquiescing, and saw the small, approving inclination of his head before he got out of the car.

Darkness had come almost unnoticed, and the lanterns glowed gaily across the gardens. Some of them were nestled in the branches of the trees, others were strung like a radiant necklace above the patio, and a cluster of them were reflected in shimmering rose and green and pearl on the surface of the pool. They lent a magic to the night, transforming the silent, deserted gardens into beckoning havens for romance, and a tiny sigh escaped Hilary as the Conde cupped a firm hand beneath her elbow as she alighted from the car.

The clasp stayed, warm and guiding as he walked with

her towards the house, and suddenly she was experiencing a strange confliction of impulses. One was to find something to say, quickly, wittily, and with laughter; the other was to stay silent, stay close, and simply enjoy this delightful intimate nearness to a man who was proving to hold a much more subtle attraction than she had realized. Not yet prepared to analyse her thoughts, she waited until they had passed out of the shadows under the pergolas and had reached the patio before she stopped. 'Señor . . .?'

'Yes?' Perforce, he also halted.

'I just wondered . . .' She sought the shadowy planes of his features and was aware of diffidence as she encountered his questioning gaze. 'May I ask a favour, señor?'

'It depends what it is,' he said lightly.

'About the flamenco. I wondered – could Juanita come with me?'

She held her breath, wondering if it were her imagination or if his dark eyes were hardening with displeasure. Then she saw the glint of very white teeth as he smiled.

'I think that could be arranged. Especially as I too have a request to make of you.'

'Me?' Half prepared for anything from downright suspicion to outright refusal, she felt a sense of relief that was quite out of proportion. It made her laugh softly as she exclaimed: 'Thank you – but of course! Anything – as long as it doesn't include taking Joaquin to the *corrida*!'

'No, it has nothing to do with the *corrida*.'

He looked down at her unguarded expression of pleasure and some of the amusement faded from his face. He touched her arm, indicating that they enter the house. 'But it can wait for a little while. I only trust that the flamenco will find favour with you, señorita. Perhaps,' he added in low mocking tones, 'it may prove more appealing than the skill of the matador – and the misdeeds of my renowned ancestors!'

CHAPTER FIVE

RAMON was the first person they saw as they came into the light of the outer *sala*. He looked surprised, then flustered, and hurried forward.

'*Señor!* We were not sure if you were – they have commenced *cena*. But I will tell Señora Navarre that—'

The Conde checked him with a brief gesture. 'No need, thank you, Ramon.' He turned to Hilary with the small gesture of indication that she was coming to know so well, and wordlessly she moved at his side in the direction of the dining-room. Somehow it was easier to follow where he led and as he decided . . .

There was much chatter and gaiety in the big dark-panelled room. The sombre tones of heavy carvings, aged ebony and ancestral oil paintings were contrasted strongly by the glittering jewellery and colours of the ladies' gowns. At least twenty-five people were gathered at the long polished table that gleamed with silver and crystal, and Hilary was suddenly conscious of the voices stilling and eyes turning to her as she entered. Instinctively she felt that they noted that she still wore the sleeveless coral slip of a dress she had donned to go to the *corrida*, and the Conde his lightweight town suit. But if he were conscious of any such notice he did not allow it to disturb his assured bearing. Still with the little prompting touch on Hilary's arm, he steered her firmly to where Doña Elena and her hostess, Señora Navarre, were sitting.

He took each of their hands, raising them in turn to his lips and smiling a smile which would have taken an extremely hardened feminine heart to resist, and said smoothly: 'A thousand pardons, *señoras*. You will forgive us that we arrive so. But the *señorita* was indisposed at the *corrida*, and so it was necessary that she seek calm for a little while. And now, she is much distressed that we have interrupted *comida*, attired as we are.' He bowed his head, and his closing words were lost in the two ladies' instant response.

All smiles for him, nevertheless there was genuine concern in their expressions as they made voluble protestations to his apologies and turned to Hilary. They were deeply grieved that she had felt indisposed. It was of course the heat and the noise. The little *señorita* was not yet used to the climate. Was she sure she was quite recovered . . .?

It was a little overwhelming and Hilary began to feel like a fraud. However, there was nothing she could do but smile and thank them, and take the place at table that was made for her.

The ebb and flow of conversation was resumed, and, probably because of convenience in serving the food, she found the Conde seated next to her, almost immediately on the right of their host and hostess. A fresh carafe of wine was brought and a scalloped silver dish of seafood to begin with, and this was followed by barbecued chicken and mounds of white fluffy rice with a rich spicy sauce.

After a small, polite interchange of pleasantries with her table neighbour to her left Hilary fell silent. She had a great deal to think of now as she looked back over the day, and already it seemed ages since it began. But she suspected that it was really beginning now for the assembled company. According to Bruce Gilford there was to be dancing and high jinks! Quite a party. Now she realized that the siesta had its benefit!

'You are very quiet!'

The Conde's voice made her start guiltily. She said, 'I'm sorry, *señor*. I was thinking. Did you say something?'

'No.' He reached for the carafe and topped up her glass. 'Do not apologize. It is quite a refreshing change to find a woman who can appreciate silence.'

She felt the warm colour of pleasure come to her cheeks and looked down into her glass.

'Fruit?' he queried softly.

She hesitated over the heaped basket he drew forward, looking wonderingly at the exotic strangers among the more familiar grapes and peaches and glossy scarlet apples.

He said gravely: 'You wish to sample the things new and strange that our land has to offer. Try *chirimoya*, it has white, very sweet flesh. Or this, the *granadilla*, it is the fruit of the passion flower.'

The sense of word association was suddenly a little quelling and she selected a *chirimoya*, discovering that it was as he said – very sweet and white, almost too sweet.

The Conde took a peach for himself, peeling it deftly with the small silver fruit knife by his plate. Again, as when in the car, she found herself watching his hands, the long dexterous fingers, the fine-boned lines and beautifully kept nails. The fingers stilled, and something made her glance up.

Her own survey was being returned, and there was a quality in the dark, considering eyes that met her like an impact. Unsteadily, she forced a smile and exclaimed: 'I – I could never peel a peach like that – not without getting bathed in the juice.'

'There are more agreeable mediums in which to bathe, I agree,' he said with a hint of amusement, 'but a man must never allow himself to be mastered by a mere globule of fruit.'

She smiled again and rather hastily reached out for an apple, which was easy to deal with, and firmly refused to allow her gaze to be drawn back into that disturbing orbit. Perhaps it was the wine that was having this heady effect, or maybe she'd had too much sun today, she decided with an inward giggle at herself. She sought to attract the attention of Juanita, who was sitting farther down at the opposite side of the table, but Juanita seemed to be elsewhere – at least in spirit – as she stared dreamily at the peach she was slicing.

Hilary's eyes went tender with understanding as she looked at the young, sensitive face; she was looking forward to seeing Juanita's delight when she told her that the assignation was arranged . . . . Hilary sighed softly. How wonderful was the transformation love could work in a person! Only a few hours ago Juanita had been downcast, not caring what the day might bring, but it had brought joy after all. Somewhere, chance had decreed an emergency in a stranger's life, he was unable to keep a business appointment, and so the Conde decided to meet his family and friends at the *corrida*. And Ramon came too . . . It put the week-end in an entirely new perspective . . .

When the long leisurely meal was ended at last Hilary

was tense with a pleasurable feeling of anticipation. The tension snapped, gave a strange little kick over her heart and tightened again as the Conde stood when she did and drew her chair out of her way.

'You are going to join in the dancing, *señorita*?' he asked.

'Yes – the moment I have changed and made sure that Joaquin is safely installed in bed,' she smiled back.

'Till then, *señorita*.' He inclined his head gravely and waited until she slipped past him before he turned to another guest.

Hilary's cheeks were glowing and her eyes were brilliant when she faced the tiny mirror in her room. It was going to be wonderful. She need never have had a moment's doubt about her decision to take this job. And the possibility for which she had prepared herself – that she might be treated like a servant – showed no signs of arising. She had heard some *au pair* tales that were hair-raising, but this time her instinct hadn't let her down. No employer could have been more kind or considerate, even though a somewhat dictatorial element was present at times . . . The only fly in the ointment was Consuelo – thank heaven Consuelo wasn't a member of the Pacquera clan!

Quickly she slipped into the white voile dress with the silver embroidery at the neckline. It was flowing and misty, and she was glad she had brought it. The Conde plainly intended to join the dancing himself . . . it was going to be a wonderful experience to be able to dance out of doors at night, under the stars . . . something that the English climate rarely allowed back home . . . What was the Conde like as a dancing partner . . .?

But first she had to find Juanita.

The strains of music floated in from the night and the scent of white roses massed on the ornate gilt gables in the wide hall rose to meet Hilary as she came downstairs. It mingled, not unpleasantly, with the rich aroma of cigar smoke coming from the open doors of the *sala* where some of the male guests were still gathered with their host. Hilary's steps flitted lightly across the parquet, and more than one male head turned to watch the slender golden-haired girl who seemed to float in a mist of white and silver towards the

76

wide doors opened to the patio.

The night air came warm and velvet-soft to her bare throat and arms, but for the moment she was oblivious to it. Juanita seemed to have vanished.

Only a few couples were dancing. Others stood or sat around on the garden terrace, and under the glow of the lanterns she saw the tall figure of the Conde, now immaculate in a cream tuxedo and dark elegant trousers that seemed to increase his height. He was talking to Sanchia and Consuelo, and biting at her lower lip Hilary turned away and made for the pergolas. A suspicion was now giving her some concern. There was no sign of Ramon, either, and it didn't require much imagination to guess what made two. But where were they? The Navarre grounds stretched a considerable distance, and once away from the illuminated section near the house they were inky dark and strange with pitfalls for unfamiliar feet.

Hilary gave a sigh of exasperation and at last turned back. She might search for hours for the young idiots. But what if someone else, not so sympathetic, came upon them accidentally? She emerged from the shadows and almost instantly she was caught by Consuelo.

'We've been looking for you,' said Consuelo. 'Or rather Bruce has.'

It seemed like the beginning of a conspiracy that night. She danced with him, twice, then was drawn into a group to have iced drinks, and left alone with him again.

It was all done gaily, by most of the guests. She was English; Bruce was English. Therefore they must have lots to talk about; they must be drawn to each other, two compatriots meeting on foreign shores. *Esta claro!*

Bruce laughed softly, as though he guessed at her thoughts, and guided her steps skilfully to the sensuous South American rhythm. 'You might as well give in,' he said against her ear. 'You're landed with me now, whether you like it or not.'

'You're landed yourself – whether you like it or not,' she returned wryly.

'I'm all for that. Shall I tell you a secret?' he whispered.

'Then it won't be a secret any more.'

Again he put his lips close to her ear. 'It's wonderful to have a cool, sweet English girl in my arms again.'

'Oh, are your arms so scorched after a succession of dark smouldering beauties?' she teased.

He groaned comically. 'I always lead with my chin. Actually, I've led so pure a life during the past three years any convent would open its doors and say welcome. It's true,' he said indignantly when she laughed. 'My God, they guard their daughters like rubies round here. And as for their wives—!'

'Maybe they've got reason to while you're around.'

'Is that supposed to be sympathy?'

'No, a search for the truth.'

'Meaning that man never tells it?'

'Does he?'

'Always!'

She laughed. He was proving terribly easy to talk to, and to fall back with into the old pattern of chaff and banter that didn't commit either party one single iota. 'Tell me about your work,' she suggested.

Nothing loath, he launched into an account of his day-to-day life as ranch manager of an estate into which his county at home could have been fitted easily and with room to spare. Listening to him, she realized that under the light, almost frivolous air he had displayed when they began to dance Bruce Gilford must be hard, capable, and immensely strong. Yet there was no trace of boasting, or the swaggering rough range rider about him, and she knew that he had a genuine love in his work and pride in his knowledge of stock.

'Of course we're mainly crop country here,' he told her. 'The Argentine's the place for herds and horses, the rolling miles of ranges and the round-up that most people imagine as soon as you tell them what your job is.'

She nodded, suddenly glimpsing Juanita across Bruce's broad shoulder. Juanita was dancing with her uncle, and in his arms she looked small, sweet and demure. As though she felt Hilary's gaze she glanced up and gave a little smile of acknowledgment. Hilary gave a sigh of relief; there was no sign of Ramon among the dancers, but the Conde was the safest alibi of all for his niece.

'I'd like to show you around, some time,' Bruce was saying, 'if you're interested.'

'I'd love to,' Hilary responded.

'Can you ride?'

'Only on four feet with tyres,' she said flippantly, and he laughed.

'You'd better not say that to any South American.' He paused, his brow furrowing. 'We must arrange something. Of course the ideal thing would be to have you come for a week-end – it's the only way you could see around at leisure. But—'

'Your place?' she broke in.

'I have my own house, with a couple who live in. Maria housekeeps and her husband Pedro does odd jobs along with working in Don Alonso's gardens. So how about a day with me?' he grinned. 'The eyebrows would rise to heaven round here if you made it a week-end.'

'Thank you – I'd love to.'

'Next week-end?' When she nodded he said, 'Fine. But you'll have to make an early start or half the day will be lost with the travelling. If I picked you up at eight . . .'

Making plans, he drew her to one of the lacy iron seats dotted round the sides of the patio and got a drink for her. Presently Sanchia spotted them and came across, her smile friendly but still holding its hint of sadness. She said, 'You and Bruce will have much to talk about. It is good that you should meet him. He will be able to show you round Lima and introduce you to his other English friends.'

She turned as her sister approached. Consuelo was accompanied by a thick-set, swarthy-featured man called Miguel whose smile was bland and did not reach his eyes. He bowed formally to Sanchia and drew her away from the little group.

Consuelo watched them, a faint frown between her heavy brows, then said abruptly: 'Where is Juanita?'

'She was here a moment ago.' Hilary tried not to be ruffled by the other girl's peremptory tone. 'She was dancing with her uncle.'

Consuelo stared across the patio. The music had stopped and there was no sign of Juanita. Fortunately, there was no sign of the Conde.

Hilary said evenly: 'I expect he's getting her a drink. Would you like me to go and look for her?' she offered.

'No. You stay with Bruce.' Unexpectedly, Consuelo bestowed a remarkably expansive smile on Hilary. 'It must be exciting for you to come all this way and meet someone who lives almost next door to you at home. *Bueno?*' she added to Bruce.

'*Bueno, señorita.*' He laughed, perfectly self-assured, and Consuelo moved away, presumably to search for Juanita herself.

Bruce looked at Hilary. '*Bueno?*' he whispered. 'You don't look very sure.'

'No, it isn't that.' She had no responding smile to his teasing whisper. She hesitated, glancing round to see if they were alone for the moment. The instinct to trust him and the impulse to confide were too strong and she said in a low voice: 'Bruce, I'm worried. You see, I'm sort of responsible for Juanita, and she keeps disappearing. And for some reason Consuelo seems to dislike her. I—'

'I know.' Bruce gripped her arm and stood up. 'You're afraid that young hearts are a-flutter and it's strictly *verboten!*' He drew a dramatic hand across his throat and led her out of the circles of illumination cast by the lanterns above. 'Come on, we'll winkle the young idiots out, wherever they are. Who's the boy?'

Hilary shook her head. That was one secret she had to keep, even as she feared that Consuelo had been in possession of it for quite some time. The music started again, and Bruce said wryly: 'I'm in need of an excuse to miss out on the *pasa-doble!*'

He seemed fairly well acquainted with the geography of the Navarre grounds – and the small secret sanctuaries that invited lovers to escape the crowd, or authority. The second one yielded Juanita, and a guilty, worried Ramon. Somewhat to Hilary's surprise, Bruce played it as though he deeply regretted such an unwarranted intrusion. With a warning aside and pressure on her arm, he drew her away and into the shadows of an arbor. A moment later the ghostly white of Juanita's dress flitted along the path in the direction of the main part of the garden; the dark figure of Ramon moved along the opposite path.

'You see,' said Bruce, preparing to move on. 'Far better not to say anything. They've had a shock and they'll be too scared to indulge in any more nonsense tonight.'

'Yes, I didn't think of it that way.' Hilary wondered why she hadn't and chalked up a mental compliment to Bruce's wisdom. Poor Juanita; she would be terrified if she hadn't recognized the intruders. Impulsively she touched Bruce's arm.

'You won't tell a soul about this, will you? I know I should scotch her little romance, but I haven't the heart. It seems so harsh, this not letting her choose her own friends. I mean, conventions are all very well, but there's a limit. How is she ever going to learn to judge human nature for herself?'

'She doesn't have to,' Bruce said flatly. 'It's done for her, as her suitors will be judged for her and she'll be expected to make the right choice.'

'I could never make a marriage that way. I'd rather not marry at all.'

'You've had a different upbringing.' Bruce took out his cigarettes and when Hilary refused put them back in his pocket. 'You must remember that in your dealings with Juanita. You have to realize that she's been conditioned from childhood to accept a much more restricted mode of behaviour than you have. Given more freedom it's doubtful if she'd be any happier. It's the old spice of forbidden fruit. If she was free to throw her hat over the windmill with this boy he'd probably not seem nearly so attractive.'

'But that's the whole point,' Hilary exclaimed. 'I'm sure being free to choose friends helps a person to judge character.'

'I agree, but if I were you I'd keep clear of any dispute and whatever you do don't get involved in their intrigues. No matter how sympathetic you feel. Because no one outside their own circle really understands just how they're going to react. You could find yourself involved in a first-class family explosion, and believe me, they're no picnic. I know.'

Something in his tone made Hilary check her step. She looked up at him. 'You sound as though you speak from personal experience.'

'I do. So take my advice, if you've a notion to help love's young liberation along – forget it.' He put one arm lightly around her shoulders to duck under a low hanging bough, and as they straightened he said in a lighter voice: 'I'll have to be getting back. When am I going to see you again?'

'I thought we'd fixed that for next week-end,' she said in equally light tones.

'Yes, I know. I wondered if you'd be in town during the week. I have some business to see to mid-week.'

'Maybe I'd better leave it till the week-end,' she said slowly. 'I'm not sure when I'll be free.'

'Next week-end, then. *Mucho bueno, señorita!*' he said in dramatic tones, giving her shoulder a shake that was almost brotherly as they passed out of the same shadowed patch which Hilary had trod a few hours earlier with a companion much less predictable in mood.

The soft radiance of the lanterns fell on her upturned face and the smile parting her mouth as she was about to make a light-hearted response to Bruce Gilford. It was never spoken. The dark shadow of the Conde fell across her path and stilled.

He said with formal politeness: 'You are enjoying the night, *señorita?*'

Her face felt stiff and she wanted to wrench free of the friendly arm round her shoulders. She made herself remain composed and said steadily: 'Very much, *señor*. It is a beautiful evening.'

'*Bueno.*' With an aloof inclination of his head towards Gilford, he moved away.

Hilary watched him, unnoticing that Bruce had let his hand fall from her shoulder.

'*Bueno,*' she whispered. *But it wasn't!*

* * *

They returned to the villa early on the Monday morning and Hilary had no regrets for the passing of the week-end. The Sunday had been unbearably hot and she had missed Bruce Gilford; it was the first time she had been conscious of being among strangers and the sensation was faintly disquieting.

She unpacked her week-end case and tried to dismiss the

trend of her thoughts. So Saturday had been a winner; despite the fiasco of the *corrida* she had enjoyed it, but why this urgency to analyse the why and wherefore of one day bringing pleasure and the next day dragging its hours through strained sociality?

A blouse slipped off its hanger as she reached into the wardrobe and she exclaimed annoyance under her breath as she stooped to pick it up. Why didn't she take out the stupid little thought and see its very stupidity? It was quite plain that the Conde believed she had been flirting with Bruce Gilford in the secret shadows of the garden; only hours previously he had issued a dictum regarding her mode of conduct in future, and she had never been left in any doubt of his opinion of femininity that did not conform. *We do not respect* . . .

But she was different! And Bruce was English. What right did the Conde have to look down that disdainful nose of his? Did he think Bruce was starting to get fresh already, just because of his putting an arm round her? He must have a suspicious mind, she thought furiously. Anyway, the way they'd all gone on they'd practically thrown her at Bruce from the moment he arrived.

'You look angry, my Hilary. What is the trouble?'

She spun round. Juanita had come to the half-open door and peeped in curiously.

She forced a smile. 'Just thoughts. Where's Joaquin?'

'At lessons – we have peace for an hour or so.' Juanita wandered into the room and studied herself in Hilary's dressing table mirror. 'Did you enjoy the week-end?'

'Some of it – most of it,' she amended hastily. 'And you?'

Juanita heaved a great sigh. 'I'm so happy. And no one saw us except you and Mr. Gilford – he will not betray us, will he?' she asked anxiously.

'He won't betray anyone,' Hilary said, too touched by Juanita's youthful trust to be amused by her love of exaggerating everything in a dramatic manner. She said, 'But you ran a risk, you know. Did you think you would have the garden to yourself for dalliance – on a moonlit night with all those guests there? What if it had been Consuelo instead of me?'

83

'*Caramba!*' Juanita giggled. 'What man in his senses would choose Consuelo for dalliance in the moonlight? She is bad-tempered – and *corregidora*! I do not even consider her to be very beautiful. You know,' Juanita lowered her voice confidentially, 'she would like to be Condesa, but I do not think Tio will choose her. Sometimes I do not think he will ever choose anyone.'

Hilary stayed silent. She looked down at the empty case and closed it rather abruptly.

Juanita said, 'Do you remember Don Miguel?'

'I think so.' Hilary cast her memory back over the many guests who had gathered at the Navarre hacienda.

Juanita, who seemed to be in the mood for confidences, prompted: 'He is not as tall as my uncle, but *mucho*' – she wrinkled her nose – '*grueso*, although he is not terribly old. His eyes are so—' Again she stopped to convey expression, and Hilary gave a gesture of comprehension.

'Yes, now I can recognize him. He is what we would call pompous, and no sense of humour.'

'He wishes to marry Sanchia.'

Hilary's expression must have conveyed a reaction of which Juanita approved, for the younger girl nodded mournfully. 'Yes, her family approve. He is vastly wealthy and when his mother dies he will inherit all her estate, for there is no one else. He has much money invested in fertilizer.'

'Poor Sanchia,' Hilary murmured under her breath.

'She has not yet decided, but it is unfortunate. She is no longer a girl and she may not have many more opportunities,' Juanita said with a seriousness that promoted Sanchia to a sereneness she certainly did not warrant. 'I do not think she has the large *dote*. Her late husband was not a rich man.'

Hilary expelled a sharp breath. 'I'm surprised they allowed her to marry him, then,' she observed tartly. 'Seeing that such store is set on material values.'

'You do not understand,' Juanita said patiently. 'It is simply that families who care about their daughters' happiness wish to ensure that the suitors they choose are able to support them. Actually, they did not fully approve of Sanchia's choice, but she refused to marry into the Romez

84

family. She wanted to marry an *americano* once, but I do not know all the details. It was many years ago and I was still a child. But I overhear little bits . . .'

'She was happy, though,' Hilary said thoughtfully. 'She told me she'd escaped into a marvellous freedom.'

Juanita sighed her agreement and wandered to the window. After a moment she asked: 'Do you like Señor Gilford?'

'Yes, I think so,' Hilary said cautiously.

'He seems very nice. It would be exciting if he fell in love with you.'

'No, it wouldn't.'

'Why not?' Juanita swung round. 'He is attractive and I think he likes you. Then you would fall in love with him and be as happy as I am.' She gave a blissful sigh. 'I have been so happy this week-end.'

'Well, you concentrate on your own happiness and leave me – and Bruce Gilford – out of your speculations,' Hilary told her in humorous tones that were, nevertheless, firm. 'Just because we're both English and found one another easy to talk to doesn't mean we're going to fall headlong in love.'

Juanita put her head on one side and studied Hilary with a thoughtful sidelong regard. 'Are you in love with anybody?'

'No.'

'Not even attracted?' The wide eyes expressed disbelief. 'You mean there's no man who makes you – how do you say it? – tingle all the way down your spine just to think of him?'

'Most certainly not.' Hilary returned briskly to putting away her make-up kit. 'And that isn't entirely love, my pet, those tingles down the spine.'

'Perhaps not, but they are very pleasant, are they not?' said Juanita, with an air of innocence that was a little overdone.

'No doubt. But one can't spend one's entire life enjoying tingles down the spine. There are other aspects. Have you unpacked, Juanita?'

'Marita has done it for me – she said to give her your laundry, by the way.' Juanita took a deep breath. 'Why do you change the subject, Hilary?'

'Love and tingles aren't a Monday-morning topic.' Hilary giggled, the conditioning of two years of the Monday morning atmosphere after the battle of the underground and the aseptic polish aroma of the office, especially on wet Monday mornings, still very easily evoked. 'But you wouldn't know anything about that.'

'I think there is some man, but you do not want to tell me,' said Juanita with unusual persistence.

'There's nothing to tell. If there were anyone special at home do you think I could bear to leave him?'

'Hm.' Juanita did not appear entirely convinced.

'And I haven't been here long enough to fall in love with anyone new.'

'No, that is true, perhaps. But who knows? We may meet someone exciting on *miercoles*,' Juanita said hopefully. 'Ramon has a friend who knows one of the singers at Las Castanuelas Rojas. Are you looking forward to our visit there?'

'Very much.' Hilary nodded and the younger girl moved restlessly. 'I wish it were tonight.'

'It will soon be here,' Hilary assured her patiently.

Strangely, despite her prophecy, the two days did drag, even to Hilary, for whom the long-awaited evening did not hold the same vital fascination that stretched Juanita's patience to breaking point.

The week began quietly and the villa had a calm more pronounced than usual, though it was probably a natural contrast to the festive air of the week-end at the hacienda. Doña Elena was tired after her reunion with her friend and the excitement and she kept mostly to her own *sala*. Joaquin managed to fall down and graze his knees rather badly within a couple of hours of returning, and the Conde left almost immediately to complete the business matters interrupted at the week-end. Ramon, of course, went with him and by the Wednesday afternoon Juanita was convinced that fate would delay them and Ramon would not return in time.

Hilary was infected by this anxiety, and found herself waiting with a curious impatience she could not dismiss. When the sleek shining Chevrolet arrowed up the drive and the tall lithe figure emerged she gave a small sigh that was almost relief.

Joaquin limped to greet him, but she stayed where she was, in the shade of the high trellis which was ablaze with scarlet blossom, and returned his formal '*Buenas tardes, señorita,*' with equal gravity.

Less than an hour later he departed again.

What was the favour he had intended to ask of her? Hilary wondered as she got ready to go out. He had told her he would discuss it later; it was now four days later. Admittedly she had had only the briefest of contacts with him during those four days. Perhaps it was not of importance. Perhaps of such little importance it was already forgotten ... She fastened tiny crystal ear-rings to her lobes and turned to pass judgment on Juanita's appearance.

She had chosen a tight-bodiced dress of sheerest ivory *panne* velvet with wrist-length sleeves and a sleek clinging skirt that flowed when she moved. It had no trimming at all, but a heavy coral and pearl choker at her bare throat was a perfect foil and gave her dark demure beauty the maturity she craved.

She waited expectantly, unconsciously posing, and Hilary said with perfect truth: 'You look beautiful. Ramon and I will have to keep you under lock and key tonight.'

'Really?' Juanita dimpled. 'I look grown-up?'

'At least twenty!'

'*Bueno!* I so often wish I were taller. And you too look wonderful, my Hilary. *Bella!*' She twirled excitedly. 'Come, let us go before someone changes their mind and stops us.'

The sense of freedom was potent. Ramon drove a small silver-blue coupé at an exhilarating speed which had the wind sporting through the girls' hair and had them laughing and breathless when they reached the tucked-away restaurant which was a favourite with the locals. It was quiet and intimate in atmosphere, and the food was superb. Ramon was a pleasant host, if a little formal towards Hilary at first, and there was something rather touching about his grave courtesy as he ensured that everything should be to her liking, almost to the exclusion of Juanita. But soon they all relaxed and forgot formality to become three young people out to enjoy themselves.

Because the evening was still young they dined leisurely, and then strolled the short distance to Las Castanuelas Rojas, which, in the tradition of most nightspots the world over, would not really start swinging until the hour grew late and the crowd poured in.

And crowded it soon became. The heat rose in waves to the balcony alcove which Hilary and her two companions shared with a party of four strangers. Hilary fanned her warm face with her programme and wondered how the dancers below kept up their pace without melting into grease-spots. The castanets clicked their rataplan, heels beat out a sharp tattoo of ever-increasing speed on the hard wood apron of stage, and the cascading frills of scarlet and yellow and orange whirled and rippled with the supple bodies of the dancers. But despite the colour and fire of the girls it was the male dancer who captured the admiration of the audience.

Tall, and almost deceptively slight in the tight, high-waisted trousers, close-fitting black bolero, and the stiff-brimmed formal *sombrero*, his movements seemed effortless as he conveyed rhythm, dignity and smouldering fire in a faultlessly executed floor pattern. Soon he was alone, centred in a spotlight outside of which there was almost total blackness, bringing sound, spectacle and fervour to a climax which held everyone breathless and captive. When the lights went up and the tumult of applause began to die Hilary turned to her companions.

They smiled at her pleasure, and Juanita said softly, 'Ah, but wait until you hear the flamenco – Manuel is the best of all – very romantic.' Her gaze strayed as she spoke, to the couple who were sitting to Hilary's left. They were talking in soft whispers over their programme and it was possible now to tell that they were visitors or tourists and English. In the seconds before the lights dimmed again the boy smiled into the girl's eyes and drew her hand into his clasp.

Hilary thought she detected a wistfulness in Juanita's expression and she sighed with understanding. No matter how envious Juanita might feel of the young couple's freedom to betray their affection for one another her cloistered upbringing would effectively stifle any temptation to do the same; Spanish people, voluble and demonstrative in so many other ways, did not express their emotional feelings towards the opposite sex in public.

The rhythm of guitars began and the first notes of song instantly evoked the plaintive, haunting sadness of old Andalusia. Hilary forgot her thoughts, and it came as something of a shock when the long story in song ended and she discovered that Juanita and Ramon were no longer at her side.

The flamenco was the last item of the cabaret and the patrons were dispersing to other amusements, some to eat, some to drink, others to dance on the ballroom floor below. Hilary moved out of the alcove and looked for a sign of her companions. Almost immediately she saw them entering from the terrace door near the head of the stairs. There was a dark feverish glow about Juanita that told its own tale of stolen ardour and even at that moment she was disengaging her hand from Ramon's. Hilary moved forward, but before she could pass through the clusters of patrons blocking her way a tall, elegant man ascending the stairway spotted Ramon and turned to him with a voluble greeting.

A sense of uneasiness she could not quite define disturbed Hilary as she reached the little group and was introduced to the elegant stranger, who, it transpired, was the mutual acquaintance of Ramon and the singer, Manuel, mentioned previously by Juanita.

Señor Pereira bowed over Hilary's hand and professed himself charmed to meet the English *señorita*. In a very short while Hilary, along with an excited Juanita and Ramon, found herself being conducted behind the scene to the singer's dressing-room and being introduced to Manuel himself. He was as romantic and charming close to as under the spotlight, and he too professed himself charmed by the English *señorita*. He spoke of his last visit to London, was amusingly modest when she said how much she'd enjoyed the flamenco, invited her to return as his guest at a later performance during his season at Las Castanuelas Rojas, and was then drawn away by his other admirers en route for a party.

A little bemused by this singling out, Hilary did not notice that Señor Pereira had attached himself to her own small party. By the time she did realize this it was too late to back out; they were seated at his table and an obsequious waiter was taking his drinks order. But the pattern of events soon became obvious after Ramon had dutifully asked her to dance and Juanita was claimed by the elegant newcomer, and then Hilary found herself with her proper partner.

I must be getting dim! she thought wryly, gliding on to the dance floor in the expert arms of Señor Pereira. Now there was a proper balance of numbers; she was no longer the gooseberry! However, Señor Pereira was an excellent dancer, so how could she back out and spoil Juanita's sweet hour? And why not? It was a superb floor, the orchestra was good, the atmosphere luxuriously beckoning, and the air-conditioning seemed to function perfectly. She said so to her partner and he smiled his approval at her pleasure.

'We have many visitors come here. Especially the *americanos* – and you know how they care for their air-conditioning and their ice. Ah, their ice! They even serve our *viño de Jerez* on the rocks!' He gave a pretended shudder of horror, and Hilary laughed.

He was the *ne plus ultra* of Latin courtesy, and after a while he had almost disarmed Hilary of her instinctive reserve. But a tiny element of wariness remained, even though she wondered if she was imagining that he held her a shade closer than was necessary whenever one of the inevitable near-collisions of a crowded ballroom floor threatened. Mentally, she made a reckoning of time, setting a limit at which, when it arrived, she was going to insist that Ramon took Juanita and herself home. But long before the hands of her watch reached that time Señor Pereira decided he had been patient long enough with this cool English miss. He inquired if she would care for another drink, frowned slightly at her polite refusal, and said: 'May I?'

Juanita and Ramon were already back on the floor and with a little sigh Hilary acquiesced. Another half hour, she decided, then they would leave. It was almost midnight. By the time they walked back to the car and drove home . . . She had no idea of the rule governing Juanita's time of being in at night; the question had never arisen and she had not thought to check . . . Heavens! Supposing it was some ridiculously early hour . . . it would be ghastly if there was a row . . .

'Please do not look so concerned, *señorita*. They are being very discreet.'

'I beg your pardon!'

Her partner's low-voiced injunction brought her back from her worried thoughts and she stared up at his suave, rather fleshy features.

'I said – they are being perfectly discreet.' Señor Pereira smiled, showing very white teeth under the dark smooth thread of moustache. 'You are taking your duties of *dueña* very seriously, are you not, *señorita*? But your English love of freedom makes you very understanding of two young people kept apart by outworn convention.'

Hilary's fine brows narrowed. 'I'm not sure what you mean, *señor*.'

'Ah, come, *señorita*! One has only to look at them to see. It is a pity it will never be permitted to flower.'

She felt a tremor of panic. How many more people had guessed poor Juanita's secret? Consuelo certainly suspected. Bruce had guessed. And now this stranger. How long before it came to the Conde's ear?

She said uneasily, 'You are quite mistaken, *señor*. Actually,' she attempted to laugh, 'Juanita is chaperoning *me* tonight.'

'You!' He laughed openly and his arm tightened. 'An English girl with a chaperone! When the world knows that an English miss does exactly as she pleases, goes where she pleases, and with whom she pleases. Oh, that is a good joke. But not to worry – that is how you say it, I believe. I shall be the soul of discretion. No one will hear of their stolen assignation tonight. How could I even notice them when I have so charming a partner to occupy my attention?'

He bent his head nearer and murmured, 'So take off that worried little frown, *amada mia*, and let us enjoy the evening.'

To her dismay he began to pay her the most outrageous compliments. In languorous, unctuous tones he admired her soft, gold-spun hair, dwelled at some length on the famous English-rose quality of complexion, let his warm gaze feast with ever-increasing ardour on all those attributes he found so appealing, until Hilary was in an agony of embarrassment.

It was impossible to escape without drawing attention to herself. He was holding her much too firmly for that, and he was also well aware of the trait inherent in most people that makes them dread causing a scene. Even so, it still did not occur to her that she might fail to deal with the situation. She had been caught by the ageless wolf-in-sheep's-clothing trick and could blame only herself for being so foolish. She would have to suffer it until this endless medley of old-time movie themes came to an end, then she would politely but firmly bring the evening to a close.

Perhaps Señor Pereira suspected that she wasn't going to be an easy victim to his blandishments. His hold tightened and his manner perceptibly changed. He said in a low voice: '*Señorita*, I trust you are not thinking of making a fool of me in front of all these people.'

'I have no desire to make a fool of anyone, *señor*,' she said tautly, 'but I must ask you not to embarrass me any further. You have made it perfectly plain that you are well acquainted with our customs, therefore there is no excuse for presuming on them. Otherwise I shall have no choice but to make fools of both of us, *señor*,' she added grimly.

She felt rather than saw his tight-lipped, indrawn breath of anger. But when he spoke his voice was controlled. 'In that case, *señorita*, we will finish the dance and I will return you to your companions.'

'Thank you, *señor*,' she acknowledged coldly.

He did not speak again, but those last few minutes on the dance floor were the most distasteful Hilary had ever experienced. No matter how she tensed and tried to keep a formal distance Señor Pereira's hot hand stayed like a clamp on her spine, bending her against him at every turn. At last she could not bear the lecherous humiliation a moment longer. Almost in tears, she saw a break in the encircling throng and tore herself free. Heedless of heads turning and the angry exclamation following her, she ran off the floor, scarcely avoiding collision with a tall, statuesque woman who turned and stared after her with disapproving eyes.

She brushed at her eyes, furious with humiliation and positive that every eye in the ballroom was looking at her scarlet face, and stared blindly across the weaving pattern of dancers. Where were Juanita and Ramon? She had to find them quickly, before . . . She gave a small murmur of distress as she failed to see either of them and bit her lip. They must be sitting out, or—'*Oh!*'

She exclaimed aloud as her arm was caught and she whirled round, fully prepared to see the deceptively charming Mr. Pereira and do battle for escape. But it was not her late, importunate partner. Her eyes widened and her distress changed to horror as she saw the tall, furious figure towering over her.

'A *charming* performance,' the Conde said icily.

Shock temporarily robbed her of speech. She could only stare up at his dark angry features and wonder despairingly what evil genie had brought him there at that precise moment.

He did not wait for her to recover from her shock. His fingers bit like iron into her arm, even as he turned his head and gave a superbly controlled nod of greeting to an acquaintance brushing past. The brief smile vanished and he said in a low, grim voice, 'We will leave now,' as he propelled her forward.

The movement brought her back to mobility. 'No!' she said wildly. 'Not yet. I have to find—'

'If you are referring to my niece and my negligent secretary you may dismiss the thought. I have already attended to that matter.'

Something in his tone made her go cold with premonition. What had happened? Where was Juanita? She started to stammer, and he cut her short with icy politeness. 'Please, *señorita* . . . Juanita is waiting in the car. Did you have a wrap?'

'Yes, but—'

'Go and get it and come back here to me.'

'I – yes, but it isn't here.' She hardly knew what she was saying. Everything had happened so quickly, and she only knew that Conde was very, very angry indeed. 'I – I left it in Ramon's car. It's so warm tonight I—'

'You have your purse.' He noted the small silvery brocade evening bag she was clutching. 'Come, *señorita*.'

The hard fingers stayed round her arm. Almost as though she were one of his chattels, to be returned to its proper place in his household – after suitable censure had been passed, she thought bitterly.

But she could do nothing except accompany him to the car, wherein Juanita was already huddled, small and apprehensive in the back seat. With a chill air of courtesy that made Hilary feel worse than ever the Conde opened the front passenger door and handed her in. He drove away instantly, heading for the road out of the city centre, and she turned abruptly to exclaim: 'But, *señor*, does Ramon know that—?'

'He is returning in his own car. One of the maids will bring your wrap to you as soon as possible,' the Conde said in clipped tones that did not encourage any further protests.

The big car gathered speed. Dismay gave way to miserable acceptance of the fiasco as she thought of the situation and liked it less with every fresh little recollection of the evening. In one way she was thankful the Conde had arrived when he did, but if only the rescue had been from *any* other than the ignominious situation in which she had landed. Her cheeks grew hot with the memory and she was thankful for the dimness of the car. How long had he watched her efforts to extricate herself from the amorous attentions of Señor Pereira? Worse, did he think she had encouraged those attentions?

There was ominous silence at the back of the car. She could only let imagination conjure with what had taken place when the Conde confronted his niece. She longed to turn and speak to Juanita, sensing that the silence of the small figure back there in the shadows was anything but happy, but the cold air of dominance from the aloof man at the wheel was an effective deterrent to her badly shaken courage. Better to wait until they were in the privacy of their own rooms.

However, there was no opportunity of seeking any reassurance that Juanita had escaped catastrophe. When the car reached the villa the Conde swung out, opened the rear door, and with a crisp command dispatched his niece indoors.

Juanita did not stop to argue. A small, muffled '*Buenas noches*' floated over her shoulder as she ran. But escape was

94

not to be swift for Hilary.

'One moment, *señorita*.' The Conde closed the car door with unwonted force. 'There is something I wish to say.'

Foreboding descended like a leaden weight on her spirits as she walked indoors and passed before him into the *sala*. Obviously the reckoning was to be demanded; she'd broken the rules – in spite of first seeking his permission – and she had offended his immutable code of convention. Feeling very much like a child caught out in some ghastly misdemeanour, she went stiffly to the great carved fireplace and stood in front of it, looking unseeingly at the intricate pattern of scrolled leaves and florets at eye level while she braced herself to face the chill, arrogant disapproval of the man coming on firm, even steps to her side.

'Well, *señorita*,' he said grimly. 'Are you still so certain that you can look after yourself?'

She started, having expected censure concerning Juanita, and felt a slight relief. 'I've always fought my own battles, *señor*,' she said with a trace of defiance, 'and tried not to make the same error of judgment a second time.'

'Error of judgment! *Por Dios!* Do you not recognize a *libertino* at first glance? Or do you set so little value on your reputation?'

The intensity of the words jerked her to face him. His eyes had deepened to glittering black and whiteness flared in the taut lines of anger at mouth and nostrils. Never had she seen him so incensed, or visualized the force and strength previously only dimly suspected beneath that polished, urbane control of his. She drew an unsteady breath and moistened dry lips.

'*Señor*, I – I do not think it – it is quite as dramatic as that,' she faltered. 'I hardly think that a couple of dances with a – with what we call a fast worker is going to ruin my reputation. After all, I made my opinion of him quite clear and left him before you even arrived, so—'

He caught her wrist as she gestured. 'You still do not understand. You are not in your own country now, *señorita*. For a young, unattached girl to be mauled on a public dance floor may count for little in London, but it certainly would not be overlooked in our society. Perhaps *you* do not care,' he snapped, 'but I certainly do.'

Hilary stared back at him, and anger stirred in her. She looked down pointedly at the autocratic hand fastened on her wrist and shook herself free. 'Aren't you forgetting something, *señor?*' she said coldly. 'I happen to be the injured party. *I* had to deal with a two-faced wolf belonging, presumably, to the society you are so proud of. *I* am the one who should be furious.'

'Perhaps you will be more circumspect in future,' he said thinly. 'You should never have allowed yourself to become so vulnerable in the first place.'

'How was I to know?' she flashed.

'Because already you have been warned about careless attachments. Or is your memory as unreliable as your sense of discrimination?' His mouth compressed as he surveyed her defiant expression. 'But you may be sure the opportunity will not arise again. I shall take care of that. Ramon should never have allowed the situation to occur; nor should my niece have become involved.'

'But she wasn't!'

'In your opinion, perhaps not.' He had regained control now and his bronze-chiselled features were set in their familiar autocratic lines. 'In future you will go out only with an escort whom I have designated, and the same ruling will, naturally, apply also to my niece. I fear she may be entertaining foolish ideas regarding my secretary. However, I shall find it necessary to send him to Huaroya for a while, which should effectively nip any such nonsense in the bud.'

Hilary's emotions were undergoing several wildly fluctuating changes. The surge of fury invoked by his imperious decree regarding herself was abruptly quelled by the statement succeeding it. Horror overcame her and she sought desperately for means to undo the damage.

'Oh, no, *señor!*' She put out her hand imploringly. 'You are entirely mistaken. You—'

'In what way?' From his superior height he looked down on her distraught face. 'Explain yourself, *señorita.*'

'You must not blame Juanita. Or send your secretary away,' she exclaimed frantically. 'It was entirely my fault. *I* asked Juanita to come with us. It was entirely my idea. And Ramon's behaviour was faultless. He—'

'It was he who introduced you to that gigolo, was it not?'
The Conde's mouth turned down with distaste.

'Yes, but he had no choice. Pereira came and spoke to us –
he – he knew Ramon slightly. Surely, *señor*, it would have
been in bad taste not to introduce him to us. And *I* was taken
in,' she rushed on, almost in tears by now. 'He seemed a
delightful person at first, and – and if he hadn't danced with
me there'd have been an odd one out. Ramon couldn't partner me and leave your niece sitting alone. It—'

'You went to hear flamenco, not comport yourselves on
the dance floor.'

'Yes, I know.' She shook her head and let her hands fall
despairingly. 'But I love to dance, and the band was super,
and it's a lovely floor, and it just seemed the natural thing to
want to join in. Can't you understand?'

'Not entirely. I have never heard of three people setting
out to dance,' he said dryly.

'But it just happened.' She turned away hopelessly. 'I can
only repeat that it was entirely my fault. Please do not
blame your secretary, or your niece.'

There was a silence and at last she turned, to find he was
watching her with unreadable eyes. 'Please, *señor*,' she
begged. 'Don't hurt Juanita – or blame Ramon.'

After an almost unbearable pause he raised dark brows
rather puzzledly. 'That thought distresses you, *señorita*?'

'Very much.'

'Such concern does you credit.'

'No.' She took a deep breath. 'I dislike injustice. That's
why I ask you not to judge too hastily.'

There was another brief silence, then abruptly he moved
towards the door. 'Very well, I will think it over. But remember, *señorita*. Never let me find you in such company
again, do you hear?'

'Oh, yes, *señor*!' she breathed fervently, suddenly knowing that this time it was going to be all right. 'I don't think
I'll ever be quite so stupid again.'

He paused, his hand reaching to open the door, and the
first glimmer of a break in his stern mien disturbed his
proud mouth. He raised one hand and touched an unruly
wisp that curled over her brow, and his searching gaze
missed nothing of the overbright sparkle in her eyes or the

unhappy spots of colour still clouding her cheeks. He said softly: 'The lessons of experience are invariably the most painful, are they not, *pequeña*? Especially when one is forced to admit the lesson has been learned.'

'Yes, *señor*, the admission is the most painful of all.'

He inclined his head and held open the door. All the way up the great curving staircase she was conscious of him standing below, watching until the sweep of the gallery above cut her off from sight. She was considerably shaken when she reached the privacy of her room and could allow tension to relax. Thank heaven she seemed to have convinced him that his suspicion about Juanita's 'ideas' were unfounded. The sense of relief made her smile tremulously as she made preparations to retire. But when she was lying in the darkness the swing to relief had lost its impetus and her eyes were troubled.

She nestled her face against the pillow and crept one hand under her cheek. It was proving very difficult to banish the imprint of a certain autocratic face from her memory. Not only those particular features but a voice as well, and a certain conversation that the bank of memory was throwing up; one phrase especially, spoken quite a long while ago.

You have a quality of honesty that is rare in a woman. It is for that quality I make my decision. I trust it will be a happy one . . .

Honesty . . . was she betraying the quality that at times in her life had seemed less a virtue than an inconvenience? The cheek resting against her hand felt uncomfortably hot. This sense of shame was a new and strangely disturbing bedfellow.

CHAPTER SIX

THE uneasy week drew to its close. Although Ramon was to be seen about the *quinta* and the Conde had made no further reference to his threat of banishing his secretary the suspicion seemed to hang in the air, or so it seemed to Hilary.

He had obviously bestowed a stern scolding on his niece – the pains she took to avoid him were extreme – but exactly what he had said remained curiously confused in the somewhat heated and dramatic account she poured out to Hilary. The main gist which emerged was that the matter of the Swiss finishing school was in the air again. The idea horrified Juanita, and she said so volubly and at length every time she remembered it – which was several times a day.

'I do not understand why he wants to punish me!' she said in outraged tones. 'It was not my fault. You do not blame me, my Hilary, do you?'

'Good heavens!' Hilary stared. 'What for?'

'That is what I ask him. But he go on and on about my – my lack of discretion and Ramon's and who is the Señor Pereira and how did you meet him. At first I am so thankful that he does not seem suspicious of me and Ramon, and I dare not say a thing lest I make a mistake.' Juanita paused for breath. 'Then he say am I sure that was the one and only time we all go out and meet that – that *dago*. And then he start on about sending me to school. Oh, Hilary, he won't send me away, will he? Not now that you are here?'

'He probably thinks you would benefit by the company of girls of your own age,' Hilary said slowly. 'It would be a change for you and a wonderful chance to go to Europe.'

'Well, I do not wish a change. Nor do I wish to visit Europe – yet.'

'Then you'll have to behave yourself – and so shall I – until this blows over,' said Hilary with a return to her old humour. 'You'd better pass the word on to Ramon.'

Juanita nodded fervently. 'I think we make sure we do not encounter your passionate Pereira – and keep out of Tio's way until he comes out of his *mal genio*.'

Hilary agreed with equal fervency. Now she thought it over she decided that the Conde had handled the situation with extreme cunning. He had not risked planting any more foolish ideas in his niece's head by threatening to banish his secretary; instead, he had threatened to banish *her*, and the effect on that young lady was all that any concerned guardian or parent could wish.

All the same, even though he was as cool and polite as ever in his attitude towards Hilary she was sure she detected an air of disapproval behind his glance whenever it encountered her. Or was it disappointment?

Hilary wasn't sure, and was somewhat surprised to discover that it mattered. Once, his censure or his disapproval would have stung her to defiance and resentment, but now it didn't. Gradually she was building a picture in which the background was taking shape, and only now was she beginning to grasp the immensity of the responsibility he shouldered. Technically, his mother, the Condesa, had assumed parental care of the two orphans, but the elderly Condesa was Chilian born. She did not care greatly for Lima's moist, sub-tropical climate and since the death of her husband three years previously she spent a great deal of her time with her brother and sister-in-law on the family estate near Valparaiso, returning for family occasions, holidays and an extended stay during the winter months. But this did not prevent her from demanding full reports of all family events, of the Huaroya estate, and the many business affairs her husband had added to his already considerable holdings in real estate. Then there was Doña Elena, also widowed and in indifferent health, and her not inconsiderable affairs as well as herself to be cared for. There were the tenants, and the workers at Huaroya, all of whom he knew by name, and now there were the children of his sister to care for. No wonder he exuded authority – and automatically extended it to herself . . .

She wasn't sorry when the sun set on Friday and she was free to look forward to the week-end. Bruce was picking her up immediately after an early breakfast and she would be away for the whole day, and she was planning to spend Sunday exploring – alone.

Immediately after the evening meal she made her excuses

and retired to her own room, intending to shampoo and set her hair before she went to bed. But first she would decide on what to wear tomorrow in case she had to go downstairs again and seek the loan of Concepta's iron for a last minute pressing. She wandered out on the balcony, mentally going over her wardrobe. It was the old problem of staying fresh and crisp and cool all day in a hot, humid climate. The synthetics didn't crease but tended to get clammy; the cottons were most comfortable but went limp so soon . . .

The night breeze was gentle, bringing a cool whisper of the sea and coaxing and sweetness from the sleeping blossoms in the darkness below. Hilary sighed and leaned on the rail, the dress problem fading from her mind and the niggling sense of guilt returning. Perhaps it was silly to remember all that business about honesty; she hadn't really connived with Juanita to hoodwink her uncle. The tender little romance was harmless enough, she was sure. But there was another important aspect which had completely escaped her memory until tonight, and now that she contemplated it she had to admit that it made a difference; the matter of Juanita's inheritance. Certainly the Conde would not forget it, and it was only natural that he should suspect the fortune-hunting motive in any young man who took interest in his niece.

Poor Ramon; his chances seemed remoter than ever. Hilary was positive that he genuinely cared for Juanita, but would the Conde ever believe that? The ghastly barrier of class was bad enough – obviously the mere thought of Juanita marrying the Conde's secretary would rock the foundations of the *quinta*, but Juanita being an heiress put it into the realm of impossibility.

Hilary shook her head wistfully, a slight smile curving her mouth. She was beginning to take it as seriously as Juanita, yet back home it would be so light a flirtation it would scarcely stir a leaf. It all came back to Juanita being so sequestered. She ought to have lots of friends, both boy and girl, of her own age, then she wouldn't make a grand passion of the only personable young man with whom she came in frequent contact. Anyway, whom had the Conde lined up for her marriage partner? There would be some young man somewhere, of good family and sufficiently well endowed to be above any suspicion of seeking a wealthy bride. The courtship would be chaperoned in the old tradition, there would be a tremendous wedding celebration to which the families would come from near and far, and only then would Juanita be left alone – to begin getting to know her husband. The smile had gone from Hilary's lips; even though there were advantages to an arranged marriage – if one looked at it from the viewpoint of the skilful family matchmakers – the very idea was repugnant to Hilary. To be taken for life, jealously guarded, with the chance of true love relegated to very long odds indeed . . . Was it true that love did enter these arranged marriages? That time after time they turned out very happily? Perhaps they did, she conceded reluctantly; propinquity could wield a strange wand. But it could also engender hatred. Nothing, she thought vehemently, could ever compensate for the freedom of choosing one's own partner, and for the wonder that could be born in the meeting of a stranger's glance, that could happen when one least expected it; anywhere, any time, across a crowded room or . . .

A sudden movement below tore into her reverie. She saw the shadow still, and the glimmer like a firefly spark through the velvet darkness. Too late she drew back.

'Señorita . . .?' The Conde had paused in his leisurely stroll. He was looking up, his dark head catching a bluish glow of radiance from some unknown source. It was lending new angles to the fine-boned contours of his features and a polished swarthiness with the rich tones and highlights of a superb portrait in oils. The vivid picture rose in Hilary's mind, merging with one remembered from that first morning, and the power of glinting eyes forged its compulsion.

Then he laughed softly and broke the tenuous cord of magnetism. 'You were far away, señorita – until I disturbed your pleasure of the night.'

The aromatic drift from his cigar coiled softly in tiny spirals, a sensuous challenge to the innocence of the blossom scents, and strangely tantalizing to Hilary's nostrils. She said, 'Yes – it is a beautiful night.'

'Almost as beautiful as the mornings, *no es verdad, señorita?*'

The firefly spark winged again and she wondered if she

imagined the hint of devilry underlying the light tones. Or was it the wickedness of a satyr that was making her recall that first morning when she had found joy of the morn in this very place? *En deshabille!*

She said unsteadily: 'I'm not sure, *señor*. I do not think they can be compared.'

'Yes, that is true,' he mused. 'No more than one could compare the radiance of a beautiful woman as she greets the first rose caress of dawn with the mystery of the same woman when night veils her beauty and her eyes reflect her lover.'

The rich timbre of his voice made the observation into a strangely sensuous communication. It was not without considerable power to disturb and Hilary moved quickly, almost as though by doing so she could dispel the odd sensation his voice had evoked.

'You seem to know a lot about how we look first thing in the morning and last thing at night,' she remarked acidly, then rued the words the moment they were out. 'But of course you speak of goddesses – not mere ordinary mortals,' she amended hastily.

He laughed, deep rich sounds, and his sweeping upward glance seemed to challenge. 'Poetic observation, *niña fresca mia!* And certainly not of goddesses. Do you always take everything so literally?'

'Sometimes it is safer to do so than read between the lines,' she said carefully, a tinge of rose deepening in her cheeks. *Fresh!* Was she? Hastily she sought a more expedient topic and almost instantly her brain supplied two alternatives. '*Señor* . . .' she leaned forward a little, 'there is something I wished to ask—'

'Ah, yes?' he interrupted, one hand rising. 'But I am about to suffer a crick in the neck, as I believe you describe it. Would you care to descend to this more comfortable level of conversation?'

She looked down at the shadowy lines of him and again there came that ghost of a deep chuckle. She hesitated, just a second too long.

'You are not afraid of the dark, *señorita*?' came the soft taunt.

Hilary stiffened. 'Not in the least!' Pausing only to snatch a filmy scarf for her shoulders she went down the curving shallow stairs, deliberately checking her steps when she reached the foot and moving slowly across the dim, echoing hall.

He was waiting for her on the terrace, lounging negligently against the ghostly white marble of a pilaster. He took the scarf from her arm and with unhurried movements placed it round her shoulders.

'Thank you,' she murmured, obeying the light touch that compelled her to fall into step with his leisurely stroll forward. The slight pressure of his hand fell from her shoulder and as it did so his sleeve brushed her bare forearm. He was wearing a smoking jacket of maroon-coloured velvet. In the subdued glow of the terrace lamps the material took on the rich fathomless depth of a sea of crimson wine, and its touch on her skin was like a sleek caress. With an almost involuntary movement she drew away from the contact, and he turned his head to look down at her.

'There was something you wished to ask me, *señorita*?' he said in suave tones.

For some reason she felt flustered. It made her stumble a little over the phrasing of her words as she said, 'Yes – this week-end. I just wanted to check—'

'Ah, yes. Your leisure time.' The dark sculptured head flipped back, and the movement revealed his profile, silhouetted like bronze against the blue-misty radiance cast by the white wall of the villa. Abruptly he swung to her again and his brows winged high. 'You sound a little concerned, *señorita*. Are you afraid I may suddenly curtail your freedom?'

'No.' She hadn't expected anything of the kind and her response betrayed her surprise. 'I only wanted to let you know I would be away all day tomorrow and Sunday, and remind you about Joaquin—'

'You are staying somewhere tomorrow night – where?' he demanded with that disconcerting abruptness.

'Oh, no – I shall be coming back at night, though I may be late,' she said quickly. 'But I was wondering about Joaquin . . . He was to have gone to visit his cousin Ruy at Miraflores – the children were going to the beach – but Señora Mendoza telephoned this afternoon to say that little Ruy has a sore throat and she thinks it wiser to cancel Joaquin's visit. He is very disappointed, so . . .'

She hesitated, and he said sharply: 'So?'

'He's going to be a lonely little boy, so,' again she hesitated, 'I could take him out with me on Sunday if it would help – everyone at the villa has arrangements of some sort for this week-end.'

'I have not – would you care to sit down, *señorita*?'

He touched her arm and she saw that their indolent paces had taken them along the path to the vinery. Its entrance was screened by an *enramada* which held a rustic seat, and it was this the Conde gravely indicated.

The cool waxen ivory of sleeping magnolia blossoms stirred softly nearby and the scent of unseen garden sweetnesses caught subtly at the senses. A certain tension of sudden awareness made her glance at him and make no move towards composing herself in those scented shadows beneath the magnolia. It was impossible not to be instantly conscious of the Conde's magnetism and her own femininity in an atmosphere such as this . . . Impatient of the trembling instinct, she dismissed it as quickly as it came; how foolish could imagination make one?

He did not sit down after she had sat stiffly on the extreme edge of the seat. Instead he raised one foot and rested it idly on the edge, leaning his arm across his knee. From this careless stance he looked down at her. 'You are a most conscientious young woman, Miss Martin. I appreciate your concern, but I could not dream of allowing you to spoil your arrangements.'

'It wouldn't spoil anything.' Her surprise at his reversion to the English formality was tinged with something like disappointment; suddenly she wished he would use her first name – almost everyone at the villa did so now. 'It wouldn't spoil anything,' she said with unconscious aloofness. 'I was planning to take the train up into the mountains. I've been told that the funicular railway is an excitement that mustn't be missed.'

'True – for a tourist. You were not planning to sample this excitement with Mr. Gilford?' he asked sharply.

'No.' She gave a small shake of her head to underline the

negative. 'Tomorrow – yes – but not Sunday. That's why I thought—'

'You are going sightseeing tomorrow?' he broke in as she hesitated.

'No,' she glanced up. 'He's showing me over the ranch.'

'Ah.' The Conde flexed his well-shaped hand and looked down at it. The fingers relaxed, then curved under as he said lightly: 'And then you will dine at his house, delightfully free of conventional restraint. You will reminisce on your home country and your backgrounds, discover a common interest which you both adore, and then he will flirt with you.'

'He won't.'

The Conde smiled slightly, his teeth glinting very white. 'Pardon me my contradiction, *señorita*, but you delude yourself – if you believe that!'

Hilary smoothed a fold from her dress. 'But I do believe it.' She did not look up.

'And I prefer to believe the evidence of my own eyes.'

Her head lifted sharply. She frowned. 'Evidence, *señor*?'

'The good Bruce Gilford wore the look of a man who does not quite believe in his good fortune last week-end,' the Conde observed evenly. 'I think he had forgotten what it was like to relax with one of his most charming country-women.'

My Señor Conde see too much! she thought with a flash of shock. His perception made her recall Bruce's words as they danced; it also caused her to remember a moment later that same evening in the garden at the hacienda. Hilary's mouth firmed and her clasped hands tightened a fraction. The Conde's determination to keep tabs on her had induced annoyance, resentment, defiance and amusement in turn; now it brought a sudden need to change the subject. In any case; what business was it of his if she did flirt with Bruce?

'I'm sure that was *all* it was,' she said firmly, 'and speaking of last week-end reminds me . . .'

'Yes, *señorita*?' He straightened and sat down at her side, crossing his knees to conclude the swift lithe movement. 'What about last week-end?'

She looked directly in front of her and kept her voice casual. 'You mentioned a favour you wished to ask of me, *señor*.'

'A favour? Ah!' he snapped his fingers, 'I remember. It was almost a bargain we made, wasn't it? This side of it concerns my nephew.'

Bargain! Joaquin? Beneath curiosity she felt a small sense of flatness as she inclined her head and waited.

'It will be his birthday soon, next month,' went on the deep, velvet smooth voice out of the shadows. 'You probably know that it is our custom to celebrate our saint's day – that is the saint after whom we are named – rather than the anniversary of the actual day on which we were born. However, Joaquin's parents died only a week before the little celebration that was planned and in the circumstances we decided to postpone it until his birthday, for this year, anyway. The other will always be fraught with sadness, I'm afraid.'

He paused, and Hilary turned her head. 'You are very wise, *señor*, and very understanding. How can I help?'

'In view of your arrival in our midst, I thought an English style birthday party would prove an innovation. A friend of mine has recently imported an English technologist in connection with new plant he is installing, and I believe the Englishman has brought his family with him. We will invite the two children; it will be an opportunity for them to make new friends in a strange city and it will also help to bring the right birthday atmosphere.'

Hilary nodded. 'You would like me to be on hand, and translate and help with the children? Of course I will.'

'I wish you to organize the entire affair, *señorita*, if you will be so kind.'

'The whole thing?' she exclaimed, somewhat startled.

'Yes. I would like you to arrange everything. The menu, the amusements, and whatever else is necessary. I will give you *carte blanche* and instruct the staff to follow whatever orders you give them. In brief, *señorita*, imagine you are arranging a birthday party for a seven-year-old boy in your own home and then put theory into practice.'

She was silent so long that he moved, leaning forward to look into her face. 'You do not wish to arrange this?'

'Oh no – that is yes – I should love to,' she said hastily. 'But are you sure it'll work? I mean, will the children like it?'

'You have doubts?'

'Well,' she took a deep breath and smiled wryly, 'Joaquin may have his own ideas for his party.'

'That is the English way, perhaps?' The Conde's tone sharpened. 'The children are allowed to arrange their own celebrations?'

'Yes, very often. A lot depends on the parents, of course,' she said thoughtfully. 'If they're the understanding type they'll supply masses of grub, lock up all the breakable stuff, and leave the kids to enjoy themselves their own way.' There was a silence, and she was instantly sensitive to the definite aura of disapproval in the air. She added quickly: 'But that's older children, of course, not little ones.'

'I should hope not!' He leaned back, resuming his former relaxed position. 'However, there is some time. Perhaps you will think it over and then we will discuss it more fully in a day or so. *Si*?'

'*Si, señor*,' she agreed absently, her mind already turning over the possibilities his idea had suggested. She could bake and ice a birthday cake herself for Joaquin, with seven blue candles . . . how would sausage rolls, cheese dip, trifle, and treasure hunts go down with Joaquin and his little friends? Perhaps she could— She heard the Conde's voice and looked up. 'I'm sorry, *señor*. I was thinking. What did you say about concern?'

'I was inquiring, *señorita*, if you were upset by *el señor* Pereira's ill-breeding the other night?'

'Oh . . .' a little surprised, she switched her mind from party plans to the memories of the night of the flamenco. 'Yes, a little, at the time,' she said reflectively, 'but I've forgotten it now – and written it off as experience.'

'Experience.' The Conde's mouth compressed at the corners. 'I would not be inclined to write it off so cheaply and forget it.'

Hilary stiffened. '*Señor*! Are you insinuating that my behaviour was cheap?'

'No—' his hand fanned the air – 'not cheap. Foolish, perhaps, indiscreet even, naïve certainly. But not cheap in

108

the sense that you use the word.'

The firm lines of her mouth did not quite regain their normal sweet curves, despite the suppressed vehemence she detected in his tone. She drew the filmy blue folds of her scarf more closely round her shoulders and made to rise; this was certainly a moment to exercise discretion!

But discretion lost to a grasp of light, deceptively steeling fingers round her wrist.

'*No, señorita* – you are not to run away in pique.' Warmth lingered on her skin, held her wrist captive. 'I fail to understand your reactions. You will submit to the most blatant passes from a stranger on the dance floor – for fear of making a scene, perhaps – yet you will read unpleasant insinuation in a perfectly innocent, if angry observation from myself. Why?'

'I–I'm sorry.' A little ashamed now, she looked at the dark supple hand outlined against the pale sapphire luminence of her dress. 'I didn't mean it that way. It – it's just I'd prefer to forget it, that's all.'

'That you were taken in by a *libertino*?'

'Something like that.' Rather tremulously she raised her head and met the shadowed power of his stare. A small rueful sigh escaped her. 'I know how you think of these matters, and – I'll be honest – I'd hate you to think I might have encouraged him, and—'

'Your very presence would be an encouragement to that *chacal*.' The clasp slackened abruptly and fell away from her wrist. 'You see, as I've already tried to explain, such a situation would be unlikely to happen to one of my own countrywomen. A girl of good family would not be allowed to disport herself on the dance floor with any casual pick-up, and once married her husband would certainly ensure that such embarrassment did not befall her. That is why young foreign girls, especially those who enjoy a great deal of liberty, are particularly vulnerable to the attentions of men such as Pereira.'

'Yes, I know what you are trying to explain,' she said quickly. 'And we do realize that no matter what the nationality it will include men of courtesy like yourself—'

'Thank you, *señorita*,' he interposed gravely.

'—and the other kind. But it isn't always so easy to recognize them away from one's country,' she admitted ruefully. 'It's that aura of Latin glamour.'

'Is that how you think of us?' He sounded amused.

She looked away. 'But all the same, we'd prefer it that way. To be free to discover people's – a man's character – for ourselves. To be free to accept or reject. That way we learn to judge.'

There was a short silence. She knew he was not convinced, yet his interest was still caught. She thought of Juanita's cause and suddenly thought: why not? An opportunity for a little propaganda should not be missed. She turned and said earnestly:

'You see, *señor*, what happened to me was a kind of lesson which taught me to be wary in future. Mr Pereira was charming at first – disarming, in fact! – but it wore off soon. How do we know that he is not betrothed to some sweet little innocent like your own niece, who believes in that charm, in the limited sociality she is allowed with him? So she'll marry him, and discover that he's a regular Don Juan. He'll be unfaithful, he won't have any charm to spare for her then, and she'll be unhappy for the rest of her life. But *she* won't be able to take a lover and find a little happiness.'

She paused, and so far there was nothing in the ensuing silence to deter her from continuing. Encouraged, she went on: 'In our society we mix freely and reputation takes on a much clearer and fairer definition. Word gets round more freely and we're forearmed.'

'You judge on hearsay, then?' he said coolly.

'No. We judge as we find, but our freedom helps us to be more discriminate in forming serious relationships.'

'I see.' The Conde shifted his position and studied her more closely. 'So it is exactly as I have heard: you are in favour of more free and easy relationships between the sexes.'

She hesitated. 'Yes, in a way. That's what I'm trying to explain. If a boy and girl make a lot of friendships it all helps them to know human nature and make comparisons. Then they are less likely to make a mistake when they choose their life partner.'

'Go on,' he prompted as she paused.

'One learns how temperaments can clash. So it's better to

have a friendly relationship first, get to know each other, before entering into a more emotional, or – or formal relationship,' she said cautiously suddenly aware of a slight shift of intensity in the atmosphere. 'Temperament is extremely important to a happy relationship, so it's far better to discover incompatibility before it's too late,' she ended more firmly.

'Yes, I think I follow your line of reasoning.' The Conde's dark brows rose over his intent eyes. 'So it is perfectly permissible for a man to engage a girl's interest, even make overtures to her, without committing himself in the least?'

This wasn't quite what she had meant, and she frowned, uncertain how to parry the undoubted modicum of truth in this cunning ambiguity. The suspicion was born on her that he was amused behind that intent gravity – and not above encouraging her to discourse on the subject. She said indignantly: 'It isn't quite as cold-blooded as you make it sound. The girl understands that when a boy asks her to go out with him and—'

'Date is the term, I believe?' His mouth did not flicker.

'Dates her, perhaps makes a small gift of sweets, or a record,' she went on steadily, not looking at him, 'it doesn't mean that he immediately becomes her special property or she his. They're both perfectly free to form other attachments. But usually they do break away from their circle of friends and date each other exclusively for a while, if they've become very attracted to one another, but even then—'

'There appear to be a great number of buts and ifs involved in these non-committed relationships,' he observed with utter gravity. 'But I am sorry – I interrupt. Please continue. This is most interesting.'

She glanced at him, then away, her mouth tightening a fraction. 'It still doesn't mean that they automatically expect the relationship to end in marriage, and even if they do decide to get engaged, only to discover that they've made a mistake or quarrel too much, they're still free to break it off. It's their decision, and even if the parents are upset it's understood that it's the couple's decision. Because it's their future happiness that's at stake and no one else's.'

'I see.' He leaned one arm on the back of the seat and

stroked his chin musingly. 'But what about the girl's parents? Don't they object?'

'Object?' She stared at him. 'Why should they? Not if they love their daughter. They want her to be happy.'

'No, you misread me, *señorita*. Do they have no objections to their daughter being subjected to amatory advances from these casual male acquaintances?'

His dry phraseology invoked a gleam of amusement in her eyes and a desire to giggle. But it also masked what might have been a twinge of warning instinct and made her miss a certain intentness in his tone. She said firmly: 'Not at all. They don't look at it from that viewpoint. Not if they know the boy and – and trust their daughter.'

Silence fell, broken softly only by the stirring of the leaves and the secretive murmurs of some unseen insects. The skies were very clear, ablaze with stars, and the edges of the shadows were crisp now, making a bright latticework among the leaves. She stole a glance sideways and could discern the Conde's lean, aristocratic profile quite clearly. It was thoughtful, unmoving, and he stared at the night scene for quite a while before he turned to her, almost as though he had reached some decision.

'I understand now,' he said coolly.

She smiled. 'I hope it has helped you to see our viewpoint, *señor*.'

He inclined his head. 'I understand that two young people may encounter one another quite casually, as total strangers, even. Perhaps in a café or theatre and without introduction by a mutual acquaintance. And then the man is quite free to make an advance if he feels attracted. To which the girl, if she is also initially attracted, will not object. It is all in the name of learning to judge human nature if he should put out his hand – so – and touch her hand. Or caress her – thus . . .'

The warm steely fingers had stolen along the curve of her cheek almost before she realized his intention. They cupped her chin, turned it so that she was forced to meet his intent gaze, and imprisoned her even as they had imprisoned her wrist a short while before.

His voice came softly but quite clear: 'He may then proceed to embrace and kiss her.'

Hilary heard the gasp of her own indrawn breath as she moved to break the dangerous little spell. Instantly he released her and drew back.

'I have overstepped the permitted line? There is, after all, an invisible boundary which must be crossed with care?'

She managed a smile. 'I don't think you *do* understand, *señor*. We don't all start making love the moment we meet a stranger.'

'I would hardly say *we* are still strangers,' he said suavely.

'Oh, no, but that isn't quite what—' She stopped, wondering how to extricate herself from the dissertation which had taken an unexpected turn. She attempted to laugh lightly. 'We do stay fairly level-headed, you know, and try to keep our emotions from getting *too* out of hand.'

The moment the words were out she realized their foolishness – and regretted them bitterly. The Conde's eyes glimmered with the light of challenge accepted – and returned!

'Now who is cold-blooded?'

'N-not cold-blooded.' This time the dangerous little spell was not so easily broken. She gave a helpless shake of her head. 'It's just a matter of being sensible.'

'*Sensible*!' He was clearly astounded. 'You really believe in so cold a theory? You—'

'But it isn't a theory! It—' She tried to argue, to get back to safer ground, but his impatient gesture swept aside her frail protest.

'You foolish *chica*! You really believe you can play around and still keep emotions within hand. It is my belief that you do not know the meaning of the word!'

Denial rushed to her lips, faltered, and was lost in a gasp as the Conde effectively routed it. That sensuous touch of velvet came against her again, and in its turn was lost in the crushing strength of his embrace. Fresh impressions assailed her senses, wildly and overwhelming; a tang of spiced lotion lingering on his skin, the scent of the dressing that sleeked his black hair, the trace of warm smokiness in his breath, all mingling with the sheer impact of his personality to bring a power that reached every part of her being. Then the assailing impressions in their turn were lost in an oblivion in which nothing existed except his mouth on her own.

By the time she sought to recover shattered senses he was drawing back, looking down at the pale tremulous oval of her face. A light of satisfaction glinted in his dark eyes, and the mouth that could wreak such total devastation curved in a slight smile.

'I have a mind to teach you that meaning, my so cool little English miss.'

He was still holding her in the warm captivity of his hands, and Hilary was discovering an alarming weakness had robbed her limbs of their independence. Only her brain functioned wildly. . . . *take flight . . . stay . . . protest . . .*? All questions . . . no answers . . . *Why?*

'But you tremble! Surely one kiss is not so great a shock!' His voice was soft with amusement and the suspicion flared in Hilary that he was considering further shocks.

Furious at her loss of composure, she pulled away and averted her face. 'I–I certainly didn't expect such a shock from *you, señor.* I—'

'Me?' There was astonishment in the exclamation. 'Do you think I am impervious to the call of the senses, *señorita?*'

It seemed safer to agree and she shook her head dumbly.

'Or proof against feminine appeal – especially that of a charming and modest little ice maiden who dares to lecture me so solemnly on my outmoded attitude to the lack of decorum in society today?'

'Oh, but I wasn't!' She started back, then stood up frantically.

'But *I* think you were.' His own movement was no less swift but considerably more composed. He placed his hands on her shoulders and said in a low voice against her ear: 'And I begin to think that you did not expect so sudden a conversion.'

'Nor did I expect a practical demonstration of word definition,' she managed with commendable insouciance considering the circumstances. Wishing her heart would stop its wild capers, she spun to face his mocking gaze. 'And please remember, *señor,* that— *Oh!*' Her words ended with a gasp that was echoed almost immediately from behind the

Conde's tall figure.

It was too dark to see clearly the face of the girl standing there, but Hilary had no difficulty in recognizing Consuelo – or her anger.

'*Con perdón!* – but we have waited fifteen minutes already!' she cried furiously. 'Or had you forgotten, Romualdo?'

He turned to face her and bowed his head with a brief, icy courtesy. 'My apologies, *señorita*, I did not know.' He moved forward, then checked Hilary as she would have fled. 'No, *señorita*. I will see you indoors.'

'We are going to be be terribly late,' Consuelo grumbled as the Conde guided the two girls towards the terrace.

Hilary scarcely heard her; a complexity of new bewildering emotions was besetting her already shattered composure as she saw the Conde go to the waiting Sanchia and take both her hands to his lips as he murmured his apologies.

The corpulent Don Miguel hovered in the background, and as all three newcomers were in evening attire it was obvious that a social foursome was in the offing. The Conde greeted the other man and then excused himself, a brief gesture brushing his lapel indicating that he must change from his informal jacket, otherwise he was ready.

He appeared to have forgotten Hilary's existence, and after an automatic acknowledgment of Sanchia's friendly smile she made her way upstairs, back to the shampoo preparations which seemed to have been begun aeons ago. She stood for a long time, staring unseeingly into the mirror and running long finger-strokes through her loosened hair. Already the past hour was taking on a curious dreamlike quality – except that no dream left after-effects like this! Nor did any dream leave this sudden surge of unreasonable hatred of Consuelo.

Why had fate brought her along at that precise moment? How much had she heard of that bizarre little exchange? Hilary's mouth quivered; it *had* been a bizarre little lecture on her part! Then her mouth tightened again. How much had Consuelo seen?

Suddenly Hilary jammed the wash-basin plug in place with unnecessary force. There was nothing bizarre about it at all; it simply proved the Conde was human after all, and she would be deluding herself to pretend that he wasn't one of the most fascinating, exciting and attractive men with whom she had ever exchanged a kiss. *Exchanged?*

The oval face in the mirror was glowing a distinct pink. Abruptly she plunged her head into the water and upended the bottle of shampoo too wildly to be accurate. Knuckling the liquid stream away from her eyes, she pushed the thought out of her mind. What did it matter if Consuelo *had* witnessed that kiss?

CHAPTER SEVEN

A SENSE of normality returned with the advent of Bruce
Gilford the following day. As promised, he arrived very
early driving a large white tourer, and Hilary found it
pleasant and relaxing to ride through the cool, misted morning to reach Bruce's house before the heat of noon sapped
energy.

As the day wore on the scene of the previous evening grew
more dreamlike in retrospect, yet the memory of it persisted
in returning, to bring secret quivers of amusement at the
Conde's supposition regarding Bruce.

In all but one respect the Conde's forecast was extremely
accurate. Bruce *did* show her over parts of the ranch, in-
cluding some of the most magnificent horses she had ever
seen, and pointed out the main house and superb garden
which was Don Alonso's country home. He *did* tease her
with nonsensical quips, entirely free of conventional restraint during a pleasant meal in his own more modest but
extremely comfortable house, and after his housekeeper
brought coffee and withdrew he invited Hilary's remi-
niscences to intermingle with his own anecdotes of his life
and travels. But not once during that long and pleasant day
did he make any effort to flirt.

The Conde was of far too suspicious a turn of mind, she
decided when a companionable silence fell between herself and Bruce during the drive home under the silver-
dusted purple night. Anyway, he had no room to talk, in
view of his own guileful performance in the garden last
night. An increasing awareness of how skilfully and craftily
outplayed she had been brought, surprisingly, no anger, only
a small secretive curve to her mouth and a warm sense of
anticipation of the next time she should cross swords with a
conquistador – when she would be well and truly on
guard!

'What's so amusing?'

Bruce's voice recalled her errant attention and she realized that the car had stopped. She saw the outline of the

villa silhouetted against the deep velvet sky, and turned guiltily to the man in the driving seat. He shook his head admonishingly.

'I don't believe you heard a word I said!'

'I'm sorry – I *was* off the wavelength,' she said contritely. 'What did you say, Bruce?'

Her apologetic smile disarmed him instantly. 'Nothing profound,' he said lightly, 'only to ask what were you planning for tomorrow?'

She told him, and he raised quizzical brows. 'Mind if I join you? I'm an expert guide.'

She hesitated, then laughed. 'Are you afraid I get lost in the mountains?'

'Exploring's more fun with two. So we'll call that settled.' He reached for the car door. 'I'll see you up to the house.'

Her small demur was lost in the closing of the door. He tucked an escorting hand under her elbow as they strolled along the arbor walk and up the terrace steps. At the patio door Bruce stopped and looked down at her for a moment, still cupping her arm in the warmth of his hand. Hilary experienced a moment of wry doubt. Perhaps Bruce was about to make a belated start at a mild flirtation, or . . . Why did men invariably expect a reward for taking a girl out? An exchange of endearments should happen naturally, she thought, not because it had become a tradition. Suddenly she knew she didn't want to kiss Bruce, even the goodnight kind of kiss that could be a pleasurable exchange without counting a jot to either party. Then she felt her hand taken into his warm clasp, and heard him say lightly:

'No, I don't think you're the kind of girl who dispenses goodnight kisses to all and sundry. Am I right?'

She was so surprised she could only stare up at his quizzical features.

'Unless of course you'd be affronted if I didn't pay you the compliment?' he added softly.

'Oh, Bruce, you're an idiot!' she laughed. 'Thanks for a lovely day.' Impulsively she reached up and gave him the kiss that a moment ago had seemed an unwilling token.

She was smiling to herself when she ran lightly upstairs to her room a little while later, after making the arrangements for the next day with Bruce. The big villa was still and silent, as though deserted, and she gave a small exclamation as the staircase lights flipped out just as she reached the top.

The culprit was Juanita, just closing the door of her room. She re-emerged and looked curiously at Hilary.

'I am sorry – I didn't hear you – but I could not sleep with the light shining under my door. Have you had a good day?'

'Wonderful.'

'He is very attractive, the English Señor Gilford, is he not?'

'Yes, he is rather nice-looking,' Hilary agreed after a moment's reflection on Bruce's undoubtedly attractive physical appearance. But Juanita was shaking her head.

'I do not mean in only his looks,' she said wistfully. 'It is the way he accepts a woman as an intellectual equal and companion, yet is still protective towards her in the way that an escort should.'

'I didn't think you knew Bruce well enough to notice all that,' Hilary said with some surprise. 'But most Englishmen are like that now, although there are pockets of resistance,' she added wryly. 'Quite a lot of them have decided that we can't have equal pay and all the rest of it and still expect them to give up their seats in buses and open doors for us. Which is fair enough, I suppose. So,' she regarded Juanita with merriment in her eyes, 'think it over carefully before you go all out for complete emancipation.'

'But you would not give up your freedom now you have won it, I think.'

'No, not our freedom to choose our lovers.' Hilary sighed, sensing Juanita's desire to exchange confidences, and leaned against the door jamb. She smiled at the younger girl. 'Anything exciting happened here today?'

Juanita closed her eyes and gave an exaggerated sigh of boredom. 'Nothing exciting ever happens here, and today has been even duller.'

'Bad as that?'

Juanita nodded. 'Joaquin was peevish because he could not visit Ruy, and so I had to amuse him. Tio was in a bad temper as well, and then Consuelo and Sanchia called to see Tia Elena, and even Sanchia was in a disagreeable mood.'

Juanita lowered her voice. 'She is talking of going back to Europe and taking a post with Carlo's firm, and everyone is trying to dissuade her.'

'I don't see why she shouldn't go back to Europe if she wants to,' said Hilary, 'or why she shouldn't take a job with her late husband's firm. After all, she is bound to have made friends over there. I think it's a very good idea.'

'Yes, but there is Don Miguel. Actually, I think she wants to get away from him,' Juanita giggled.

'I'm not surprised.' Hilary did not lower her voice to a secretive whisper as Juanita had done. 'The family seems determined to push her into some man's arms.'

Juanita nodded sagely. 'And then Consuelo can – how you say it – set her cap at Tio with her conscience clear.'

'I should have thought Consuelo would be the epitome of correctness,' Hilary said tartly. 'Surely it's for your uncle to decide who should do the cap-setting.'

'Ah, but we have our ways of helping them decide.' Juanita giggled softly. 'Do you think we are entirely without wiles?'

'No, I didn't.' Hilary straightened, an automatic prelude towards departure. 'But if he must marry one of them he'd be wiser to chose Sanchia,' she added flatly.

Juanita rested her chin on her cupped hands and looked up soberly. 'I think so, too. For her, Consuelo would stand aside – but for no one else. That one should have been the oldest sister. She is too bossy – but Tio will tame her tantrums,' she added with a quirk of malicious glee.

The thought did not bring the satisfaction it might have done. Hilary frowned, decided it was time to bring the discussion of Consuelo and the Conde's marriage prospects to an end, and Juanita broke in suddenly:

'They were talking about you this afternoon, my Hilary.'

'Really!'

'They are hoping that you and Señor Gilford will become drawn to one another. Consuelo is certain that he is attracted to you.' Juanita leaned forward confidingly. 'Already they are planning to invite you and him to join the party for the fiesta. You have never seen a fiesta, have you? Oh, it is wonderful – especially for lovers – and when—'

'It's getting late.' Hilary moved abruptly. With an effort she hid her anger until she bade Juanita goodnight, but when she reached her own room she was seething.

How dared they discuss her and couple her name with Bruce's? Apart from the sheer stupidity of it – with a man she'd known so short a time and been out with only once! – it was sheer impertinence. What on earth would Bruce think if it got to his ears? Probably he would only laugh, but it wasn't funny. And the Conde . . . Surely *he* had not partaken of the stupid speculations about . . .

Suddenly she wished she had not arranged to spend the rest of the week-end with him. It would certainly give them cause for further conviction. Oh, why couldn't they mind their own rigid convention and not apply it to her? They just didn't understand . . . Wild thoughts of cancelling the arrangement for the following day raced into her angry brain, only to be dismissed by the reaction of logic. She would have to let Bruce know, which meant telephoning him tonight, and that would mean hanging around for another hour to give him time to get home.

She sat on the edge of her bed and thought of the phone in the little alcove under the curve of the stairs. This was the one for the general household – the Conde had his own personal line in his library, and Doña Elena an extension in her suite – and its situation did not exactly make for privacy. Hilary felt a marked reluctance to venture down there at so late an hour to make a call which, if overheard, could give rise to further misleading impressions.

A fresh spurt of resentment made her shoulder out of her light jacket and slam the door of her wardrobe. Why should she worry? When was she going to get it into her head that her personal life wasn't beholden to the Conde and the rest of the Pacquera clan? If she went out with half the English colony in Lima it was no affair of *his*, and neither he nor his friends had any right to couple her name with anyone's. She was free, she was British, and Spanish protocol had no part in her life – thank heaven! She would ignore the whole silly business . . . All the same, she would tell Bruce tomorrow, before somebody else had a chance; they would have a giggle – hadn't he once warned her never to get involved in the family quarrels? He might have warned her of their liability to involve her in their matchmaking gossip . . .

But although her anger had abated to a wry acceptance of it all by the next morning it had uncovered an odd sense of depression she could not shake off as she got ready to meet Bruce.

She tried to define it, telling herself that it was natural now that she knew there was speculation about herself and Bruce. It was bound to spoil what had promised to be a very happy friendship. For it was only a friendship. She wasn't going to fall in love with Bruce, and instinct told her that he wasn't going to fall in love with her. It was simply that they were both temporary expatriates and Bruce was attractive and good fun. But how could she expect the Latin mind to see it that way?

Somehow, once she was with Bruce, she found she couldn't bring herself to mention it to him, and instead of the shared amusement she had visualized there was only the annoying little depression to sober her spirits as she boarded the train with Bruce. However, once the journey commenced and the first few miles through the cottonfields were passed her interest was caught and the mountains began to exert their spell.

The tiny village stations were fascinating, each one with its purveyors of fruit, wares and refreshments for the travellers, and the climb itself, high into the heart of the Andes, was breathtaking and at times almost terrifying.

The train roared and hurtled round bends and over switchbacks that left the heart several beats behind, only to slow and puff at the next incline while the heartbeats caught up with it and the eye could take in the spectacular vistas of mountain scenery. One moment a precipice of steely grey shale would loom ahead, then the world would fall away into a fathomless green ravine while the train seemed to sway on two slender silver threads and the rhythm of the wheels roared over the spidery steel span bridging the wild foaming torrent below.

At each swooping bend Hilary was pressed against Bruce and his hand would reach out to steady her until centrifugal force released its grip. The most hair-raising moment came at one point where the train turned abruptly, by means of its rear engine, and began a steep climb that made Hilary feel slightly giddy when she looked down at the drop of hundreds of feet immediately below.

Bruce gripped her hand reassuringly. 'This is nothing to what's at the top,' he said cheerfully. 'Peru has the highest passenger rail station in the world. They come along the train with oxygen to revive the passengers – those that survive that far, that is.'

'Bruce!'

'Don't worry, honey, we're not going there today,' he said in assuring tones. 'We wouldn't have time. It takes best part of the day to get there. Besides,' he added, gathering up their belongings, 'I'm not going to risk your suffering an attack of *siroche*.'

She frowned, puzzled, and he explained: 'Mountain sickness. It gets you if you're not used to high altitudes. The Indians, who are born to it, have a far greater lung development than we have. They'd never work and survive on the high plateau if they didn't.'

He helped her down from the train and paused to select a flower favour from one of the vendors whose wares were set out along the side of the track.

He tucked the small posy behind her ear from where it immediately fell out. Hilary caught it and laughed as she met the wide-eyed gleam of amusement from the Indian girl who was watching.

'When the man does this in a film and tucks a flower in the girl's hair it always stays put at a perfect angle,' Bruce grumbled, 'but when I try it look what happens.'

'Yes, but they probably do about fifty takes in a film to get that one casual little incident to stay put,' she laughed, searching in her bag for a pin to fasten the posy at the neck of her dress. 'Where are we going?'

'There's a market here – nowhere near as famous as the one at Huancayo but quite interesting – and a spiral track winds up the mountainside to the church. There's a little bridge up there – that's if you feel like walking and looking at views. Or would you rather go to the market?'

'You're the guide,' she said demurely.

'We'll walk just a little way first,' he said, taking her arm to guide her, 'then we'll go to the market, by then we'll be ready for some grub. And there's a nice little spot I know of where we can picnic.'

His prosaic tones had not prepared her for the sheer grandeur of the scene that awaited when they left the little wayside halt and turned to the narrow path that wound up the hillside and overlooked the whole valley. There were terraces of carefully tilled crops, from the distance looking like long green steps edged with pearly grey pebbles, and the long straggle of little houses clinging to the steep hillside like a widening swathe through the patchwork of smallholdings. And for the first time Hilary saw the Andean *Indios* in their colourful traditional dress.

They were returning from church, the gay colours of their striped ponchos and the women's full skirts making a picturesque frieze of reds and blues and pinks against the skyline as they crossed the bridge by the church and wound their way down the path to the village.

The air was thin and clear, and the colours seemed to glow, but it was the peaks beyond, far in the distance, that brought an almost overwhelming sense of awe and made Hilary shade her eyes and stay silent as she gazed at the scene.

An enigmatic sun cast a film of gold and apricot across the snow-capped peaks and threw the cruel grey crags into sharp relief. That day there was little cloud to soften the starkness of those peaks and the bland blue of the sky under that great sun only served to emphasize the might of the mountains and the punity of man. Suddenly Hilary shivered. Her gaze strayed to the neat green terraces of maize, quinoa, and tubers, hard-won by patient toil from the thin, unyielding soil, and she perceived how harsh was the life of the Andean Indian.

Bruce touched her arm and she turned away, to take his guiding hand and pick her way down the steep, uneven path. A short walk brought them to the village and the central square which was the hub of village life. They spent a leisurely hour wandering through the market, fascinated by the infinite variety of crafts displayed by the stall-holders. Hilary admired the gay textiles hand-woven from alpaca wool, and the pottery formed to traditional designs that had come down through the centuries. After a great deal of indecision she chose a piece of silver-work in the form of a cross-

shaped pendant to send to her mother and after a brief argument desisted gracefully and allowed Bruce to buy her a
scarlet-fringed poncho.

'You'll feel as though you belong here now,' he grinned,
slipping it carelessly across her shoulders before they moved
on.

The market place was thronged now and noisy, the bar-
tering voices shrill through the thin dusty haze hanging in the
air. Bruce had brought a small picnic basket and when he
shot an inquiring glance at Hilary she nodded, conscious of
thirst if not hunger.

They found a secluded spot by the winding path and unpacked the lunch Bruce's housekeeper had prepared. There
were small, deliciously crusty rolls stuffed with herb-
seasoned minced meat and tiny sharp-tasting onions, plump
gherkins and golden tomatoes, avocado pears and little
sweet seedless grapes that spurted juice as the teeth sank
into them, and a bottle of sparkling wine to complete the
menu. Bruce laid the bottle of wine in the stream and they
watched the clear mountain waters ripple over it while they
ate. By the time they were ready for the wine it was deliciously cool and sharp.

Solemnly Bruce filled two glasses and inspected one
frowningly before he handed it to Hilary. He held up his
own and quirked inquiring brows. 'To what? The mountains? The old country? Bacchus – or just us?'

This last was uttered in a lower, more meaning tone, or so
it seemed to Hilary. The scarlet fringe of the new poncho
made a gaudy necklace on the grass near her feet, and suddenly she was conscious of all the troublesome thoughts of
the early morning. She looked down, and Bruce said evenly:
'Have I said something I shouldn't?'

'No, not at all.' Her mouth curved tremulously as she
tried to regain the light-hearted mood of moments ago. She
held up her glass. 'To us – and all those other things you
said.'

Bruce responded, but the carefree mood had vanished and
she was painfully conscious that Bruce himself was aware of
it. She sipped her wine and looked at the crystal peaks,
trying to summon up a pert remark that would restore normality. Before she could do so Bruce said quietly: 'What's

the matter?'

The perfect cue to laugh off the very thing that was the matter, but now she was unable to meet his gaze, still less to begin explanations. How could one tell a man that people were coupling his name with that of a girl he had met only twice previous to this day? And that the people concerned were making no secret of their match-making plans? Bruce would be furious, as furious as she had been, and suddenly she knew that his friendship mattered a great deal to her. Perhaps she was not so seasoned a traveller as she had believed; but Bruce was of her own kind and the thought of not having his reassuring presence near at hand was oddly disturbing. She forced a smile. 'Nothing's the matter, you idiot. It's a perfect day.'

'Sure?' Bruce looked unusually serious. 'I had a notion that something was bothering you this morning and decided that I was imagining things. Now I'm not so sure.'

'That's my natural early morning expression – I can't help it,' she fended quickly.

But his expression did not lighten. He leaned back on one elbow and regarded her with a level glance. 'Are you quite happy here?' he asked abruptly.

'Here?' For an inane moment she took the question too literally, believing he meant the immediate moment, then her half-smile of surprise faded. 'Yes, of course I'm happy,' she said. 'The country's fascinating and there's so much to see and discover.'

'I didn't mean that.' Bruce's mouth compressed. 'I mean your job. Are they treating you okay?'

Her surprise returned. 'So far, I can't complain. But what makes you ask?'

He shrugged. 'You're still a slip of a kid, and I wouldn't like to think that things weren't turning out as well as you'd hoped.' He sighed and relaxed back. 'I've been out here a few years and I've heard of a few cases of wide-eyed innocents coming to grief – not that anything like that will happen to you where you are at present,' he interjected as he read shocked comprehension on her face. 'But putting it at its mildest I've known of girls coming out here and to the States, lured by salaries that sound like riches compared to what they can earn back home and fabulous apartments

thrown in, then when they've got here they find a home-
sickness they didn't bargain for, and very often the job
proves far more demanding than they'd ever imagined. But
by then it's too late and they have to stick out the year, or the
two years, whatever they've contracted for, or repay their air
fare, which in most cases is out of the question for them.'

'Yes, but employers have to insist on that,' Hilary said
gently, 'or the more irresponsible types would take the job as
an excuse for a jaunt abroad and pack it in after a few
weeks.'

'Which is all the more reason why the girls like yourself
shouldn't be victimized,' he said grimly, 'and while the Pacquera family is above reproach in the obvious ways there are
scores of more subtle aspects that could affect their treat-
ment of you, simply because their way of life is different.'

Hilary was touched by his thoughtfulness, even as
memory threw up a strange little paradox to illustrate
Bruce's words. Unbidden came recall of the day Joaquin had
'wounded' her with the conquistador's sword, and the
sequel; then memory made its second instant leap to a sultry
afternoon at the Plaza de Toros. Strangely enough, that had
been the day when she had instinctively looked to Bruce for
understanding – only to find it from a source where she least
expected . . .

She said softly, 'It's nice of you to care, but everything's
fine. And they aren't so different really, not once one dis-
counts the surface trappings of convention and tradition.'

'Don't you kid yourself,' he broke in, so abruptly she was
startled. 'You'll never fathom the Latin mind as simply as
that, and if you're wise you—'

He stopped at the sound of voices, and Hilary looked
round. She could hear the sounds of people approaching,
although the steep curve of the path hid them from view.
Then she stiffened. The child's voice was unmistakable. It
rang clear on the still air and was plainly indignant:

'But it is! I tell you it *was* the Señorita Martin! She is
with Señor Gilford. And round here you will see that
I—'

Joaquin's small dark head appeared above the screen of
silver-leafed shrub and he saw Hilary. He stopped, plainly
torn between wanting to rush to greet her and staying to

state his triumph. The latter won.

'It is!' he proclaimed, turning towards the as yet unseen figures making their leisurely way up the incline. 'I told you, Tio. They *are* here!'

With that he came exuberantly across to Hilary and Bruce and began a volley of questions. Bruce responded with indulgent amusement, but Hilary's responses held a certain mechanical note. She watched the tall figure of the Conde come into sight and offer a courteous hand to Sanchia and Consuelo in turn as they stepped over the narrow verge of the path. Only then did he move across the small shaded clearing where the picnic things still lay waiting to be re-packed.

His greeting to herself was formal and faultlessly easy, and she could not help wondering at that blend of arrogant charm, imperious bearing and sheer masculine appeal that he wore with the carelessness he would don a favourite garment. He instantly became the central point of any radius he entered, she thought with a flash of inexplicable resentment. Why had he decided on the same outing, this same day? Certainly it did not strike her as the kind of outing that either Consuelo or Sanchia would have chosen.

She became aware of the Conde's gaze resting on her, and thought she detected aloof disapproval flickering in its dark depths. To her annoyance she felt colour warm her cheeks and she turned aside.

Consuelo gave her a cool smile. 'I am glad that you have found Bruce to show you around. It is not always pleasant to go alone around a strange country.'

'I'm jolly glad I found her to show around,' Bruce put in with a firmness that seemed rather exaggerated. Hilary had a fleeting impression that he also was hiding annoyance, then she decided she was imagining things as he looked down at a demanding Joaquin and grinned. 'Now what is it, *amigo*?'

'My birthday party. You will be receiving a formal invitation, but I wish . . .' Joaquin drew him aside importantly to make explicit explanations.

Consuelo smiled again. 'It is a pity that Lima is such a long drive away for Bruce to meet you. You know,' she paused, her sloe-dark eyes considering, 'I do not see why you should not stay overnight with us should you wish to spend a long weekend in the country. Is that not a good idea, Sanchia?'

'You would be most welcome,' Sanchia affirmed, but her tone was automatic. Her gaze had fallen on the scarlet-fringed poncho where it lay on the ground beside the picnic things and suddenly it seemed to flaunt there with a thoroughly abandoned air.

Hilary looked up, to meet the Conde's gaze again, and his silence seemed to underline everything that Juanita's confidences had imparted. She could not tell what he was thinking, and suddenly the warm discomfort of colour came into her cheeks again. Her mouth tightened and abruptly she turned away, murmuring a brief acknowledgment of Consuelo's invitation before she began to gather up the picnic things.

Joaquin had discovered that some wine still remained in the bottle, and under Bruce's amused gaze was about to drink it. She glared at Bruce and took the bottle from Joaquin. Uncaring of his little-spoilt-boy protest, she thrust it into the hamper then took the glasses to the stream. A shadow fell across the ripples.

'You do not approve of children taking wine, I suspect.'

'No, *señor*,' she did not look up and continued to rinse the glasses very thoroughly, 'it is not that entirely. The weather is warm and the wine will be sad by now.'

'Like your afternoon, perhaps?'

Now she did glance up, and glimpsed beyond him Sanchia sitting on the grass at Bruce's side while Joaquin chattered and Consuelo stood looking on. 'I am not in the least sad, *señor*,' she said coolly. 'Why should I be?'

'Question – and question.' The sardonic note she knew so well lingered behind the cool little rejoinder. Then subtly it altered, to a note not so easily defined, as he added more softly: 'Do not worry. I shall remove the intrusion very soon and endeavour to direct my nephew's powers of observation elsewhere.'

She polished the glasses carefully. 'It is no intrusion, *señor*. Joaquin would have been very welcome to join us today. I thought I made that quite clear two days ago.'

'Ah, yes, but the circumstances have changed since then.'

The inference to be drawn was quite clear. 'Not at all,' she said coldly. 'Joaquin likes Bruce's company. He would have enjoyed the day with us.'

'Perhaps.' Aloofness returned to the Conde's expression. 'But it is hardly a suitable arrangement. I thought I had made my wishes quite clear in that respect.' He turned and called sharply to Joaquin.

But Joaquin merely responded with a careless, '*Si*, Tio – come and look,' and returned his attention to something across the valley.

There was a rough rail at one side of the clearing and a single plank of timber spanning the stream. Joaquin was standing on the tiny bridge while Bruce moved to lean over the rail, and the two girls went slowly to stand one at each side of him, to follow the pointing directions of the small boy.

Bruce said something, and Sanchia laughed softly, then Joaquin's small voice piped a comment Hilary didn't quite catch and brought smiles from the trio, followed by an exclamation of annoyance from the Conde. He moved across the clearing and laid an admonishing hand on Joaquin's shoulder, and the boy lapsed into silence.

Hilary fastened the lid of the picnic basket, then straightened and moved slowly to the rail to see what had caught everyone's interest. From this vantage point the valley could be seen spread out below, stretching down to the grey and white huddle of the village about the dark patch of the market square. It was a picturesque scene, but did not appear to hold anything of undue fascination for a small boy in his native land. Hilary rested her hands on the rail and surrendered herself to an odd little mood of discontent normally foreign to her nature. She wished the others hadn't turned up, and she wished they hadn't seen her with Bruce, and she wished they hadn't guessed that Bruce had bought her that poncho – and the Conde was bound to have noticed the wilting flower at her throat . . . *He* would know that girls didn't usually buy themselves a posy . . . But what the devil did it matter if he *had* noticed? And why on earth did she have to keep blushing when he looked at her . . .? Then abruptly she was jolted out of her angry little musings by a blinding flash of light.

She blinked, and exclaimed aloud as it came again from a small shadowy hollow under the crags some distance down the valley. She looked away, thinking that a car windscreen was catching the sun down there, then another flash scintillated from the same spot and she realized it could not be a car as there was no trace of any road or wide enough track to be seen. The flashes began again, this time a dazzling series in rapid succession, and she exclaimed aloud: 'It must be a mirror!'

Bruce leaned forward and looked along to her, smiling, He nodded. 'It's an Indian boy. He's trying to attract the girl of his choice. You can't see her at the moment, but she's down there quite near to him. He's trying to catch her face in the reflected sunrays to tell her he wants to court her.'

'Some of these customs are charming,' Sanchia said in her gentle voice. 'He will turn her hat inside out when she has answered him, then they will make a little model of the house they hope to build and they will take it to the church to put it on consecrated ground.'

'That's right,' said Bruce. 'And they'll add effigies of the children they wish for, the llamas and cattle that will bring them prosperity, and they'll plant corn round them. If the corn grows high over them their wishes will come true; if it doesn't . . .' he opened his hands, palms upwards.

'You seem to be well versed in the *Indios* superstitions,' Consuelo observed dryly. She glanced at Hilary. 'Have you brought your own mirror in readiness?'

'Only a compact – probably the same as your own,' Hilary returned in tones equally dry, and was secretly delighted to see the smile fade from Consuelo's face.

The tic-tac of mirror play began again, and Hilary was suddenly aware of the Conde at her shoulder. She tensed, certain that some sardonic comment was about to come, but it did not, and a moment later Bruce said quickly:

'Look – there she is. And she's given him her answer.'

Hilary almost missed the small shy flash of the second mirror, but she saw the movement and picked out the bright blue colour of the Indian girl's poncho and her dark red skirt.

'She'll run away from him now,' Bruce continued his commentary, 'and he'll pursue her. Then he'll probably try to snatch her hat or scarf. Once he does that she'll never escape him. His possession of something that has touched her hair gives him power over her, a kind of magic spell, for as long as he keeps it.'

Hilary could see the little Indian girl quite clearly now. As Bruce had foretold, she was running up the hillside, her laughter and her cries ringing through the crisp air, and the boy was bounding over the craggy slope. His entire mien expressed the purpose of pursuit and very soon his quick agile steps narrowed the gap between himself and his quarry. Then the girl's laughing cries changed to a squeal as she caught her foot in a fold of her long, voluminous skirt and went sprawling.

The boy's shout of triumph rang out and the next moment he had seized her wide-brimmed hat and darted away. From a safe distance he watched as she picked herself up and turned uncertainly in his direction. There was a little more by-play that made it quite clear to the onlookers that the girl wasn't trying as hard as she might to regain her property, and at last the pair went swinging down the hillside towards the village, no doubt to break the news of the betrothal to their families and friends.

'A pretty custom!'

Hilary whirled, startled by the voice close to her ear, and met the Conde's dark, sardonic gaze.

'You find these superstitions romantically appealing, I see,' he added sarcastically, replacing his dark glasses with a casual movement of his hand.

'And why not?' Conscious of the others turning towards her, she held the enigma of his masked gaze with defiant eyes. 'Since you ask, I do. I think it's a very romantic and appealing custom, and I hope that when they plant their corn for their future children and llamas and their little home that every grain of it grows strong and tall – and I hope she doesn't steal her hat back, either!' Hilary paused and drew a deep breath. 'But of course, you, *señor*, would not deign to believe in magic spells.'

For a moment he stared down at her and the chiselled lines of his mouth betrayed no hint of his inward reaction to her outspoken remark. Then the corners compressed slightly.

'To win a woman, *señorita*? Is that what you mean?'

She made no reply, and he allowed himself the ghost of a smile. 'But is not the whole concept of love a kind of spell? And one, alas, *señorita,* that does not always keep its magic.'

While she looked at him, quelled by the cool, imperious tensity of his manner, he inclined his head mockingly and turned to the others. Almost before she realized what was happening he had drawn his small party together and departed after the briefest of leave-takings. Almost as though he were keeping that stupid promise, Hilary thought wildly. *Removing the intrusion!*

For the moment Bruce was forgotten. She rested her hands on the rail and listened to the gritting sounds of footsteps gradually fading down the dry, stony path to the village. Then there was silence, broken only by the slight sounds of Bruce gathering up the things, and suddenly the valley seemed empty.

CHAPTER EIGHT

THE preliminary arrangements for Joaquin's birthday occupied a fair amount of Hilary's attention during the next few days. Everyone in the household from Doña Elena to Concepta, the little maid, began to evince a fervent interest in the subject, which was, apparently, something of an innovation to them all.

'He will be demanding this every year,' observed Doña Elena when Hilary went to consult her over the invitation list.

It was here that the first problem arose. Joaquin demanded printed invitation cards. He also stipulated that they should be printed in English. In vain they all argued with him, and even when Hilary tried to convince him that specially printed cards weren't an essential feature of a British child's celebration he refused to listen.

'We usually buy them ready-printed,' she assured him. 'It's only practical to have them individually done if you're having an enormous affair with lots of people.'

'I want them with my name on,' he said stubbornly. 'And I shall fill in all the guests' names myself.'

'You can't write in English, silly *niño*!' Juanita taunted.

'Their names are exactly the same in English.' He turned such a withering, small-boy glance on her that she giggled and raised a defensive hand to shield her face.

Doña Elena decided it was time to settle the argument. 'I should have them printed,' she said with a fond glance at her young nephew, whom she tended to spoil outrageously.

But Hilary was unable to find a printer who could do the rush job in the short time that remained. She came back that afternoon, exhausted after a shopping tour in town, and was overtaken by the Conde's car just as she reached the drive.

He surveyed her numerous parcels and her heated face. 'You did not use the car, *señorita*?' he said rather sharply, taking her shopping bag and parcels out of her tired arms.

'No, *señor*.' She gave a sigh of relief at being relieved of her burden. 'I went by bus.'

He looked down from under deep lids. 'But I do not expect you to use public transport when there is a household car at your disposal.'

'I use public transport to go to work at home, *señor*,' she responded evenly, 'so why shouldn't I use it here when necessary? Besides, Rico has gone home early today, so he couldn't have driven me. His wife is ill.'

'Yes, I remember.' The Conde frowned. 'I must inquire into that situation. But you can drive, *señorita*?'

'Yes, *señor*.'

'Then in future use the Renault. But be sure to take utmost care on our roads.'

She smiled and thanked him, and he looked down at the largest of the parcels. 'Have you been buying souvenirs, *señorita*?'

'No, they're for Joaquin's party. Little gifts and prizes for the games, and various other things.' She dropped her handbag on the patio seat and took the biggest parcel from the Conde. 'This is his birthday present – I want to sneak it in before he sees it. It's such an obvious shape he might guess what it is.'

The Conde studied the rose-pink cheeks and glowing eyes above the curiously shaped package and shook his head. 'I should never guess. May I share the secret?'

'Of course! It's a kite. Silver and blue. Do you think he'll like it? I couldn't think what to get for him.'

'I am certain it will become his most treasured possession,' the Conde assured her, then raised querying brows. 'The preparations are going according to plan?'

'Oh, yes. Except . . .' Suddenly it was very easy to confide the present difficulty, and when she had finished he said briskly: 'I will arrange that. Let me have a note of the required wording straight away, *señorita*.'

Unexpectedly he smiled at her exclamation of pleasure. It was a smile untinged by cynicism or guile, or the mere politeness that lacked the depth and warmth only spontaneity can give. The softening it brought to his strong, rather austere features was quite remarkable, and it evoked in Hilary a response that took form in a request far from her mind the moment before that unusually sweet smile flashed warmly.

'Please, *señor*, why don't you call me Hilary? Almost everyone else does now.'

The moment the impulsive little exclamation was out she felt her cheeks glow with fresh colour. He did not respond instantly, only that smile settled in the curves at the corners of his mouth and lingered there briefly before his normal graveness reformed. He inclined his head.

'I shall be delighted – I could not very well suggest it previously – Hilary. And now, if you will let me have a note of the printing requirements . . .'

She hurried in search of pen and paper, a strange, secret little source of pleasure guiding her steps. Later, when she was stowing away her purchases she relived the small interlude on the patio and could not help comparing his mood then with that of the previous Sunday. *Why can't he be consistent?* she wondered wryly, her face sobering as she recalled the afternoon in the mountains. The advent of the Conde had snapped the smooth thread of the day with Bruce and left her with a restlessness and feeling of irritation that persisted all the rest of the day. Once acknowledged, it was not so difficult to define. The Conde had an uncanny power to needle her and it was all the more infuriating when she considered the ease with which he could disarm her and make her forget all those other disturbing occasions.

It's that Latin charm! she told herself wryly as she stowed the big kite at the back of her wardrobe. *He can turn it on like a tap!* But it shouldn't worry Bruce, she mused, her memory ranging back again to the outing.

Bruce had been rather withdrawn during the journey back, and this had surprised her. He did not appear to be a moody type, at least not at first impression. When they had got back to Lima late in the evening and collected the car he had driven rather aimlessly through the city and then stopped near San Cristobal hill and looked down at the lights twinkling in the old part of the town. Suddenly he had said, 'Do you want to go straight back? I'd like to go for a drive.'

Sensing this echo of her own restlessness in him she had

agreed to the extension of the trip and he had jabbed at the starter, saying vehemently: 'Good! I've a yen to get right away from the Latin temperament just for one night.'

He had headed south, passing the moonlit pleasure beaches down the coast from Lima, and then let the powerful car have its head on the broad stretches of the Pan-American highway. The speed was exhilarating, if at times a bit hair-raising when other speed-masters roared out of the night, headlights ablaze, and the blare of car radios turned up full volume merged with the throb of engines and left the echoing strains of music on the midnight blue stillness.

It had been long after midnight when Bruce finally dropped her at the villa. The fast drive seemed to have restored his good humour and he had bidden her a cheerful, 'So long, honey – sleep tight,' apparently unperturbed by the prospect of the long lonely drive back to the Verdano Valley and the hacienda.

'I hope he didn't drive as madly over *that* road,' she murmured aloud, experiencing a twinge of concern as she remembered that she hadn't heard from him since then.

However, he telephoned the following evening, to say he would be down in Lima on business at the end of the week and could they meet for a meal and a drink?

So that was all right; and the Conde had fixed the invitation problem. How he had overcome the *'mañana'* trait so characteristic of the South American she did not know, but the neat little pack of engraved cards arrived three or four days later and the job of sending them was done immediately.

Joaquin personally wrote each one out, and was persuaded that his flourishing signature was not needed as endorsement. A menu of true English fare, sausage rolls, cheese dip, crisps, savouries, icecream and trifle was decided on; in secret Hilary made a birthday cake which she would ice and decorate, and, much to Juanita's delight, Ramon was co-opted to help make out a programme of games and entertainment for the great occasion.

They spent several happy evenings concocting clues for a treasure hunt and planning out the locales of the clues, and then, one morning about ten days before the day, Juanita rushed into Hilary's room and broke into a storm of temper and tears.

Hilary listened, at first not sure if she was grasping the right gist of the angry, incoherent account Juanita was pouring out. It seemed that the Conde had sent for her immediately after breakfast and told her he had just received a letter from his mother, the Condesa, whom he was going to visit during a business trip to Valparaiso that week. Unexpectedly, the Condesa had expressed a wish to see her granddaughter – and the Condesa's wishes were not usually ignored. But that was not all.

During the visit Juanita was to be introduced to the man who might become her husband.

'His name is Carlos. His father owns the Hacienda Ariposa – they are distantly linked by marriage to my grandmother's side of the family.' Juanita wandered to Hilary's bed and sank down on it, her small oval face a study of despair. 'He has just come home from university. *Ay de mi!* If only he had stayed there!'

Hilary was silent, concern clouding her eyes as she considered the best way of consoling without encouraging the outright defiance she suspected was very near the surface. At last she said slowly: 'How can you be sure that they're going to arrange this marriage? After all, you haven't even met him. Your grandmother may hope that you'll like him and it'll lead to marriage. But if you don't . . .'

'They will.'

'Did your uncle say so?'

'No, but I could tell.'

'Now how?' Hilary instilled lightness into her tone. 'How could you tell if he didn't say so?'

'Because he tell me to go shopping today – I am to take you with me to help me choose dresses – and I say I do not want any new dresses just now,' Juanita said brokenly. 'And then he laugh and say, "Oh yes. Who knows? You may come back *prometida!*"'

Still convinced that Juanita was over-dramatizing something that might never happen, Hilary shook her head. 'He was teasing you. Even if Carlos does fall violently in love with you he's hardly likely to propose marriage at first sight. How do you know he didn't meet a girl at university and have her in mind for his bride?'

'No! Oh, you do not understand!' Juanita flung out her hands. 'Tio was not teasing. How can I explain how it happens with us? No one will say: "Yes, you must marry Carlos, and he must marry you." It is more subtle than that. But in a hundred different ways they will convey to us that our marriage would be eminently suitable and make both families supremely happy if we chose one another. Till we know we will hurt them and bitterly disappoint them if we refuse, and so, because we love them and we have been brought up to believe that they know best for our happiness, we conform. And everyone is so happy we believe we are happy too. That is how it is, my Hilary.' Juanita got up and went sadly to the window. She stared out and repeated tonelessly, 'No, Tio was not teasing.'

'I see.' Hilary sighed, at a loss to know what to say. 'When are you going?'

'We are flying down tomorrow evening. Tio is returning next week, but I have to stay with Grandmother until – until–' Juanita's voice broke, and she whirled round. 'Oh, please! Can you not help me?'

Startled, Hilary backed a pace. 'But how can I? You know I'd do anything I could. But what can I do?'

'You could talk to Tio. Tell him you have something planned.' Juanita was improvising desperately. 'Tell him you have planned something educational for me and Joaquin. And – and it is too late to cancel it, so that I have to come back with Tio. And then—'

'Juanita!' It was Hilary's turn to make an impassioned gesture. 'How can I? I can't interfere in your personal family affairs. As for *that* little idea . . . do you really think he would buy it?'

'Oh, yes. Yes, he would,' Juanita said feverishly. 'He would take notice of *you*.'

'Me?' exclaimed Hilary incredulously. 'Not in this case, I'm afraid.'

'But he has told me so. He told me I must be tolerant of differences I would find in your outlook because despite this you possessed certain admirable qualities I might learn much from.'

'Really!' Hilary did not know whether to laugh or be affronted. In her mental ear she could almost hear those autocratic tones and picture his expression. 'And what are these qualities he's suddenly discovered in me?' she could not resist asking.

'You are calm in face of emergency—'

—What emergency? thought Hilary. *Must have been during some of Joaquin's tantrums.*

—'but you have much courage and honesty.'

'Have I?' Hilary pretended amusement, but not very successfully. 'Go on.'

'I can't remember any more.' Juanita's dark eyes narrowed. 'Your cheeks are very pink. I should not have told you these things. But I wish to make you understand that Tio will listen to you.'

'It wouldn't say much for my honesty were I to tell him a pack of lies,' she said flatly.

Juanita's shoulders rose and fell with her sigh. 'It would not be lies if we did arrange something.'

For a moment Hilary studied her, and then she shook her head. 'It wouldn't work, and even if it convinced your uncle he would simply expect us to cancel it.'

'I see.' Juanita's head came up and she turned stiffly. 'You do not wish to help me.'

Hilary sighed, knowing that Juanita's idea was utterly futile, and as for the possibility of the Conde taking any notice of herself, should she summon the temerity to question his decision regarding his niece, well, it was so remote as to be impossible. The impulse came to tell Juanita of two occasions when she had ventured to air her opinions to the Conde; neither of them could be said to have been exactly successful in selling him a picture of liberated womanhood, she thought wryly, especially the most recent occasion.

The pink deepened to scarlet as the recollection of his kiss came back so vividly she could almost experience the touch of his mouth on her own, and she knew she could never bring up the subject of his plans for Juanita. His answer was almost predictable, but the outcome regarding herself was not . . . She looked at Juanita and took a deep breath.

'Listen,' she said firmly, 'you're taking this far too seriously. You're barely seventeen. Go and stay with your grandmother and meet this Carlos and enjoy yourself. He might be gorgeous for all you know. You might have forgotten Ramon by the time you come back.'

'Never.' Juanita's mouth curled with scorn. She flounced to the door and cried, 'You don't care! Nobody cares!' before she slammed it behind her.

For the rest of the morning Juanita stayed in her room, pleading a headache, and when she did emerge, mute and wan-faced, she took herself to the seclusion of a shaded arbour in the most remote part of the villa grounds where she was not discovered until it was almost sundown.

Hilary, even while she was deeply sympathetic, suspected that Juanita's malaise was due more to temper and sulks than actual physical cause, and it seemed she was not the only one with that suspicion.

The opportunity that might have been golden presented itself late that afternoon when Hilary was on her way to the pool. A gay towelling jacket demurely covering her bikini-clad figure, she was slipping out the side door when a shadow barred her path. The Conde did not immediately stand aside.

His brows arched. 'You are going to swim?'

'Yes, señor.' She thought of the unhappy Juanita and wondered if she dared broach an appeal, and her heart began to beat uncomfortably fast. While she hesitated, he said:

'Was the shopping expedition successful?'

'N-no.' There was no option but to explain – without adding that at present poor Juanita was refusing to speak to her at all.

The Conde's brows narrowed. 'I have a suspicion that my niece is not relishing this visit to her grandmother. Is this so?'

Suddenly Hilary knew that far from being courageous she was utterly craven at that moment. 'I – I think she would prefer to be here while the preparations are going on for the party,' she said after an agonized pause.

'Is that all?'

She could only make a helpless gesture, and he smiled grimly. 'I do not think so, señorita.'

The return to the polite formality brought an absurd stiffness into Hilary's throat.

Her head came up proudly. 'You are quite right, Senor Conde. Your niece is not very happy, and you seem to forget that she is still sad at the loss of her mother. She needs love and understanding – lots of it.'

She turned away abruptly, but not swiftly enough to escape steely fingers that closed round her wrist.

'One moment, *señorita*. I feel it is time we reached understanding on the matter of my niece.'

His tone had sharpened with the hardness of frost, and the line of his jaw was taut. His gaze held her as unrelentingly as the hard grasp about her wrist while he went on: 'I am well aware of the lack of discipline among the young of your society, even as I am aware of the self-confidence and ability you undoubtedly possess, but I should be extremely angry if I discovered this to be influencing my niece towards disobedience.'

'She is not disobedient!' Hilary flashed. 'Nor would I dream of encouraging her to be so. Is it disobedient to desire a little say in one's own life?'

'In the case of my niece – at present: yes,' he said coldly, 'and unless I'm greatly mistaken she has already acquainted you with a certain fact concerning this visit to Valparaiso.'

At the small gasp Hilary could not repress he gave a grim, humourless smile and released her wrist. 'I thought so. And as we have already had discussions regarding this certain aspect I am well acquainted with your feelings on the subject. I may also add that I am not entirely blind to a certain romantic interest harboured by my niece for some time, nor to the identity of the object of it and it is not one I wish to encourage.' He paused and looked down at the pallor of shock his icy statements had brought to her face. 'Have I made myself perfectly clear, Miss Martin?'

'Perfectly clear.' It was an effort to force the words past her trembling lips while her brain reiterated the words: he knows! *He knows!*

'Therefore I do not need to add that any further encouragement of that interest is strictly forbidden?'

A whisper of wind tugged at the scarlet creeper behind the Conde's dark head and made soft rustlings amid the blossoms. Then the little wind-whisper fell silent and the blossoms drooped again in the still, humid air, and the heavy stillness seemed to emphasize the leonine power in the man.

She forced her petrified limbs into motion and backed a

pace. From some deep hidden source she found strength and that same courage he had once apparently been moved to commend. Facing him, she said quietly:

'There is one thing you have forgotten, Señor Conde: Sometimes it is only the forbidden things that are most desired. Once they are attained they are no longer wanted. Your niece is waking to love, and to forbid that awakening is akin to trying to turn back the tide. To the only eligible subject within your household is a predictable step. Had you not considered this?'

'Not, it seems, until it was almost too late, but it will most certainly be taken care of now. And you, I trust, will remember that, señorita.'

He inclined his head with that icily controlled salute and stepped to one side.

All desire to swim had gone now, but she would not turn to precede him indoors. She heard the patio door close behind him with a soft click, and she ran blindly to the edge of the pool. She plunged in, almost as though the waters closing over her could quench all memory of that interlude for which she had been totally unprepared. But there was no such magical assuagement and when she climbed out she was biting her lip to control its trembling, while the droplets glistening on her wet cheeks intermingled with escaping tears.

*　　*　　*

The Conde and his niece departed on the evening flight to Valparaiso the following day. Juanita was mute and sullen, and the Conde grim of visage. Ramon drove them to the airport and returned with the car, and a message to the effect that Hilary was to call upon him for any assistance she might need in coping with the preparations for Joaquin's party.

Ramon looked moody and unhappy, and Hilary could only guess at what the Conde might have ordained now that he was aware of the situation between his secretary and his niece.

The days dragged by miserably. A curious sad tranquillity descended over the villa and even Joaquin lost interest in the party, now only a week away. There was no word from Valparaiso, and no one knew if the Conde and his niece would be returning in time for the celebration.

Hilary iced the cake, adding Joaquin's name and seven small blue candles, and wrapped up his gift and after that there was nothing to do but wait. She wished she could confide in Doña Elena, but despite the shrewdness of those keen eyes searching her unhappy face reserve and pride kept her silent, and Doña Elena did not ask. Probably she guessed, Hilary thought, and there was little likelihood of sympathy forthcoming, even though her manner remained kindly and unchanged. Even Bruce's consolation was denied her.

At the end of the week he rang up, full of apologies, to cry off the trip planned earlier.

'I'm terribly sorry, honey, but something unforeseen cropped up, and I've a whole list of things to clear up before my leave.'

'Leave?' she echoed, her eyes shadowed above the receiver. 'What leave?'

'Didn't I tell you? My long vacation's due next month. Three months.'

She gasped softly, and he chuckled. 'Hey! It's the first in two years. I reckon I've earned it.'

'Yes, of course.' She swallowed hard and forced lightness into her words. 'I expect you're planning to go on the razzle. Where are you going?'

'Don't know yet. Miami, maybe. I've friends there. Or I may even go home.' He paused, as though he had heard her silent sigh, and exclaimed: 'What's the matter? You sound down.'

'Yes, I am a bit, but I can't tell you over the phone.'

'Bad as that! Never mind, it'll soon be fiesta – we'll take a ride on top of the world. Is that a date?'

Panic stirred in her, and a sick sense of disappointment. She needed someone now, even though she knew that no one could do anything other than give the solace of friendly companionship.

An unutterable sense of loneliness closed in on her as she stood in the dim, oak-lined alcove under the staircase. For the first time since her arrival she felt lost in an alien atmosphere and conscious that outside the Conde's household and acquaintances linked to his circle she knew no one except Bruce.

She said, 'But Joaquin's party . . . have you forgotten?'

A muffled expletive at the other end of the line told her he had. He said ruefully, 'It had gone right out of my head. Yes, of course I'll be there. Anyway, I think I promised to escort the girls – there's some frolic for the oldies as well, I believe.'

This was the first Hilary had heard of it, but she made no comment, and after a few more of the aimless pleasantries that tend to creep into phone conversations she rang off and went sadly in search of Joaquin.

Two days later there was a letter from Juanita. It was rather stilted and somewhat guarded in content, but it brought a measure of warmth to Hilary. She would not have been human if she had remained unhurt by Juanita's sulky silence, but deeper perception told her that Juanita was similar in one respect to herself; when she was hurt or angry she was incapable of putting on a false face. However, she was obviously capable of the non-committal phrase on paper, and Hilary smiled wryly over the long, rather wooden account of the events and people amid which she had arrived and the mention of a certain Don Carlos was given no more emphasis than a casual reference to an elderly Señor Lorenz who had distinguished himself by falling asleep during liqueurs and a rather specialized discussion on Chilean contemporary art, which had not exactly amused the Condesa, who was something of an authority on the subject. The Condesa . . .

Hilary reached the final paragraph in Juanita's small, neat script and gave a small exclamation. At least Juanita would be back in time for Joaquin's party, as would the Conde. They were returning on the eve of that day – and the Condesa was coming back with them.

This news wrought a startling effect on the household.

The air of tranquillity vanished overnight; the maids stopped gossiping, the cook ceased her arguments with old Ernesto, the *portero*, and a frenzied spate of activity swept through villa and gardens. Lawns took on the soft smoothness of a sheet of velvet newly unrolled, the odd creeper with a tendency to stray free was ruthlessly pruned, and the tiles of the patio floor shone as though they'd been polished. Indoors it was exactly the same. The scent of waxes emanated from dark carved oak and the crisp honey and tan and sepia of marquetry. Silver and copper sent warm glowing rays from alcove and corner, and the great mirrors in *sala* and hall reflected the burnish of gilded frescoes and the dark sweep of polished parquet.

All this for one person! Hilary thought as she surveyed the setpiece below from the vantage point of the gallery outside her room. The exclamations of 'The Condesa will . . .' 'The Condesa won't . . .' had ceased to float anxiously from various lips and the staff were now gowning themselves in freshly starched aprons so white they dazzled and newly cleaned livery.

Joaquin and Ramon went to the airport to meet the returning family and Hilary felt tension grip her as the moment approached for their arrival. She had helped Doña Elena to her chair on the patio and now stood by her side, a little uncertain. Doña Elena propped her silver-knobbed cane in a niche conveniently within reach and glanced up at the silent girl. A quirk of humour touched her mouth.

'Do not look so concerned, my dear. She cannot eat *you!*'

'Does she usually eat people?' Hilary asked wryly.

'My sister-in-law?' Doña Elena permitted herself a somewhat enigmatic smile. 'No, but she has a way of dismissing those who displease her with a mere glance that makes them cease to exist in her presence – though I suppose I should not say it.'

Hilary sighed. It did not sound very propitious for the future. Then she sensed the older woman's glance and turned her head, to read something not unlike sympathy in those fine dark eyes.

'It sometimes helps, when one is vulnerable, to forge the shield of forewarning,' Doña Elena said softly. She nodded as a small exclamation formed on Hilary's lips, and went on: 'Yes, I have watched you during these past days and I understand. It has been difficult for you. You have a kindness and the kinship of youth which would make you indulge Juanita against the sense of duty you feel towards our wishes. I'm afraid my nephew is unsparing of censure

146

should his wishes be ignored, and I think, perhaps, you have taken it a little too much to heart.'

Confusion bathed Hilary's cheeks in scarlet, as much from surprise at Doña Elena's perception as at her sudden broaching of the subject. It did not occur to her at that moment to attribute that warm flush of embarrassment to any other cause, and she began to stammer, but Doña Elena made a small negative gesture.

'Do not worry any more – it is all being taken care of now.'

The sound of a car came through the stillness. Doña Elena sat up straight, reaching for her cane and composing her thin, fine-boned old hands about the engraved silver top.

The car stopped and the next moment the patio seemed filled with people.

Joaquin scrambled out and rushed to hold out his hand to his grandmother as she stepped out of the car. Juanita stood still for a moment, looking round her before she came towards Doña Elena, and Ramon was opening the boot and starting to unload what seemed a mountain of pale blue and cream dress cases. Then the cries and the gesticulating and the exuberance of a Latin family reunion began.

But Hilary was seeing only one person.

For the moment no one was seeing her and she could stand aside, looking.

He seemed taller, his smooth olive skin more burnished, his hair thicker and more darkly attractive than ever, his lithe movements lazier yet more suggestive of the effortless strength of an idly prowling tiger. He was wearing dark glasses and a slim, sleek shirt of the same enigmatic dark shade of the lenses with tight-hipped cream pants, and as he turned the movement rippled down the length of him in a way that made Hilary catch her breath.

He was looking straight at her and she felt a strange, bewildering pulsation throb through her senses, and a crazy feeling of suddenly paralysed limbs holding her fast on the spot while a warring little instinct bade the rest of her to flee. Then the long shadow darkened over her and his voice flowed into her. Through the strange, dreamlike trance she heard another voice, cool, gracious, saw dimly a woman, and felt the hand she must have put out taken lightly and then released.

'So this is the little English *señorita*,' said the Condesa.

*   *   *

The Condesa was tiny and slender, with an air of fragility that was completely misleading. Her exquisite blouse of snowy guipure lace and suit of deep rose silk cut in soft, feminine lines aided that impression of delicate femininity, and it was not until she spoke and Hilary encountered the full impact of domination behind the outward façade that the true Condesa could be assessed.

She was decisive, authoritative, and formidable. The servants were terrified of her, Juanita and Joaquin in complete awe of her, and only Doña Elena maintained her normal serenity in face of her sister-in-law's more dominant personality. The only person in the household who seemed unafraid of her was her son, and behind the impeccable deference it was natural he should accord to his mother it was soon easy to discern where he inherited his autocratic assurance – and his charm. For undoubtedly the Condesa could be charming, and she was not without a certain somewhat acid vein of humour.

That evening she summoned Hilary when the long evening meal eventually ended and the family drifted out into the coolness of the patio. The Conde touched Hilary's arm, a formal escorting gesture which nevertheless burned like a caress, and placed a chair for her beside the Condesa.

For a long moment the cool, aristocratic gaze surveyed her, then unexpectedly the Condesa chuckled. 'I suppose I must beware how I speak to you, Miss Martin. Not as I speak with my own family, or the servants, for you hold a rather different position, and you are English.'

Hilary stayed silent, and the black eyes glinted with a light of wickedness which was uncannily like one Hilary already knew too well.

'You will probably put that pale little nose up in the air and tell us what we can do with our job. *No es verdad?*'

'Not entirely,' Hilary said quietly. 'Despite all reports, some of us are still amenable to discipline – provided it is a fair discipline.'

She could not help glancing up at the Conde as she concluded, to find his regard steady and unreadable. The Condesa missed nothing. She looked at her son, then back to the taut, youthful face.

'I think perhaps that has already been questioned – the *señorita* has the cool, wary shell within which the English tend to hide their true feelings. Is that not so, Ruaz?'

'I do not believe that is a trait entirely peculiar to the English, Madre,' he observed coolly, his eyes ranging Hilary's outwardly calm expression. The small compressions at the corners of her mouth betrayed, however, something of unsteadiness held under control and he added smoothly: 'I suspect you are embarrassing Miss Martin. She is not yet used to such directness.'

'Nonsense!' snapped the Condesa. 'She is merely sensitive to a man who would stand in over women's chatter. Take away your cigar and your wine and leave us in peace to get to know one another.'

The Conde's mouth twitched, but he made no response other than a grave inclination of his head to Hilary and the customary salute to his mother.

Somehow Hilary succeeded in avoiding one single glance towards the tall figure moving across the patio. She answered the Condesa's questions, took up her cue where the conversational gambit led, and tried to pretend that the Conde was a thousand miles away instead of some dozen yards distant, knowing all the while that one unguarded glance could betray the turmoil of emotion that had raged in her heart ever since the moment the Conde stepped out of the car that morning.

The Condesa's eyes were like needle-points and her perception as sharp. She wanted to probe Hilary's reactions to the job and the family, and it was unavoidable that the Conde's name should occur with predictable frequency during the course of the discussion. The Condesa plainly adored her only son and liked to talk about him, which was quite natural, but it was agony to Hilary, when every mention of his name was enough to send a small shock through her.

She longed to be alone to try to come to terms with the

shattering discovery that she'd apparently lost her heart where she least expected. *This* was the explanation of the inexplicable touchiness she'd suffered at the slightest sign of censure from him; this was the reason for that joyous elation with which she'd responded to him in lighter moments – and the sadness that had flattened her spirits during the past ten days. She knew now why it was a sheer physical difficulty *not* to look at him and keep on looking at him, and why every instinct urged her to seek his nearness, to seek for some answering sign of response . . .

She was crazy! Hilary told herself in every waking moment over the next twenty-four hours. It was some kind of madness – perhaps her hormones were working overtime or something! He was an attractive man, a very attractive man, and once a woman became aware of that attraction, allowed herself to be drawn into that magnetic radius, it would be easy to imagine herself in love with him.

But none of these desperate little arguments rang true and she was thankful that she had the responsibility of the birthday party on her hands; the last-minute preparations and then the influx of some twenty small boys and girls of diverse temperaments kept her fully occupied for most of the day.

At first the adults tended to hover, with the inevitable dampening effect on the children, who were obviously well primed with admonishments regarding their behaviour, and Hilary began to despair of ever breaking the ice. Also, it seemed that the idea of having the two English children was not so good after all. They proved to be older than Joaquin's contemporaries, their tastes were somewhat sophisticated, and the games Hilary had planned so carefully for six and seven-year-olds were obviously going to prove much too tame for them. The boy offered to help Joaquin fly his new kite and for a moment it looked as though the party was going to lose its host, until Ramon reminded him that he could fly the new kite any time but his party was a once-a-year event. So Hilary was both thankful and perturbed when the Conde entered the big *sala* and immediately assessed the situation.

He crossed to her, noting the chattering groups of adults and the inhibited little ones forming up decorously for musical chairs, while Juanita stood by the record player, and said gravely: 'You are having difficulties. Is there any assistance I can give?'

She shook her head, longing to say: *Yes – come and join in*, and instead said aloud: 'Thank you, *señor*, but it is going to take a little while for them to lose their shyness.'

He nodded and moved away, and then suddenly the adults seemed to melt away and the children were left in possession.

The two English children then decided to take on the roles of helpers and at last the party got under way. Half an hour later Bruce arrived, instigated a hilarious version in Spanish of '*Simon Says*', which broke down the final barriers of reserve and ended in cries of '*Otra vez!*' from the small guests. After that they adjourned to the buffet tea and Joaquin solemnly blew out the seven candles before the cake was cut.

The party had been a great success after all, Hilary thought with relief when the children had been borne away by nursemaids and chauffeurs. True, there had been one crying match, two arguments that almost came to blows, and a sad case of too much excitement combined with too much to eat, but Bruce had been wonderful. Although she was exhausted she was feeling happier when she bathed and changed for dinner and the informal party to follow.

When the dancing started on the patio she was bright-eyed and pink-cheeked as Bruce swept her into the circle. The Conde was not yet dancing. He was standing in the shadows talking to the Condesa and Sanchia, but he would dance later, she was sure, and surely he would choose her for his partner for *one* dance. Hilary's heartbeat quickened and she spun in Bruce's arms and dreamed the tender little dreams of new love. Hadn't he once taken her in his arms and vowed he had a mind to teach her the meaning of emotion?

She imagined his arms round her and a tremor so violent passed through her slender body that Bruce stared down at her.

'Cold?' he said incredulously.

'No – I – I nearly slipped.' *How love could make one learn to lie*, she thought with a flash of compunction as

Bruce got her a drink and stood at her side for a moment.

'I'll be back — don't circulate too far,' he adjured with a grin before drawing a somewhat wistful-looking Juanita on to the floor.

She sat down, sipping her drink and feeling alone, yet quite content to await what the evening might bring. She had lost sight of the Conde, but Sanchia passed by, the faithful and hopeful Don Miguel perspiring in tow, and smiled her sad smile as she surrendered to her corpulent suitor's embrace. Hilary felt a flash of sympathy, then heard the quiet voice of Doña Elena at her side.

'How wonderful to have the staying power of the young!' Doña Elena settled herself stiffly and smiled wryly at Hilary. 'Are you not tired, my dear, after all those noisy little ones?'

'Not really — it's gone off.' Hilary was watching Sanchia, wondering how she could bear to submit to the hot, amorous embrace — for it was that rather than any dancing hold — of a man she so obviously did not love. Then she forgot Sanchia as she saw the striking head that towered above the crowd. He was exceptionally tall for a Latin, she thought dreamily. He would never run to grossness in age, or . . . A tiny sigh escaped her and chased the tenderness from her mouth. Consuelo was moving confidently into his arms, as though she had every right to be there.

'They make a handsome couple, do they not?'

The soft voice of Doña Elena sent a chill through Hilary's veins. Consuelo's gown was of a bold white with slashed insets of black lurex. Only a flamboyant personality could have carried it, and she looked sleek and superb, like a sinuous cheetah, thought Hilary, unable to avoid watching how close Consuelo's dark head was against the Conde's shoulder.

'Perhaps the Condesa's visit has a special purpose this time,' Doña Elena mused, almost as though to herself. 'Ruaz must take himself a bride some day — though we have almost despaired of ever seeing that day.'

A constriction closed round Hilary's heart, making it difficult for her to breathe. She whispered: 'The Condesa is staying for some time?'

'Until after the fiesta. She is coming with us to Huaroya —

where we go every year for the festival of thanksgiving for the crops. And I have a feeling in my romantic old heart that this year is to be the occasion we have all longed for.'

Hilary gave a choked little murmur. The music had stopped and the Conde and his beautiful partner were crossing the patio to where his mother held her court of reunion with her old friends and acquaintances. The Condesa was smiling. She took both of Consuelo's hands within her own and drew the girl down so that she could whisper something to her. When Consuelo straightened she was laughing.

Doña Elena sighed, a sigh of happiness that struck the chill of misery into the silent girl at her side. Doña Elena had never made any secret of her hopes for her nephew and the lovely daughter of her dearest friend. Now it looked as though those dreams were to come true at last . . .

CHAPTER NINE

A CALM enfolded the villa after the departure of the guests the following morning, but Hilary knew it would be short-lived. Holiday time was approaching and the excitement of fiesta in the air, not a little of it engendered by Joaquin who remained in a particularly boisterous mood long after his own party was over.

Hilary's head ached, and she was thankful when the Condesa, on her way to visit friends across town, decided at the last moment to take Joaquin along with her. But when his exuberant young voice faded with the car the listlessness of depression closed round Hilary and she almost wished him back. The villa seemed deserted, and she returned to the coolness of her room where she swallowed a couple of aspirins and settled down to write a long-overdue letter home. But the sentences would not flow from her pen. She could see only the mental image that haunted her throughout the silent hours of the night. The features that could be grave, imperious, aloof, demanding, occasionally whimsical, often challenging, but were now infinitely endearing. Was he in love with Consuelo?

It was difficult to tell; Ruaz was something of an enigma. Did Consuelo call him by that intimate family name? A flash of envy that was a physical pain stabbed at Hilary as her imagination leapt where she would rather restrain it. If he *had* to take one of the two sisters she would much prefer it to be Sanchia, whose sad smile told of unhappiness not told. Was that the reason? Had she lost one love, only to discover another that was not for her?

Hilary was so engrossed in her thoughts she did not hear the tap on the door or it opening. When Juanita looked into the room, calling a soft inquiry, Hilary turned with a startled exclamation. Instantly Juanita drew back.

'I am sorry. I did not know if— Are you ill?' Concern flowed into her small piquant features. 'Is there any-thing—?'

'No, I'm fine – it was a bit of a headache.' Hilary went to

open the partly closed shades, letting the hot silver-gilt light pour into the room. 'It's gone now.'

'Are you sure? You look very pale.' Juanita backed as she spoke. 'I will leave you in peace.'

'No, please stay.' Hilary spoke quickly, touched by Juanita's concern. During the days since her return from Valparaiso Juanita had kept her own counsel, and she had also worn a certain secretive look that did not exactly convey either the anger or the despair she had shown prior to the visit. Looking at her now, Hilary decided she could relax her anxiety over that respect; the storm seemed to have blown over. She said, 'Do you want to go out today?'

'Everyone else has, so I think we stay here and please ourselves.' Juanita struck a pose in front of the mirror and fluttered an imaginary fan. 'What are you going to wear at the fiesta?'

'I don't know. Do we dress up?' Hilary's query was mechanical; she had scarcely given a thought to the fiesta, still less to what she would wear.

'But of course! Did you not know? There are fireworks and the procession, and afterwards we have our own celebration and dance, and everyone drinks too much wine, and you cannot see the ground for flower petals, and— Oh! you must have a special costume.'

'What have you chosen?'

Juanita's lashes dropped. 'It is a secret, but I will tell you first when we get there. Joaquin is going as a soldier, a—'

'You needn't tell me. A conquistador.'

Juanita giggled. 'And Consuelo is going as Carmen, of the opera.'

Hilary nodded. She could picture Consuelo making a striking Carmen.

'She gave them the idea of choosing famous operatic characters this year,' Juanita went on. 'Sanchia is going as Violetta, and Don Miguel as Figaro, the Barber. But we must think of something exciting for you, my Hilary.'

Juanita assumed a thoughtful expression, studying Hilary's soft silky fair hair and gentle oval features. Suddenly she exclaimed: 'Why not? Come, I have the very thing.'

In her own room, watched by a wondering Hilary, she

dragged out a large box from the bottom of her wardrobe. She lifted the lid and from layers of tissue scooped out a billowing froth of creamy lace. She held it aloft and it melted softly into the form of tight bodice, long slender sleeves and a swirling fullness of skirt. 'It is eighteenth-century – I had it for a play at school last year. I think it will fit you.' She put it on the bed and delved back into the box. 'There is a mantilla . . . here it is.'

She put it over her hair, and her shining black hair gleamed bluish through the sheer lace of the mantilla. A thousand tiny jewels made it like a veil of stars, so light and fine was the material, and Hilary touched it with a gentle finger.

'It's beautiful – but I'd be afraid anything happened to it.'

Juanita waved this aside with an expansive gesture. 'No matter. I shall not be wearing it again,' She paused, her head to one side, then sniffed. 'I think you are afraid you have not the fire to be a Spanish *princesa* for one night.'

'I haven't,' Hilary admitted wryly. 'I'm too pale and pink.'

'Nonsense.' Juanita refused to listen to protests. Obviously she had decided that Hilary was to don the Spanish dress and no other. She took infinite pains to ensure that the accessories should be right, insisting on a shopping trip into town to select new shoes and then wheedled the loan of an exquisite black and silver lace fan from Doña Elena. Two nights before the family's departure to Huaroya she held a private dress rehearsal and skilfully evolved a new hairstyle for Hilary, using innumerable small jewelled combs, also bought during the shopping trip. Finally, the dress on, she showed Hilary how to hold and use the fan, then she stood back to survey her handiwork.

Certainly she had wrought a transformation.

Hilary gazed at herself in the big mirror and wondered if the radiant vision in white and silver and black really was the pale and pink Hilary Martin. A close scrutiny would have discerned the wistfulness about the soft mouth and the shadowy hint of sadness in the hazel eyes, but Juanita was too intent on achieving the picture she had in her mind of how Hilary should look. She walked round, frowning, then gave a satisfied nod.

'*Si!* You *are* beautiful. Not pale and pink. In fact you are very beautiful. Every man at the fiesta will fall in love with you.'

Hilary shook her head as she began to divest herself of the finery. There was one man who would be immune to the results of Juanita's handiwork . . . the only man who mattered, she thought sadly.

Despite herself, however, she felt her spirits lighten and her imagination caught by the excitement infecting everyone as the day of departure neared. They were flying to Huaroya, a mere two-hour flight over a distance that would entail two days of tortuous journeying by road. They were to meet the party from the Verdano Valley at the airport, and when they set off Hilary experienced a sudden sense of release.

It had been very difficult to maintain a cool and aloof air on the occasions when she encountered the Conde within the bounds of the villa, and now, with the feeling that she could lose herself in a crowd, she realized how great had been the strain.

Bruce Gilford was with the Navarre crowd, as were Don Miguel and several others Hilary remembered from that first week-end. It seemed so long ago yet it was only weeks, she thought inconsequently as she instinctively made towards Bruce.

Perhaps her greeting was a little unguarded in its warmth, betraying that she could relax in his company and use that companionship as a shield. He gripped her shoulders, held them an instant before his hands dropped, and his eyes teased. 'Hey! You're glad to see me – I guess I'll have to cancel dates a bit oftener if this is the result.'

'Hi, *amigo*!' Joaquin swaggered between them, and Bruce solemnly shook the small outstretched hand, slapping young Joaquin's shoulder with a man-to-man gesture.

'Joaquin!' The Conde's summons rang rather chill, and reluctantly the little boy obeyed, falling in with the straggling group boarding the plane.

The party occupied most of the accommodation aboard the aircraft, and as soon as they were settled comfortably the sliding doors were closed to screen them from the other travellers at the rear. When they were airborne champagne was served to the Conde's guests and by the time the plane skimmed down to the tiny airport at Huaroya most of the guests had forgotten restraint. Only Sanchia retained a subdued air, and Ramon's gaiety seemed rather forced.

Then Hilary forgot them and her own concerns for a while as new sights and scenes unfolded. Cars were waiting to drive the party to the Pacquera hacienda and in a very short time they were on their way through the fascinating old town. Its narrow streets were a blend of the ancient grey stone of Inca masonry and the flamboyant baroque of Spanish colonial. The cars were forced to crawl at times, hindered by plodding mules, heavily laden, overflowing carts and the market women with their baskets. There were disdainful llamas in the charge of an impatient small boy, girls wearing bright ponchos and stiff scarlet bowler hats carried sheaves of barley, and a solemn-eyed baby peeped from the wool shawl in which he rode, slung from his mother's back.

The narrow street widened suddenly into a square dominated by the magnificent carved façade of a church, the gilded dome of its *campanario* gleaming in the brilliant golden sunlight, and then the houses closed in again, so close that their overhanging balconies were within fingertip-touching distance overhead. They in their turn gave way to low wattle-daubed houses with scarlet-tiled roofs, and then the town was left behind and the cars began to speed down the road to the hacienda.

When Hilary had thought of it she had pictured a simpler, more rural dwelling than the ornate luxury villa in Lima's most exclusive suburb and when a twist of the road afforded her her first glimpse of the hacienda she gave a small exclamation of pleasure. It lay in a deep green fold nestled amid the hills, and it looked enormous. An ancient stone arch supported scrolled iron gates and framed the landscaped gardens and the long low shape of the house itself. She glimpsed green shutters against cool white walls, a deeply recessed entrance of dark studded timber within coloured brick nogging, and the cloistered terrace shaded under the overhang of mellowed red pantiles. Then the cars drove round the side and into a courtyard of old cobbles polished to bluish copper tones by age. And suddenly the place seemed alive with children.

Joyous cries came from them, and their little brown faces rounded with welcome. '*El compadre!*' babbled the voices, and the Conde was encircled by the small bouncing figures and eagerly outstretched hands. They fought to be the nearest when he picked up the tiniest mite and swung it aloft, and squabbled to carry his small leather personal case.

'Their beloved *patrón* has arrived,' Bruce said somewhat cynically in Hilary's ear. 'Such feudal philanthropy!'

Hilary made no reply. During those brief moments she had glimpsed a facet of the man she had not previously known. Among the children his usually austere features had softened to a tenderness she would not have believed he possessed.

The memory of the small incident kept returning as the hours passed and she gradually found her way about the hacienda. There was no trace of the poverty and oppression she had been half prepared to see among the Indian workers on the estate. The men wore the air of simple dignity that spoke of pride and achievement in their work, the women looked contented and their babies plump and well cared for. Although it was holiday time the air of well-being did not seem to be a false impression engendered by a festive occasion.

Finding herself alone later that afternoon, Hilary strolled idly through the gardens and down to the main gate. An outcrop of sunwarmed stone a little way down the winding road provided a natural seat from where she could see the cluster of neat little homes down the valley where the hacienda workers lived. Nearby was the big open area where some of the festivities would take place the next day, and already the women and girls were at work decorating their float.

The sounds of their excited preparations came clearly across the distance, and from somewhere unseen drifted the thin high notes of a flute. There was something hypnotic in the soft reedy melody and Hilary sat very still, the hot golden sun haze bathing her bare arms and head with languorous warmth. She did not hear the slow footfalls approach behind her and the long black shadow cast a sudden coolness across her an instant before the voice brought her to startled alertness.

'You are looking forward to the festivities, *señorita*?'

She raised her eyes to the dark imperious features and clenched her hands to stop the quivering that seized them like an ague.

'Very much, *señor*,' she responded formally.

She thought she saw a flicker of anger glint in the full-lidded eyes but thought she must have imagined it, for he changed his stance and with the movement his eyes came out of the shadow. Their scrutiny was quite open on her up-turned face in its frame of soft ruffled hair, and the slender, tightly clasped hands. To her dismay she felt the blushing tide of colour steal into her cheeks and almost jerked her head away.

'I think we have surprised you today,' he said suavely.

'In what way?'

'Let us walk, *señorita*.' For the moment he evaded her sharp retort and held out his hand to help her from her perch.

She tried to avoid it as she slipped off the worn old stone, but his hand caught her wrist and held it until she regained the smoother footing of the verge. When he released her she experienced the strange sensation of her wrist being the only part of her that was fully alive.

The path he indicated led round the outer boundary of the hacienda for quite some distance. He remained silent until they came to a small gate and another well trod path to a new-looking single-story building with wide windows and flowering shrubs in gay-coloured pots dotted along its broad veranda. The Conde stopped at the door and it gave to his touch.

Puzzlement parting her mouth, Hilary obeyed his gesture and slowly entered. She saw small chairs and low tables, bright pictures pinned along the walls, neat piles of books on low shelves – and a long blackboard on the wall at the far end of the airy room.

'This is our new school.' He was pacing with long leisurely strides, pausing by a particular section of the children's paintings. 'What do you think of our promising young artists?'

'They're very good.' She studied the bold colours of the paintings, their subject matter instantly recognizable and uncluttered, as seen with the directness of a child's vision. 'I did not know you had a school here, *señor*.'

'We opened it five years ago, and built this larger extension last year.' He watched her move away to examine the colourful examples of traditional handwork with which the children had decorated their schoolroom. He came to look over her shoulder. 'I suspect you are surprised again, Hilary.'

Her lashes dropped to shield her glance and she made no reply, recalling again the spontaneous welcome from the children when he arrived. The memory of his tenderness with them evoked a tenderness in her own heart, one which she must not betray. She sensed rather than saw him pick up a clay model of a llama, then put it down before he said coolly:

'This is your first glimpse of our more remote country. We are now on the eastern side of the Andes, in the heart of the *Indios*' country, as far from Lima in character as from the moon.' He moved on a pace, then turned to face her. 'I realized right at the beginning that you had done your homework pretty thoroughly, and that today you were prepared to see semi-starving *peons*, *coca*-chewing *Indios* eking out their miserable lives as they toil to expand the wealth of the grasping *hacendados*. Is that not so, *señorita*?'

The sardonic note in his voice stung her, more than the fact that he had come dangerously near the truth with his surmise. She said sharply: 'These conditions *do* exist, *señor*. The Indian has been exploited for centuries – ever since the Conquistadors took his land. I have seen the *barriadas* on the hills outside Lima, where they come to seek work and strive to make homes out of nothing. And the indenture system is infamous,' she added hotly.

'I do not dispute it, even though some of us are endeavouring to become a little more enlightened,' he said sarcastically. 'On certain haciendas the experiment of *cooperación* is proving most successful, and the Agrarian Reform Bill was a major step towards our aims.'

He touched her arm and turned to leave. As they retraced their steps she sensed the subtle shift in his mood and by the time they reached the cool violet shadows of the *cenador* Hilary's brief spate of defiance had flown. The slumbrous air of evening was already stealing across the golden-hazed garden, and the scents of roses and jasmine drifted to enchant the senses.

The Conde raised one hand to the looping tendrils of the heavy vine enlacing the sun-blackened old timber supports until she had passed, and the heady scent of the sap rising in the thick stems came to tantalize her nostrils. His jacket brushed her arm, fleetingly, yet enough to bring the shiver of contact. A sigh trembled in her throat, making unsteady her soft murmur acknowledging his courtesy. The spell of the man had enfolded her again, reminding her of her helplessness to contain her errant responses to his every mood. The sigh escaped her as he paused, his profile aquiline against the golden sky beyond the dark vine, and said quietly:

'But you must know, *pequeña*, that even with the best will in the world we can't put rich arable soil where it can never exist.' He turned his head and the dark regard falling on her face was a warm, physical sensation. 'Our mountains are inhospitable and our deserts barren, but one day our will shall prevail against poverty.'

'There is so much,' she sighed.

For a moment he looked down at her, then the sights and sounds of other people within the house spilled through the open doorway, breaking the strange little circle of understanding they had shared, and suddenly he smiled. 'Run along – you will want to make ready for the fiesta. It will soon be here.'

'Yes, *señor* . . . it will.' Almost like a child she turned at his bidding and ran indoors.

His smile stayed with her as she went to her room to shower and change for the evening meal, and even though the pattern of the evening's sociality allowed her only two brief moments of casual contact with him a pulsating glow of happiness lived buoyantly within her until she fell asleep that night. It was still there, warm and secret beyond analysis, when the fiesta began its reign next morning. Even the superb confidence of Consuelo could not rob her of her gladness that the dark mood of the past two weeks was at last dispelled. She did not have to avoid him any longer; she did not have to fear that he still held anger for her sympathy with his niece . . .

He was the single dominant motif for Hilary during the kaleidoscope of colour and impressions that crowded the senses that memorable day. Afterwards she retained many vivid isolated memories, even as others blurred and were forgotten almost instantly afterwards. She could not remember the ride down to the town or where the house was with the broad carved balcony on which she stood with several of the others watching the colourful procession wend its way along the narrow cobbled street below. She remembered the float passing, and Joaquin throwing stream after stream of coloured ticker-tape, but she could not remember whose voice it was who told her that the two players enthroned on the flower-bedecked float represented Manco Capac, the first Inca ruler, and his queen.

Later came the performance by the masked dancers. The sun blazed down on the bizarre ensemble, glittering on the silver decoration and gaudy beadwork encrusting the dancers' costumes. Their fantastic headdresses swayed and dipped, and the painted masks seemed to take on a strange travesty of human expression as the dance worked up to a frenzied climax. The drums throbbed and the pipes wailed, and the heat shimmering in hazy waves above the sunbaked earth added its own hypnotic effect on spectators already intoxicated with the spirit of fiesta.

Hilary was bemused by the heat and the noise and the drums. She could feel the echo of their throbbing rhythm when she was back in the welcome coolness of the hacienda. She lay on her bed for a while, waiting for the strange sense of unreality to ebb away, and closed her eyes. Almost instantly she fell asleep.

The sound of car doors slamming awakened her and she sprang off the bed. It was after sunset, the guests were already beginning to arrive, and she had to bathe, change, do hair and make-up . . . and how was Joaquin coping with his miniature armour and sword? And Juanita with the costume that was still a closely guarded secret?

The astringency of a cool shower brought her fully awake and restored the tension of restless energy. Suddenly she was looking forward to this evening more than she'd looked forward to anything for a long time . . .

She found that Joaquin had coped extremely well. The tiny leather breastplate and sword belt were securely fixed over tunic and pleated breeches, and the stiff snowy ruff framed his small imperious face. Hilary stifled an urge to kiss him and complimented him solemnly, then left him strutting up and down the long gallery while she hurried along to Juanita's room.

There was no response to her first tap, and she called softly, only to hear a muffled response that made her frown. Surely Juanita had not called: '*Go away!*'

Hilary stood for a moment, indecisive, then she heard the unmistakable sounds of weeping. Abruptly she opened the door, exclaiming softly: 'It's me – Hilary,' and closed the door behind her.

The shutters were closed, making the room dim, and it took a moment or so for her eyes to adjust themselves. When they did she caught her breath and ran to the small curled-up figure on the bed.

'Whatever's the matter, *querida mia*?'

The slender shoulder heaved under her hand. 'Nothing – go away.'

'Can't I help?' Distress made Hilary bite her lip. 'I can't leave you like this. Oh, what is it, darling? Are you ill?'

'I wish I were. I wish I were dead!' Juanita's face remained buried in the pillow, and she groped for a soaked little handkerchief.

Silently Hilary reached to the dressing table for a couple of tissues and tucked them down on the pillow. Juanita took them, blew her nose violently, and sobbed: 'Oh, Hilary, what am I going to do? I – I am so miserable I could die!'

'Is it Ramon?' Hilary said quietly.

There was a small convulsive movement against the pillow. 'He is going away. For ever. Tio is sending him away. He . . .' Bit by bit, punctuated by heartbroken sobs, the story came out.

It seemed that the Conde was dismissing Ramon from his job. He would be leaving immediately after the family returned to Lima, and the following day he was flying to Santiago where he was beginning a new job in the employ of a

Chilean *vinedo* owner.

'It is a vineyard – what does Ramon want with *grapes*?' Juanita cried. 'Oh, my uncle is cruel to send him all that way away from me. I hate him! Oh, Hilary—' her small features crumpled and she flung herself into Hilary's arms, 'I shall never see him again. Ever!'

'Hush – you will. Never is a terribly long time.' Hilary tried to soothe her, even as her own heart grew heavy. Disillusion welled in her as she recalled the Conde's icy statement on the eve of his niece's departure to Valparaiso. So this was what he had meant when he had said: '*It will most certainly be taken care of now . . .*'

It took all Hilary's powers of persuasion to make Juanita get up and face the evening. Even so, she refused to don her costume – that of an Inca princess – and put on a semi-formal dress of deep purple silk with a plain round neckline.

'I do not feel festive,' she said flatly, and indeed she did not look it. More than one comment was passed on her wan little face when eventually Hilary succeeded in getting her downstairs to the big *sala* where the buffet tables were loaded with every kind of canapé, savoury, and sweetmeat.

The wide windows at the end of the room were opened wide to the night and the glow of the lanterns strung above the patio. Fortunately, in a crowd of some forty or fifty guests, some of whom had not seen each other for some time, it was fairly easy for Hilary to lose Juanita and herself when incautious looks at Juanita's tell-tale eyes threatened to bring a further outburst of woe. Ramon was circulating unobtrusively, in that awkward position of being neither guest nor servant exactly, watchful that the guests were being looked after and all arrangements were proceeding smoothly.

He looked weary and unhappy, and Hilary's heart ached for the young lovers, but there was nothing she could do except offer sympathy and understanding, and make a shield of herself between poor Juanita and interfering, if well-meaning, curiosity on the part of others. Unfortunately, this could not last indefinitely. Hilary herself drew quite a measure of attention in her beautiful Spanish gown, exactly as Juanita had forecast. Her cool English fairness under the white and silver mantilla brought many admiring male glances, and when the music for dancing began she knew she would have to desert her protégée. She begged Bruce's indulgence when he approached, knowing intuitively that he would understand, but she could not beg the Conde's. Nor in her heart, despite everything, did she want to.

In full traditional dress he was devastating, and this was the first time he had taken her in his arms to dance. She might have known that he would dance superbly, guiding her steps till they flowed and merged with his and it was as though they danced as one. Over his shoulder, she glimpsed Juanita, sitting stiffly where she had left her and talking to an elderly woman, then she forgot Juanita when the Conde said softly: 'You look charming tonight, my little *señorita inglesa.*'

'Thank you,' she acknowledged softly, 'but I should really thank your niece, for she is responsible.'

'Ah yes' – she felt the subtle change in him – 'why is she not in costume?'

'There – there was some difficulty – it was not comfortable – to dance in,' she said hastily, and hoped that he would leave it at that.

But he didn't. He made an intricate turn and said evenly: 'I think not. I suspect my niece is in a pique because I have chosen to put an end to this ridiculous situation concerning her and my secretary.'

Hilary stiffened. 'I wouldn't call it pique, *señor*, or describe it as ridiculous. She's heartbroken.'

'I doubt it,' he returned calmly. 'She is young. She will soon recover from this – what do you call it? – flash-in-the-pan infatuation, once the object of desire is no longer within her reach.'

'You believe it's as simple as that. A flash-in-the-pan!' Hilary exclaimed, looking up sharply. 'When she's l—' Just in time she bit back the word 'love', realizing that she had almost told him that the affair – if affair it could be called – had lasted a full two years.

He was looking down at her, his eyes slightly narrowed. 'Yes, *señorita*?'

'You don't understand, do you?' she said despairingly.

'Even if it is merely infatuation it still has the power to bring heartbreak.'

His brows arched. 'I am not denying it. But it is one of the penalties of adolescence very few escape. I believe that one has to experience heartbreak before one can appreciate the joy of full and true love.' He slowed his steps until they were barely moving and his arm held her curved very closely against him. Her heart was pounding unnaturally fast and she felt sure he must sense it over the low, languorous throb of the music. Her lips parted, seeking to break the painful enchantment, and his own mouth curved with irony. He said softly: 'Somehow, I think *you* have yet to experience this tempering of the emotions. Like Juanita, you would seize at the shadow because you are too impatient to wait for the substance.'

'I don't understand what you mean,' she stammered.

'I am well aware of that fact, *señorita*.' A muscle flickered at the corner of his mouth. 'In matters of the heart you are as innocent as my niece.'

'You think we are children!'

'Not quite. But I would wish my niece to retain her innocence a little while longer. For you yourself, *señorita* . . . do not seize too hastily at the shadow . . .'

He gave a small inclination of his head and stepped back. She realized that the music had stopped and the mingled sounds of voices flowed into the silence it left. Suddenly his words were echoing in her brain and bringing a dreadful fear. What did he mean by seizing at the shadow? Did he mean . . .? Had he guessed that she was attracted to him? Had she betrayed herself? She swayed, hardly knowing that she moved automatically towards the place where she had left Juanita. He did know! What else could he mean other than—?

'Come on. My turn now.'

She looked dazedly at Bruce, hardly hearing him, and went into his arms as though in a trance. She did not know whether she danced waltz, quickstep or *pasa doble,* or what Bruce said as they circled the floor. Suddenly she felt Bruce's clasp tighten round her fingers. 'You're very quiet,' he said.

'Yes – I'm sorry.' She took a deep breath. 'I – I don't

want to talk – please don't ask questions, Bruce.'

The pleading expression in her wide eyes was more telling than she knew, and he said lightly: 'It *is* getting a bit warm. Let's go and cool off and I'll get you a drink.'

He guided her to a secluded spot outside the pool of amber radiance cast by the lamps and brought her a glass of lime and lemon laced with the stinging velvet of Bacardi. He leaned on the glimmering white bar of ranch fencing and stared up at the stars. 'Ever tried to count them?'

'No.'

'It's guaranteed to take your mind off anything.'

'Is it?'

'You've got involved, haven't you?' he said without changing his casual tone.

Her long sigh conveyed a great deal, and he looked down into his glass, tipping it gently and studying the broken sparkles of reflected gold. 'You know, Hilary,' he said softly, 'you learn patience as you get older. Don't rush at a problem. Sit back and wait. Very often time provides the answer.'

'I didn't know you were a philosopher, wise man,' she said with unsteady flippancy.

'I'm not.' He tipped up his glass and drained it. 'You're listening to the voice of experience.'

'I'm not sure if your kind of wisdom would work for me,' she said sadly.

'Only if you want it to work.' He turned to face her, and she saw the faint lines of cynicism round his mouth. 'Listen, honey, there's an antidote to most things, even the impossible combination of stiff-necked convention and explosive temperament of the Latins,' he said with sudden violence. 'Very often an antidote's the opposite, the neutralizing agent. In your case it's the good old British tradition of minding your own business. Take my advice and remember it.'

With a start she realized he meant Juanita and that she had completely forgotten about her during the past space of time. She said, 'We'd better go back – so you've heard? About Ramon?'

'Yes.' Bruce took her arm as they began to retrace their steps. 'Quite frankly, I've expected something like this for

some time. Ever since that weekend at the Navarres'
place.'

'You're not surprised?' Hilary stared up at him.

'No.' Bruce's mouth tightened. 'I'm only surprised that
the Conde didn't remove the source of temptation sooner
than he has. You've got to face it, honey. To the Conde
Ramon is nothing, as we're nothing when compared to their
ancient, blue-blooded lineage.'

Hilary felt shock. She had never heard the easy-going
amiable Bruce sound so bitter. She wondered what to say,
and at that moment Sanchia and one of the other guests
appeared.

Sanchia glanced rather curiously at Hilary and Bruce.
Her eyes narrowed. 'There is something the matter?'

'No – I – I'm looking for Juanita.' Hilary said the first
thing that came into her head and saw Sanchia's frown
relax.

'Ah, yes. The little one is not herself. She has gone to her
room. She asked me to tell you that she had a headache.'

'Oh dear.' Hilary bit her lip. 'I'd better go and see if she's
all right.'

Concerned, and not sorry for the excuse to escape and sort
out her own troubled thoughts, she went indoors and
stopped at her own room to collect aspirins in case they
should be needed. When she tapped gently on the door of
Juanita's room she was prepared for a response of tears,
anger, or genuine indisposition, anything but a blank silence.
Hilary stood there indecisively. If Juanita was asleep she
didn't want to disturb her; on the other hand ... A sense of
something wrong was nagging at Hilary, a sense she could
not define, and at last she obeyed it and quietly opened the
door a little way.

The shades were drawn and the room was in darkness.
Hilary hesitated, waiting for her eyes to become accustomed
to the gloom, then she distinguished the dark little shape on
the bed, and a sigh of relief ran through her. Juanita was
asleep. She had probably taken aspirins before she lay down
... Very quietly, so as not to disturb her, Hilary tiptoed out
again and drew the door soundlessly shut.

The first person she encountered as she returned to the
festivities was the Conde. She would have passed, but he

barred her path and his expression was aloof.

'My niece appears to be missing,' he said coldly. 'Have you seen her within the past hour?'

'She has a headache. She's resting,' Hilary returned in equally cool tones.

'You have seen her?' Somehow he did not appear satisfied.

Hilary's head came up. '*Señor*, I have just left her room. She's sound asleep, and I should not disturb her.'

'If that is the case, I should not dream of disturbing her.' His expression relaxed. 'But it is time for the firework display and I would not wish her to be left behind. Come, *señorita*, some of the guests are riding and some are walking. Which do you prefer?'

'Is it very far?'

'A little way beyond our domestic boundary, that is the private grounds of the house.' He glanced at the fairy lace and delicate embroidery of her dress and then shook his head. 'No, I do not think that beauty is suitable for traversing our dusty track, even though the night is warm and dry.'

Obviously she was intended to accompany him. He opened a side door, motioned her through, and indicated the big sleek car gleaming under the carport awning. Feeling as though she was losing control of her free will, she found herself in the car and a moment later the Conde was enclosed with her in the dark intimacy of the interior. He drove round the rear of the house, through gardens and shrubberies she had not known existed, and then rejoined the main drive. She recognized the dim outline of the little school, and then the car skimmed down towards the big open area where the masked dancers had performed. But this time the Conde did not drive right down to it as in the afternoon. He stopped the car on a high, natural rise about half-way down the hill and got out.

'Do not go down into the crowd – your dress may get torn – and stay near the car,' he instructed. 'If you feel a chill sit inside. You will still be able to see.'

He moved away, and obediently she stayed where she was, looking down on the colourful scene. If it had been exciting and colourful that afternoon it was doubly so now by night.

A large area had been roped off, and round it were gathered the children, the estate workers and a motley crowd from the village and nearby Huaroya. A ring of bonfires smoked and sparked against the opposite hillside, torches flared, impromptu dancing swayed the crowd, firecrackers glimmered and snapped, dogs yelped and got underfoot, and young men chased the girls, trying to tempt them away to the cover of the hillside.

Other cars were converging on this natural vantage point, and the laughing groups of more energetic guests who had made their way down on foot. Sanchia arrived with Bruce and Don Miguel and Joaquin. The Condesa's big Mercedes swept down, its headlights illuminating the night, and her chauffeur got out folding chairs so that she and Doña Elena could sit comfortably. Then the first glittering rockets shot skyward, and a great roar came from the crowd.

It was the most spectacular firework display Hilary had ever seen. Golden rain cascaded from the sky, fiery rockets sped to the heavens, catherine wheels whirled, set-pieces winked out their intricate patterns, starry showers of pink and blue and gold challenged the distant enigmatic stars, and the whole scene was electrified by a constantly fizzing and sparkling panorama of brilliance. Enrapt, Hilary did not know the moment when she was no longer alone, and she started violently when hands closed lightly around her shoulders.

Their warmth was potent, and her breath clung in her throat as the Conde said softly: 'You are not cold, *señorita*?'

'No, *señor*.' *How long had he stood there?*

'You are enjoying the display?'

'It's magnificent.' She was acutely conscious of his warm clasp. She wanted to break free of the dangerous spell, but she was powerless as long as he chose to hold her his captive. The glare of the bonfires and the flickering torches lent a wild quality that fired the imagination. The wild skyline and the long valley would look much the same four centuries ago when the Conquistadors invaded and plundered the strongholds of the great Inca Empire. And the chain of heredity stretched link by link, unbroken, down to the present day – and the man whose breath even now was warm against

171

her ear, a whispered compulsion.

'It is sad that so many things of beauty are so transient and intangible, is it not, *señorita*? That shower of stars, but one has scarcely time to hold the sight of them. And the cold light of dawn will reveal all that is left; a few tawdry rags of charred paper, the colours lost in the moistness of the dew. All that glowing magnificence – just so many spent matches.'

'Like the shadow and the substance, *señor*.'

A tremor ran through her as a line of rockets shot up simultaneously to release a falling curtain of stars. Abruptly the clasp on her shoulders fell away and even as she trembled again two warm dark wings opened and stole round her. Unbelievably, she was standing enfolded within the Conde's cloak.

She stood there, hardly daring to breathe, held in a bitter ecstasy she wished could last for ever. But it was almost over; the ring of roman candles flickered into darkness and the torches were burning low. She was acutely conscious of the lean strength of him behind her, a temptation urging every sense to relax and melt back against that strength. She tried to pretend that she sensed a reluctance in him to release her, and knew she was going to feel bereft of joy when he drew away and the heavy dark folds no longer made their delightful prison. He said softly, 'There is a rug in the car. I will—'

He never finished what he was going to say. A shrill voice demanded his attention. Consuelo was hurrying up the rise towards him, and at first Hilary could not take in the angry spate of words. Then horror swept over her as she heard Juanita's name – and Ramon's.

'I tell you I saw them!' Consuelo stormed 'The deceitful *muchacha*! And we believed her tale of a *dolor de cabeza*!'

Silence had fallen on the other guests. Some of them hovered on the fringe of the circle round the tempestuous Consuelo. Others, about to get into their cars, looked at each other, the shocked murmurs running from lip to lip.

The Conde's expression had frozen into icy disapproval. He snapped out a qustion to Consuelo and she tossed her head defiantly. 'If you do not believe me go and see for yourself. Your niece and Ramon are down there – I saw them with my own two eyes, *señor*. They were behaving like *Indios*!'

Ramon! and *Juanita!* A gasp of disbelief trembled on Hilary's mouth. Suddenly she rushed forward. 'But you must be mistaken! Juanita was in her room. I saw her asleep.'

'That is what you say.' Consuelo's lip curled. 'I believe you make it all up. You have encouraged her to be disobedient. To imitate your own wanton society. And tonight you cover up for her. Why do you deny it?'

'But I do deny it!' Staggered by the sudden turning of the attack on herself, Hilary flung out her hands in despairing appeal. 'It isn't true!'

'Of course it isn't.' Silently Bruce had come to her side. His arm curved round her shoulder and squeezed it comfortingly. 'Take it easy, honey. No one can blame you for this.'

But they could. Hilary licked dry lips and forced herself to look at the tall forbidding man who had wrapped her within his cloak only minutes ago. He was staring at her with a chill intensity that struck ice into her heart. He *did* believe Consuelo. And he did blame *her!*

CHAPTER TEN

'ALL we wanted was one hour together – to say our good-byes. Was that too much to steal?'

Hilary sighed hopelessly. 'In my world – no; in yours – yes. But why choose such a public place? Right in the middle of the festivities. You knew the entire family would be gathered to watch.' Hilary sighed again and stared unseeingly across the garden.

'Because we thought the crowd was the safest place. No one would think of going down there while the fireworks were on, and then we could slip back unseen before they returned.'

'It would have been better if you'd stayed indoors. I doubt if there was a single person left in the house.' Hilary turned from the balcony and wandered back into the room, to flop dispiritedly into a chair.

Juanita remained standing there, picking at a blossom and shredding the soft white petals with angry fingers. She flung the mutilated flower away and said furiously: 'I could kill her. Why did she not stay with you all? Instead of walking down the path, right into us. And the things she say to Tio afterwards, about you. That you had schemed and told untruths. Oh!' Juanita stamped and whirled petulantly. 'I wanted to kill her. I know it not true, and I wanted to bring you, so that you could explain, and Tio would not let me. *Por dios!* I have never seen him so angry.'

She paced round the room like a little caged cat, her oval features dark with bitter anger. 'I do not know why she hate us so much. We have done nothing to her. If she had not spied on us when we went riding none of this would have come to pass. And now Ramon is gone, and Tio is sending me to that school in Switzerland. He will not let me go back with Grandmother. But I do not want to go to Europe, and I will not stay here. I will run away! I will—'

She stopped, seeing Hilary bow her head in her hands, and the fire died from her face, to be replaced by the dawn of remorse. She ran to the side of Hilary's chair and looked down at her with worried eyes. 'What is the matter? You – you are not crying, my Hilary?'

'No.' Hilary shook her head and got up abruptly as she made the choked little denial. 'Come on, Juanita, let's swim or something. It – it's no use going over and over it again, making ourselves more unhappy.'

She began to hunt out swim things, and Juanita watched her.

'It has made you very unhappy too. I – I'm sorry, my Hilary.'

Hilary said nothing. Unhappy expressed it mildly. The three days since the return to Lima had dragged like a leaden eternity, and she still felt a stab of sick despair every time she remembered that fateful evening. She would never forget the icy condemnation in the Conde's eyes, or his silence. Sometimes she wished he had lashed her with stinging censure, with his anger and accusations. But he hadn't. He had merely excluded her from the family row that took place behind closed doors when the errant young lovers came guiltily back to the house. And the following day he had bidden his guests farewell as though nothing had happened.

If it hadn't been for Bruce's quiet sympathetic support that awful day Hilary doubted whether she would have maintained a semblance of control. As they'd parted at the airport he had taken her aside and tried to reassure her. 'It'll blow over,' he had whispered. 'Try not to take it to heart. I'll ring you tomorrow.'

With a rush of fresh despair she had remembered that he was leaving that week. 'I'll see you before you go?'

'Yes – we'll fix something. Don't worry.'

But how could she not worry? If only she had looked more closely at that dim curled shadow on Juanita's bed. She would have seen it for what it was: a housecoat lying untidily where Juanita had tossed it, but in the dimness it had been easy to assume that it hid the outline of a small huddled figure. She had expected to find Juanita in an upset state, and so when a glance seemed to confirm a sleeping girl the last thing she wanted to do was disturb her . . . And then an evil fate had chosen to bring the Conde across her path . . .

She had seen him only twice since they came back, and the length of the dining table might have been the length of the South American continent, so cold and remote was his manner.

Juanita continued to wander around the villa like a wan little ghost and refused to be comforted. Now that Ramon had gone she seemed to have one desire, to return to Valparaiso with the Condesa when she departed at the end of the week.

'I thought you did not like going there,' Hilary said, trying to jolt her out of the apathy which had followed anger and despair.

'I have more freedom there,' Juanita said, somewhat surprisingly. 'Chile is a very modern country now.'

'You never told me about Carlos,' Hilary said suddenly. 'What was he like?'

Juanita shrugged. 'He is but a boy,' she said indifferently. 'He means nothing to me. If only Tio would allow us to go with Abuela.'

'You mean Joaquin? I didn't know he wanted—'

'No – he has much studying to do,' Juanita said impatiently. 'I mean you, my Hilary. I asked Abuela if you might come also. After all, you *are* my *compañera* and *dueña*, so why should you not accompany me?'

'I'm afraid I haven't been a very successful *dueña*,' Hilary said sadly.

'*Quia!* Do not say that! Abuela said that certainly you may accompany me. But Tio must give his permission.' Juanita sighed deeply. 'He will be back tomorrow. Perhaps he may relent.'

Hilary did not share this faint optimism. The Conde returned from his business trip, remained at the villa long enough to change and collect Joaquin, and departed for a day's fishing. Joaquin returned boasting of a magnificent battle with a tuna, but the Conde did not deign to endorse the report. The following day the Condesa left on the morning flight, Doña Elena was indisposed and remained in her own suite, and sheer bleakness closed in on the two girls. One of Lima's periodic grey mists descended, a further depressant of the spirits, and suddenly Hilary felt a stirring of her old defiance. She could not bear this icy limbo a moment longer. Before her courage could desert her she went with fast-beating heart to the forbiddingly closed door and tapped firmly on the heavy panel.

'*Si?* What is it?'

Her hands trembled as they turned the ornate gilt door-knob and almost refused to obey her will. But the door swung silently inward at her touch and she saw the Conde seated at his desk at the far end of the big room. His cold expression betrayed no flicker of surprise as his gaze lighted on her taut face. He stood up. 'You wish to see me, *señorita?*'

She swallowed hard and whispered, 'Yes, *señor*,' quelling the craven instinct to turn and run. She came forward, aware of the painted eyes of the great portrait above him, and ignored the chair he indicated with a brusque gesture.

'Well, *señorita?*' he said after a moment of silence.

She put her hands on the desk and took a deep breath. '*Señor*, you must know why I've come. I— We can't go on like this indefinitely. It—'

'We?'

'Your niece – it doesn't matter about me. Won't you try to understand? She's suffered enough. Won't you change your mind?'

He stared. 'What is it you wish, *señorita?* That I should announce the betrothal?' he said icily.

'No!' Her eyes showed bewilderment. 'Let her stay with the Condesa for a few weeks as she wishes to. Surely you can't question the correctness of her staying with your own mother.'

'Not at all.' The frost did not thaw in his tone. He walked from behind the desk and pointed at a map hanging near the ebony cabinet. '*Señorita*, either you are incredibly naïve or you imagine me to be so. If you will step over here . . .' He raised his hand to the map of South America and traced a line down it. 'Here is the Central Valley in Chile. There is Valparaiso, and there is Santiago, near which is the *vinedo* where Ramon is now employed. It is not exactly within walking distance of Valparaiso,' he said sarcastically, 'but it is a great deal nearer than Lima.'

'And you think . . .' She took a step back and stared at him with pain-filled eyes.

He stalked back to the desk and said in peremptory tones: 'Sit down, Miss Martin.'

Suddenly she knew with a sense of fatality that a crisis was at hand, one it seemed she had provoked by her own rashness in seeking this interview. She wanted to refuse to obey his curt order and defy him across the width of the desk, but a trembling in her limbs forced her to back a pace and then, quelled by the dominance in his dark gaze, sink on the velvet padded chair.

His mouth was grim as he watched her and he remained standing. 'I do not care to make mistakes, still less to have to own to them,' he said deliberately. 'But I am forced to own to this one. When I brought you here I was prepared to swear by my judgment of character; now I am not so sure. I believed that you possessed qualities of honesty and responsibility which would make you leave behind you that aura of permissiveness on which your society prides itself, and that you were sufficiently perceptive enough to realize that total freedom to indulge one's every desire is not always an unblemished ideal. I also believed that you understood quite clearly what was required of you. Now,' he paused and his mouth compressed, 'I have no alternative but to admit that my judgment has never been so sadly at fault. My niece's behaviour has been inexcusable and I have no option but to attribute it to the adverse influence you have brought to bear. Defiance I can understand, even forgive,' he said heavily, 'but the one thing I can never condone is deceit.'

The silence after he finished speaking seemed to press round Hilary. Shock robbed her cheeks of every scrap of colour, and for a moment she could only stare back into those dark accusing eyes as though to implore him to tell her it was all a dreadful nightmare.

But the hurt and the bitterness was all too real, as was the choking rush of emotion that tightened her throat and stung her eyes. It was all she could do to keep the tears back as she summoned the frail defence of pride and straightened her trembling shoulders. She stood up and faced him.

'Very well, Señor Conde. I will save you the trouble of dismissing me. Naturally you will not want so bad an influence in your employ a moment longer.'

'You admit to being at fault?'

'I admit to nothing,' she said in a thin voice, 'but I can see it would be useless to protest, or expect you to listen. I—' Her voice broke and she knew she was going to break down if she didn't escape. She turned away. 'I'll leave as soon as it's convenient.'

'One moment, Miss Martin.'

The icy command halted her.

'Do you always break agreements so carelessly? You entered into a contract, remember?'

'Yes, I remember,' she stared blindly past him, 'but you have me at a disadvantage, Señor Conde. Whatever I do now is bound to be wrong or – or unsatisfactory,' she added bitterly.

'That is true,' he said cruelly, 'but I will need to make other arrangements before I release you. Until then, you will do me the courtesy of remaining.'

Through the blur of tears she saw the outline of him move to open the door. She forced herself to move slowly, keep her head high, until the sound of the door closing released her from the need for control. She ran, so blinded by tears she did not even see Juanita stop on the stairs. The Spanish girl's startled exclamation went unheard as Hilary stumbled past and reached her room. Five minutes later, having bathed her hot face with cold water and snatched up her jacket and bag, she was running downstairs, surrendering to the overwhelming need to get away from it all.

The Renault was in the long carport, alongside the enormous sleek monster belonging to the Conde. Just the sight of it was enough to start the ache in her throat again, and she dashed her hand impatiently across her eyes; she was a fool, every kind of a fool, to waste tears and heartache over a man who could misjudge her so cruelly. The Renault was unlocked and the keys in the ignition. She switched on with trembling fingers, trying to force herself to be calm as she checked over the position of the controls. She had not had occasion to try out the car since the day he had told her to use it when she wished, and the anxiety of not making any mistakes as she backed it out on to the drive helped to drive emotion into the background. Although she had not driven since she left home she soon became accustomed to the feel of the car and discovered that everything was positioned similarly to that of her father's car.

When she set off it was with no definite idea of where she was bound. Within a very short time she found she was nearing the busy section of the city and the familiar horn-blasting of Lima's many impatient drivers. Abruptly she took the next turning, instinctively seeking to by-pass the city centre, and suddenly she knew where she was going.

It took two misturnings before she got on the right route, but once she was on the broad coast highway she knew she would recognize the turning for the Verdano Valley. A small sense of relief soothed her and made her relax as she gathered speed. She had to talk to someone, even if she could not confide everything, and Bruce Gilford was the only person she could turn to who would understand. Some two hours later, when she drove into the valley and cast bitter glances at the Navarre hacienda in the distance as she passed, it had still not occurred to her that it might have been wiser to telephone before she set off. She had thought only of getting to Bruce and hoping his friendly understanding would restore a little of her bruised pride. So when she drove up the track to Bruce's house she did not notice that his big station wagon wasn't in its usual place at the side.

The veranda door was open and she ran eagerly up the three steps, calling, 'Bruce ... ?' as she tapped on the panel.

There was no response, only silence, and the desperate hope ebbed from her eyes. She tapped louder and shouted again, and then heard a breathless, 'Have patience – I am coming!' A moment later Maria's plump figure came hurrying from the garden behind the house. She stopped when she saw Hilary and threw up her hands, breaking into a torrent of explanation Hilary had difficulty in following.

Then her face paled as she began to understand. Bruce couldn't have gone already! Not until the weekend. And what was this about a letter? And the Señora Alvado? Sanchia?

'But come inside, señorita,' Maria said breathlessly. 'I start to clean, you understand. All to be painted new while Señor Gilford is gone.'

Weakly, Hilary went indoors, conscious of dismay as she looked round the room Maria had already stripped of all loose covers and curtains. The housekeeper tipped a heap of papers off a chair and bade her sit down, while she went to bring the letter. 'He ask me to post it, you understand, *señorita*. He in so big a rush and he say the letter may still be in his pocket when he gets to England. Here it is.'

Hilary stared at it, her face wan with lost hope. Bruce gone. The only person who might have advised her how to escape the heartbreaking situation in which she was caught. Her mouth parted and trembled as she began to thumb open the envelope. How could Bruce go without even letting her know? She drew out the two sheets and even as she scanned the first few sentences her eyes darkened with shock. Her lips framed the words silently as she read: *'By the time you get this you'll be able to congratulate us – I hope. Sanchia and I are leaving on the morning flight for London, where we're being married. How's that for the best kept secret of the century? We were tempted to tell you, but Sanchia didn't want to risk it – we were both determined that nothing should interfere with our plans. I've loved Sanchia for a long time, ever since she fell in love with my buddy from Montana. We were a couple of penniless young vaqueros in those days and Pete never stood a chance against her family – I guess that's why he packed in and went home to fall in the arms of his old childhood sweetheart. So now I've persuaded her to say "Si" I'm taking no chances until I've put the ring on her finger. Wish us luck, honey, you'll never know how much you helped us keep them in the dark, and forgive us. Bruce.'*

There was a hastily scribbled postscript on the back. It was a note of the name and phone number of an English couple Bruce knew in Miraflores; if she needed friends any time she was to contact them.

Hilary looked up into Maria's plump concerned face.

'It was a shock, *si*? I make you some coffee?'

'No, thanks, Maria – you're far too busy.' Hilary stood up and wandered blindly outside. She got into the car and heedless of the hot sun blazing down on her head she read the letter again. She still couldn't take it in. Bruce and Sanchia lovers! Eloping! How had she never guessed? Now that she thought back she could remember the small pointers, the times when Sanchia had looked at her so coldly when she fooled about and chaffed with Bruce. But surely they could have told her. Didn't they trust her to keep their secret?

Hilary let the pages fall to the car seat at her side. Forlornnesss rushed over her and she couldn't help reflecting bitterly that they had used her as a blind. It was all so obvious now that she knew the truth. It couldn't have worked out better for their plans, allowing the family to believe that they were succeeding in their efforts to throw Bruce and herself into one another's company.

But nothing could alter the fact that she was too late, and only now was she realizing just how much she had been depending on finding Bruce at home today. Tears welled up into her eyes and she turned the ignition key angrily.

There was no response except a splutter from the engine and her mouth twisted bitterly as she tried again. It was hopeless! That was all she needed – a breakdown. She bowed her head over the wheel, summoning weary strength to return to the house and phone for help, and the hot tears splashed on her wrist. How was she going to get through the time that remained before the Conde released her? How was she going to face him? How was she going to forget him?

She did not hear the swish of car tyres in the dust until the dark shadow overtook and pulled across the front of the Renault. A door slammed and the tall figure loomed above her.

'So I was right,' the Conde said grimly. 'And now I suppose you are running away.'

Her lower lip quivered. She shook her head dazedly. 'It – it won't start.'

'The car?' He frowned and leaned over her, trying the starter. His sharp glance ran over the gauges and he said dryly: 'I am not surprised. The petrol tank is empty.'

The pressure of his shoulder brushing her bare arm as he straightened was unbearable. She flinched away, and he opened her door, the silent command unmistakable. She stayed sitting. 'I – we – we can't leave the car here. I—'

He dismissed the broken little protest with a brusque gesture. 'I will arrange to have it picked up. Come, Miss Martin, you don't imagine I am going to allow you to run away so easily.'

The curt tones stung an already bruised spirit. 'I am not

running away,' she retorted, 'and I – I'd rather walk than – than be beholden to you,' she finished in a desperate little rush as she made to scramble out of the Renault.

A steely grip closing round her arm arrested the hopeless little show of defiance. He held her easily, his sardonic glance running down to the slender-strapped white sandals she wore. A grim smile curved his mouth and he thrust her towards the big car. 'Do not try my patience too far, Miss Martin, or I must warn you that the consequences will be painful.'

He slammed the door on her and reached back into the Renault, gathering up her handbag and dark glasses. He saw the two blue sheets of the letter and his mouth compressed as the bold signature was instantly discernible. Almost contemptuously he tossed the missive on to her lap and looked at her set, unhappy face.

'Does he mean as much as that to you?'

Her fingers tightened on the letter, and for a moment the significance of his taunting question did not register. She looked up sharply, but before she could frame the instinctive denial the Conde turned his head and smiled cynically. 'You will get over it, Miss Martin, believe me. One day you will awake and comprehend real love, not the vapid shadow of it. You surely would never have been content with what Bruce Gilford could offer.'

The cold and heartless words stirred Hilary to an anger that overcame all other emotion. Her hands clenched and she burst out, 'How dare you! You, *señor*, will never comprehend even the vapid shadow. How dare you speak of Bruce in that way? He would offer a love and understanding you don't know the meaning of!' The words were tumbling from her now as all restraint broke free and the bitterness of hurt and unhappiness escaped. 'You would break your own niece's heart, in the name of your precious tradition. You wouldn't have cared a jot if they'd found out in time about Bruce and Sanchia. You'd have stopped them. Well, you didn't find out. And I'm glad. Glad! They've got away and if they're wise they won't come back. And if—'

Hands seized her shoulders and forced her to face his dark anger. 'So you are glad, *señorita*! Do you know what you are saying? That you rejoice because another woman has

183

won his love and you spite your own heart merely so that you can exult in their defiance of this tradition you despise?'

'Yes – I'm glad!' She was in tears and on the verge of hysteria. He was shaking her and she fought to break free. 'You're wrong, you see! I don't love Bruce! And he never loved me. It was only—'

'You foolish little *amada*! Calm yourself!' He seized her flailing hands and held them imprisoned in the sheer force of his male strength. 'Why do you always fight me? Why do you weep over a man you do not love and who does not love you? *En que quedamos?*' he cried despairingly, and before she could move, his dark head blotted out the sun and she was caught in a fierce embrace. For an instant frozen in time his dark eyes held her wide, startled gaze and then his mouth imprisoned her own.

She did not know how many endless seconds ticked past before life returned to her shocked senses. She struggled violently against his arms and tore away from his kiss. 'How dare you!' she choked through her tears. 'Let me go! I—'

'What if I refuse to let you go?'

'You're despicable! You're just the same as all men,' she cried, 'but you're worse. You're breaking your own precious traditions all the time. You make the rules and then break them.'

'What rules?' His gaze bored into her. 'The rules of love?'

'You demand that your girls should never experience even a caress from another man before you deign to marry them, yet you would force your attentions on me whether I permit them or want them!'

Imperceptibly the steely grip had slackened, but the compelling eyes never flickered. 'Do you know what you *do* want?' he demanded.

'Yes! I want never to see you again. Do you hear?'

'It is difficult not to! Why were you running away?'

'I wasn't!' she said hopelessly, spent of strength to fight him. 'Why should I run away?'

'That is what I ask myself. Then why do you weep because you find *el señor* Gilford gone?'

'I – I wasn't. I—' She shook her head. 'Oh, what does it

matter? If—'

'But it does. Look at me, *señorita*. Could those tears be for a totally different cause? The fact that someone thinks ill of you, and that ill was completely unfounded?'

Her eyes widened. 'What do you mean?'

'I mean, *amada*' – the endearment was spoken deliberately – 'that it is important I know the truth. Could it be that you run to another man for sympathy because you are hurt? That my niece was correct in her assumption as to the reason for your abrupt flight after our meeting this morning?'

Hilary clasped her hands to quell their trembling. 'Your niece is quite mistaken, *señor*,' she said shakily, 'and I am not your *amada*.'

His lean mouth curved. 'The prerogative of misunderstanding is not solely the privilege of the feminine sex,' he said smoothly, choosing to ignore her protest. 'Fortunately, my niece was honest enough to enlighten me as to the cause of your quite genuine mistake on the night of the fiesta. I regret any concern this misunderstanding has caused, *señorita*. I know now that my judgment was never at fault, in that respect, concerning yourself,' he added.

She avoided his glance. 'It's over now, I want to forget it,' she said awkwardly. She settled back, trying to regain composure, and prayed silently that he would close the matter and commence the drive back to Lima. She could not bear much more of this agony. But he made no move to switch on the ignition. She sensed him stir, then warm fingers closed round her chin and turned her face towards him.

'Look at me, *amada*,' he ordered. 'There is something I wish to discover, so please be truthful.'

'I am always truthful,' she said in a low voice.

'Then tell me, are my attentions as distasteful to you as you would have me believe?'

She gasped and twisted free. 'You have no right to ask such a question of me, *señor*.'

'In this instance, I have every right,' he told her coolly. 'You have just accused me of breaking the rules of our tradition. I would have you know, *señorita*, that your accusation is as unfounded as my own to you this morning.'

She stared back at him, and his mouth curved in the

beginning of a smile. 'I agree that such attentions would be dishonourable should I have no intention of carrying them to an honourable conclusion: that of asking you to become my wife.'

'Your *wife!*'

The astonishment was so patent in her enormous eyes and parted lips that he shook his head in mock despair. 'My wife, Hilary. But how am I to discover if you reciprocate my feelings unless I make the kind of advance you tell me a man of your own nationality makes towards the girl of his choice? And how much longer,' he added fervently, 'are you going to fight me every time I endeavour to wake your sleeping heart to the meaning of real love between a man and woman?'

His dark eyes were warm now, the lines of his mouth curved with his ardour, and with an unbelieving gasp she tried to speak. But words would not come and he was too impatient to wait for her response. This time the hard arms closing round her were the delightful prison his cloak had been – and the bruising ardour of his mouth an ecstasy.

Between kisses he whispered endearments she had never in all her wildest dreams believed she would hear from him, until she fought free of what must be the most bewildering dream ever and put a defensive hand against his chest.

'You – you love me? You – you're asking me to marry you?' she whispered.

'I love you,' he smiled down at the stars she was unable to blink out of her eyes, 'and I have intended to make you my wife ever since ... but I will tell you of that later. Come back into my arms.'

'But I – I thought you were going to marry Consuelo.'

'*Hombre!*' He raised despairing eyes. 'Doña Elena – or Madrecita! – has been talking to you. No, my little *rosa inglesa*, I have never intended to be the instrument that will unite Pacquera and Navarre.'

She looked down. 'I was sure you were going to choose one of them.'

He tipped up her chin. 'Did that thought make you unhappy, beloved?'

She nodded mutely. 'I – I never dreamed you – you could feel like this about me. You – you were always so – so—' She stopped, unable to put into words how much his coldness and anger had hurt.

'I hurt you in my anger?' His mouth was tender and his hands gentle now. 'Do you not know that we always hurt those we love most? Always you fought me, or fended me off with that cool English insouciance that never let me know what you were thinking.'

'It was my only defence.' She moved abruptly. 'But how did you find me – and I *wasn't* running away!'

He sighed, making no secret of the fact that his lips did not want to make words at this moment. He brushed his mouth against her throat and ear as he said softly: 'It was quite simple. Señora Navarre telephoned my aunt this morning as soon as she found Sanchia's farewell note. At that same moment my niece, whom you believe to be so strictly suppressed, was upbraiding me severely for my harshness to you. The uproar was quite shattering – though quite normal – you will get used to us eventually! – but one of the servants had seen you leave in the Renault. My first thought was that you had run away and I immediately telephoned the airport to instruct them to detain you until I got there. Then Juanita reminded me that you might not know about Bruce and Sanchia. For some time I had believed you were attracted to Bruce, in a very cool way, and so I thought you might rush to him for sympathy. And so – here I come. Quite simple!' he added with such unabashed smugness that she had to smile.

Then she sobered, the shadow of memory coming into her eyes. 'It's partly true, though,' she admitted. 'I did want to run away. I – I didn't know how I was – how I–'

'Yes?' he prompted instantly, the spark of devilry glinting in his eye.

'You know perfectly well – now.' The rose colour was glowing all over her under the message of his ardent gaze.

His mouth quirked. 'Do not be ashamed of your blush. I find it delightful. I think it was one of the first things that made me fall in love with you. That very first morning when you wandered out on your balcony and raised your face to the sun. You were like a flower newly budded, and that wisp of petal pink floating about you ... I wanted to reach out and hold you, keep you where no other man might behold your slender beauty. And then, when I had regained control

187

of my errant emotions and tried to warn you, you blushed so endearingly . . .'

'But it was because of the eyes!' she said wildly. 'The eyes in the painting – your ancestor. I felt so foolish because I said you were like him, and—'

She stopped. The Conde was shaking his head impatiently. 'Already you are becoming like a Spanish woman – you talk too much!' He took her into an embrace that left her weak and helpless in his arms.

'Señor Conde!' she whispered at last when he raised his head and looked down at the warm glowing response his ardour had induced. 'You are not giving me much chance to talk.'

'Señor Conde!' he mocked softly. 'Do you not yet know my name?'

'Romualdo,' she said tentatively, loving the lean dark contours of his features under her exploring fingertips, 'or Ruaz?'

'I have always preferred my loved ones to call me Ruaz.' He took the slender fingers and touched them one by one to his lips. 'Now I am not sure . . . I like to hear your little English tongue curling round the syllables . . . you shall call me Romualdo.' He tried to imitate the way she said it, but in a way so endearingly teasing she dissolved into laughter, even as her heart ached with the sheer joy of being able to express her love for him.

He claimed her mouth again, and at last she stirred in his arms, one flaw intruding upon this new happiness. 'Ruaz . . .' she whispered, 'what about Juanita? We must do something for her, for she is desperately unhappy.'

He sighed, his mouth rueful. 'You still have a suspicion that I am a flint-hearted tyrant, *amada mia*, have you not? Listen, I have something to tell you, but it must remain a secret as though we were already trusting husband and wife.' He settled her in the crook of his arm, his hand caressing her, and told her of his plans for Ramon.

'You know that Juanita is an heiress, and that Ramon, although of good family, is penniless. You should know also that no man of honour would lay himself open to the taunt of fortune-hunter. However, things are not so black as they appear. On Ramon's mother's side of the family there is a distant relative who is what you call a self-made man. He owns one of the biggest vineyards in the country and he has no immediate issue to inherit. There is every possibility that he may select Ramon, but only if Ramon can prove himself capable of managing the *vinedo* without dissipating its wealth. It is only a matter of weeks since he intimated his intentions to me and sought my opinion as to Ramon's character. Naturally it is his wish that Ramon should not learn of this until the moment is opportune, and so I have arranged for Ramon to take this post in the Central Valley and learn what he needs to know to fit him for this responsibility.'

'And if it all turns out this way you will let Juanita marry him?' Hilary said eagerly.

'I shall consider it,' Ruaz said. 'But in the meantime Juanita must complete her education and learn to know her own heart.'

'You think she will change her mind about Ramon once she is parted from him, don't you?' Hilary could not keep wistfulness out of her tone. 'It will seem like an eternity to her.'

'Not quite. Tell me, *amada mia*, if Juanita were as dear to you as, say, a daughter, would you allow her to obey blindly the first fledgling stirring of her heart? I think you would counsel caution.'

'Yes,' Hilary's eyes were soft with reflective lights. 'If only I wasn't torn between both points of view.'

'I think you are concerned for my niece's futile months of yearning, my little tender-heart,' he said softly.

The thrill of pleasure at knowing the endearments from his lips were for her alone was too new for Hilary to be sad for very long. She smiled into his eyes and shook her head. 'I can't help imagining a whole year of wondering if I would be allowed to marry you,' she said slowly. 'I think, once knowing that I had your love, I would cease to exist for that year.'

'Nothing can stop you marrying me,' he said with a flash of the old arrogance. 'You are in my power for ever.'

'What?' Uncertain if he were serious, she looked at him with wondering eyes and thought she met sardonic humour in response. 'Ruaz – in our way of thinking marriage is a

189

wonderful partnership. Each gives and receives, honours and loves and shares—'

'Forsaking all others,' he interrupted tenderly.

She nodded, and he studied her for a moment, his eyes making no secret now of his love. Then he smiled slightly. 'Do you remember the day you were sightseeing with the good Bruce, and we saw the *Indio* boy and girl's courtship?'

'Yes?' She was puzzled. 'You mean the mirror-flashing?'

'No. I mean his stealing of her hat. Do you remember losing anything *amada*?'

'No – certainly not a hat. Why?'

He reached across her and groped in the back of the glove compartment. A murmur of impatience escaped him, then he found what he sought and drew forth the chiffon bandeau she had lost on the day of the *corrida*.

'Why, that's mine! So that's where it went to.' She made to take it, but he held it out of her reach.

'I had made up my mind even then that you were going to be mine.'

'But I *am* yours now, so . . .' her eyes danced, 'but I think perhaps I will not risk a fight for repossession of my property.'

Her arrogant conquistador frowned, then surprised her by solemnly fixing the bandeau over her hair. 'After all, I do not think I need to rely on so trite a token of magic.'

Her soft laughter bubbled, and was stilled under the claim of his lips. The bandeau slipped from her hair and Hilary caught it with one hand before she gave herself into his embrace. Perhaps it *was* magic, after all . . .

SPECIAL

Harlequin Romance Treasury Book Offer

This superb Romance Treasury is yours at little or no cost. 3 exciting, full-length Romance novels in one beautiful hard-cover book.

Introduce yourself to Harlequin Romance Treasury. The most beautiful books you've ever seen!

Cover and spine of each volume features a distinctive gilt design. An elegant bound-in ribbon bookmark completes the classic design. No detail has been overlooked to make Romance Treasury volumes as beautiful and lasting as the stories they contain. What a delightful way to enjoy the very best and most popular Harlequin romances again and again!

Here's how to get your volume NOW!

Let Your Imagination Fly Sweepstakes

Rules and Regulations:

NO PURCHASE NECESSARY

1. Enter the Let Your Imagination Fly Sweepstakes 1, 2 or 3 as often as you wish. Mail each entry form separately bearing sufficient postage. Specify the sweepstake you wish to enter on the outside of the envelope. Mail a completed entry form or, your name, address, and telephone number printed on a plain 3"x 5" piece of paper to:
HARLEQUIN LET YOUR IMAGINATION FLY SWEEPSTAKES,
P.O. BOX 1280, MEDFORD, N.Y. 11763 U.S.A.

2. Each completed entry form must be accompanied by 1 Let Your Imagination Fly proof-of-purchase seal from the back inside cover of specially marked Let Your Imagination Fly Harlequin books (or the words "Let Your Imagination Fly" printed on a plain 3"'x 5" piece of paper. Specify by number the Sweepstakes you are entering on the outside of the envelope.

3. The prize structure for each sweepstake is as follows:

Sweepstake 1 - North America
Grand Prize winner's choice: a one-week trip for two to either Bermuda; Montreal, Canada; or San Francisco. 3 Grand Prizes will be awarded (min. approx. retail value $1,375. U.S., based on Chicago departure) and 4,000 First Prizes: scarves by nik nik, worth $14. U.S. each. All prizes will be awarded.

Sweepstake 2 - Caribbean
Grand Prize winner's choice: a one-week trip for two to either Nassau, Bahamas; San Juan, Puerto Rico; or St. Thomas, Virgin Islands. 3 Grand Prizes will be awarded. (Min. approx. retail value $1,650. U.S., based on Chicago departure) and 4,000 First Prizes: simulated diamond pendants by Kenneth Jay Lane, worth $15. U.S. each. All prizes will be awarded.

Sweepstake 3 - Europe
Grand Prize winner's choice: a one-week trip for two to either London, England; Frankfurt, Germany; Paris, France; or Rome, Italy. 3 Grand Prizes will be awarded. (Min. approx. retail value $2,800. U.S., based on Chicago departure) and 4,000 First Prizes: 1/2 oz. bottles of perfume, BLAZER by Anne Klein. (Retail value over $30. U.S.). All prizes will be awarded.

Grand trip prizes will include coach round-trip airfare for two persons from the nearest commercial airport serviced by Delta Air Lines to the city as designated in the prize, double occupancy accommodation at a first-class or medium hotel, depending on vacation, and $500. U.S. spending money. Departure taxes, visas, passports, ground transportation to and from airports will be the responsibility of the winners.

4. To be eligible, Sweepstakes entries must be received as follows:
Sweepstake 1 Entries received by February 28, 1981
Sweepstake 2 Entries received by April 30, 1981
Sweepstake 3 Entries received by June 30, 1981
Make sure you enter each Sweepstake separately since entries will not be carried forward from one Sweepstake to the next.

The odds of winning will be determined by the number of entries received in each of the three sweepstakes. Canadian residents, in order to win any prize, will be required to first correctly answer a time-limited skill-testing question, to be posed by telephone, at a mutually convenient time.

5. Random selections to determine Sweepstake 1, 2 or 3 winners will be conducted by Lee Krost Associates, an independent judging organization whose decisions are final. Only one prize per family, per sweepstake. Prizes are non-transferable and non-refundable and no substitutions will be allowed. Winners will be responsible for any applicable federal, state and local taxes. Trips must be taken during normal tour periods before June 30, 1982. Reservations will be on a space-available basis. Airline tickets are non-transferable, non-refundable and non-redeemable for cash.

6. The Let Your Imagination Fly Sweepstakes is open to all residents of the United States of America and Canada, (excluding the Province of Quebec) except employees and their immediate families of Harlequin Enterprises Ltd., its advertising agencies, Marketing & Promotion Group Canada Ltd. and Lee Krost Associates, Inc., the independent judging company. Winners may be required to furnish proof of eligibility. Void wherever prohibited or restricted by law. All federal, state, provincial and local laws apply.

7. For a list of trip winners, send a stamped, self-addressed envelope to:
Harlequin Trip Winners List, P.O. Box 1401, MEDFORD, N.Y. 11763 U.S.A.
Winners lists will be available after the last sweepstake has been conducted and winners determined.
NO PURCHASE NECESSARY.

Let Your Imagination Fly Sweepstakes

OFFICIAL ENTRY FORM

Please enter me in Sweepstake No. _____

Please print:
Name

Address

Apt. No.   City

State/   Zip/Postal
Prov.   Code

Telephone No.   area code
                (   )

MAIL TO:
HARLEQUIN LET YOUR
IMAGINATION FLY SWEEPSTAKE No._____
P.O. BOX 1280,
MEDFORD, N.Y. 11763 U.S.A.
(Please specify by number, the Sweepstake you are entering.)